ROGUE

WAVE

HEATHER HANSEN

This is a work of fiction. Names, characters, places, and incidents either are the product of the author's imagination or are used fictitiously. Any resemblance to actual persons, living or dead, events, or locales is entirely coincidental.

Copyright 2021 by Heather Hansen.

All rights reserved. No part of this book may be reproduced in any form on by an electronic or mechanical means, including information storage and retrieval systems, without permission in writing from the publisher, except by a reviewer who may quote brief passages in a review.

Book Design By Zoe Mellors.

ISBN 978-1-7355637-2-5

For my husband. I could not have done it without all of his support.

Thank you so much enjoy

— Heather

1

As the daughter of one of the richest sugar barons around, she had all the latest and finest gowns. Fashion was nice, but in her heart she craved adventure. To see new lands like the ones her books, that lined the shelves of her room, spoke about.

She sat at her window seat, looking out past the lavish gardens of their grand estate; towards the soft, sandy beach that looked almost white. The tall ships coming and going in the busy docks were visible. *What would it be like to be upon one of those magnificent ships, to feel the waves roll beneath you?* She thought.

She would find a way out. A way to be free, to have an adventure, to discover who she really was. Her father would be leaving in a few days to go accompany a shipment of goods. Perhaps she could find her chance then.

During her childhood, her father was kind, but also busy. Her mother had died in childbirth and she believed a part of him had gone with her mother that day. Now, at nearly eighteen, her father held extravagant dinner parties and balls when he was home, trying to match her with a suitable young man. They were fun but she was growing tired of batting her eyelashes, waving fans, and flirtatious looks. These walls were closing in on her, becoming tighter than her corsets that she was forced to wear.

There was a quick knock at her chamber door. "Miss Benedict, your father would like a word with you. He is waiting in his study. I will have your tea brought in there." Her maid said with a smile.

"Thank you, Emma. I'll be right down." She smiled back at her maid. Emma was her closest friend and the one person she felt she could tell anything to.

With a quick curtsey, Emma turned and set off to find one of the footmen to ask for the tea to be brought into the study.

Catherine walked down the hall towards the large staircase. She skipped into her father's study with a quick, polite knock to let him know she was there. "You wished to speak to me, Father?" She smiled happily as her father turned towards her. He had been looking out the window at the gardens. One of the gardeners was trimming the rose bushes; the roses had been her mother's favorite.

"Yes, I wanted to make sure you had everything you needed before I set off in a couple days. I will be gone for a few months this time." He said with a frown. Catherine knew her father did not like leaving her for that long. It was always hard when he had to go away on business. He would be at sea and in and out of different ports for the next few months.

"Father, I am almost eighteen. Will you, I mean, that is, would you mind if I came along with you?" She had once asked her father if she could go with him, several years ago. At the time, she was still far too young but now, she did not see any reason he should not say yes.

He shook his head and looked at the ground for a moment. "I am sorry Catherine; you know I hate leaving you. I am afraid it is not proper and far too dangerous for you to come along. It will be better for you to stay here, with your friends.

It is time you start thinking about settling down, meeting a fine young man. There were several of them here the other night, did none of them meet with your approval?" Concern and love lit in her father's eyes.

"I am sorry Father. I know I must marry, but I would like to see more of the world, see new places, meet new people. You have travelled so often and seen so much. You used to come home and tell me all about your adventures at sea. I want that!" Catherine felt her anger rising. "Please Father, if I promise to choose a husband, will you take me with you?" She took a step closer to him, resting her hand on his arm.

"Catherine," He laughed sadly. "You are so much like your mother, filled with adventure. Her eyes shined with delight the day we set off from England to come here." His eyes had a faraway look in them. "It is far too dangerous on the ships. There are pirates and rogues, waiting for merchant vessels, like mine. Not to mention storms that can throw strong men from the decks or even sink one in a single night. If the ship were to survive the storm and you were not thrown overboard, then it's the fevers from the cold, wet air that would become your closest enemy."

His jaw clenched and his eyes lost their luster. The doctor had told him that Catherine's mother was weakened by the fever she had caught on the voyage from England, after a storm had struck them at sea. Her mother's body had just simply never recovered, and so Catherine's birth had been too much for her to bear.

"Oh, Father, I am sorry." Her heart broke for her father. Even though she mirrored her mother in looks and her sense of adventure, she was strong, healthy, and not with child. It would be different for her to be on a ship, it just had to be.

"Come now, Child, let us not discuss this anymore. Have some tea and a bit of the sweet cakes. What would you like me to bring you back. Jewels, fabrics, books…you think on it and let me know."

Her father gave her a small smile and she sat down in her favorite chair in his study. It practically swallowed her up. It faced out towards the beautiful gardens. Sometimes the sun would shine in directly on that chair, warming it perfectly. Often, when her father was away, she would sit and read for hours about the adventures' others had at sea. Her favorite books were about the adventures of Captain Nicholas Treadfast. He was a fierce Captain that all other sailors feared and respected. Of course, these books were not at all suitable for a proper lady to be reading, but her father, at least, had indulged her in that respect.

One time, her governess caught her reading one of the Captain Treadfast books and about fainted on the spot. Her governess insisted she should only be reading about the latest fashions in England and France, practicing her painting, drawing, music, and needlepoint. After that unfortunate event, her father asked her to read the books in secret and not in front of outsiders. He did not need to mention the servants and staff. They understood her and she was close with most of them, Emma in particular.

After tea, she decided to go for a stroll around the garden and for a walk in the stables. She loved visiting the horses and bringing them all sorts of treats. Her favorite was a beautiful Palomino, born in their stables. Ever since the day he took his first wobbly steps in the straw covered stall, she became completely smitten with him.

In the stable, she slowly walked down the long aisle of stalls, whispering soft greetings. She handed out treats and scratched the heads of the horses that welcomed her. Sunny, her Palomino was kept at the end of the stable. He stuck his head out the stall and gave a quick whinny in greeting.

"Hello, boy, you are looking well." She said as he nuzzled her. Catherine laughed and planted a big kiss on his velvety nose.

"Hello, Miss Benedict." Catherine had not even heard the stable boy come up behind her. He walked over to her, reaching his hand up to pet Sunny. "Are you wanting to take him out? I can saddle him for you if you'd like."

"Not today, thank you, Allen. I need to get back up to the house soon. We are having another dinner party tonight." She said, scrunching her nose as if she smelled something rotten.

Allen laughed, "Oh, come now Miss Benedict, the dinner parties can't be that bad. What is for dessert?" He asked eagerly. Catherine tried as often as she could to save Allen some of the fancy desserts.

"I believe Cook said she was making Apple Charlotte tonight." Allen's eyes grew wide and he licked his lips. Catherine giggled, "I will try and bring you a piece as soon as I get a chance. I should go, I better start getting ready." Sunny nudged Allen, bringing the boy's attention back to him and away from the thought of tasty desserts.

"Alaric, see to it that all provisions are made, and we are ready to sail in the next few days. I do not plan on staying in port very long." Lucas said to his first mate. Alaric and Lucas grew up on a small village in Ireland. They left at the age of 16 to sail the seas together.

As they stepped off onto the docks. Alaric gave Lucas a friendly slap on the back and grinned. "I'll see you later at the Rusty Anchor." The crew always enjoyed their time in port, no matter how short a visit. Some of the crew had family waiting for them and others simply enjoyed the time away from their duties on board the ship.

Lucas set off towards the heart of the city. He had some time to look around and get supplies before he needed to be at the Governor's estate. The Governor of Barbados had sent him a letter asking him to dine with him, as he had some business to discuss. He owed the Governor a debt. He could not think of what the Governor might need to speak to him about. He just hoped that he was not going to take away his Letter of Marque, that was what kept him safe on the waters and kept him from getting his neck in a noose. Without it, he would lose everything he had, his ship, his crew, and quite possibly his life.

Lucas walked around the different stalls and various shops. He did not need anything new; except a spy glass. His current one had a small crack in it from the last battle they had with a Spanish ship a few weeks ago. It was not a particularly brutal battle and was a relatively easy ship to take. There were only minor injuries, including his spy glass.

Lucas knew of a small shop that sold merchandise for sailors, they might have a spy glass. He stepped inside the small building that looked as if it had seen better days. It was rather worn down and the roof needed patching.

"Well, good day to you, Captain Harding. It has been awhile since you was last in here. What can I help you with?" The old sailor and his wife owned this place for many years. It was good to see a friendly face.

"Good to see you again, you don't look a day older from when I last saw you." Lucas laughed and reached out to pat the old man on his slender shoulder. "I am glad to see you are doing well, old friend. You wouldn't happen to have a spy glass I could purchase, would you?"

"As a matter of fact, we do, we recently just traded for it, a few compasses and a rather nice sextant. We also have a few new maps you can look at, though I am sure you know these waters better than anyone." He said, his smile revealing missing teeth. "Here, lad, let me grab you that spy glass while you take a look around." The old sailor walked over to the opposite wall. Reaching up, he grunted as he took a brass spy glass from a rickety shelf. "Here it is."

Lucas turned towards him, "Ah, that will do just fine, I think." He took the spy glass out of the man's frail hands. Lifting the spy glass to his eye, he looked through it, out towards the rest of the city. He spotted a brightly colored bird in a tree, far on the other end, past the shops, market stalls and shacks. He clipped it closed. "This will work perfectly."

Lucas placed several coins on the counter.

The man's eyes grew wide, "Captain Harding, my friend, this is far too much." He shook his head, his hands trembling a bit as he gestured to the coins.

"Of course not, you have always had what I needed, when I needed it and I enjoy seeing your friendly face when I come back here. You take it." Lucas grinned, shook his friend's hand and walked out, squinting in the bright Caribbean sun. It was about time he started heading back to his ship to get ready for his dinner with the Governor.

He entered his cabin, setting the spy glass on his desk. Shaking off his shirt, he grabbed a clean one from the trunk at the foot of the bed. After his shirt was on, he ran his razor over his chin and cheeks. He was not particularly looking forward to the meeting, he never much liked dressing in the starched collars and stiff dinner coats.

Lucas stepped out of the carriage and walked up the steps to the ornate door. The butler opened it, bowed as he entered, and led him to one of the many sitting rooms. "Wait here, if you will, Captain Harding, the Governor will be with you shortly." The butler bowed again and walked out. Lucas looked around the large room. The dark red walls held book lined shelves. A solitary desk stood in the corner with nothing on it but a bit of blank paper. The door to the sitting room opened. The butler led the Governor in, gave another bow then retreated from the room.

"Good evening, Captain Harding. I trust you are doing well?" The Governor asked as he walked over to the crystal glasses that sat on a small table. "Care for a glass?" He held up a crystal glass with swishing, amber liquid in it.

"Thank you, yes." Lucas smiled politely. The Governor poured them both a drink and handed one to him. "I hope you are doing well yourself."

"As well as to be expected, the air in these parts is always hot and sticky. I do not care for it much but then again, it is a small price to pay for such a grand position and estate. Wouldn't you say?" He smirked and raised the glass, taking a slow sip.

"I should think so, I suppose, though I am not much bothered by the damp. In Ireland it was always raining. And I have now grown accustomed to the heat." Lucas demurred smoothly, taking a sip of his own drink.

"When will your ship and crew be ready to sail?" The Governor asked. He rested a hand on the mantel of the fireplace.

"In the next few days, Sir." Lucas felt the conversation shift to the real reason why he was there.

"Very well, I have something I need you to deliver for me. It is a particularly important piece of parchment. I could not entrust it with a merchant ship, as they are targeted too often, and would not have the means of keeping it out of the wrong hands. I trust you will be able to get it to my man in France safely." He stared at Lucas intently.

"France, Sir?" Lucas was stunned. He very rarely travelled out of the Caribbean waters. As a Privateer, he was tasked with stopping trade between enemy merchant ships passing through the West Indies. Occasionally, he was asked to deliver goods or papers between the different ports but nothing as far as France. Certainly nothing that the Governor directly asked him to deliver with such importance. He felt cornered; he had to do as the Governor said or lose his Letter of Marque and risk everything.

"Yes, you will be meeting with a man by the name of Francois Dupont." He looked at the mantel again then back at Lucas with the same hard expression. "I expect you will keep this to yourself, no one is to know of this." He commanded.

Lucas's jaw clenched with a slight nod of his head. He did not like the secrecy or the look in the Governor's eyes. Obviously, whatever was on this piece of parchment was bound to stir up trouble.

"Come, let us dine." The Governor set his glass on the mantel. He pulled a long rope that hung against the wall, signaling to the butler to open the door and lead them into the dining room.

The meal was superb, though Lucas hardly tasted any of it. He was not sure how his crew would feel about such a trip. Many of them would be glad of a change, others would not be happy about leaving their families for so long. As Privateers, they were always sea bound, however this would be potentially more dangerous. Rougher waters, deadlier ships, and a secretive mission from the Governor. This was a risk and as Captain, he was not entirely comfortable forcing his men into such a situation. However he had little choice in the matter.

"I am thankful I have a man on this island that I can count on. There are not a lot of men that could be trusted with the task." The Governor eyed Lucas. Lucas knew the Governor could sense his hesitation and discomfort from carrying out this commission. The Governor waved a hand in dismissal as if that explanation should satisfy Lucas and ease his conscience. It only made him feel more unsettled.

Lucas inhaled the cool night air deeply. He dismissed the carriage back to the ship; he needed a walk to clear his mind. As long as he and his men were not in danger from carrying out the task, it should not matter what business the Governor had with Monsieur Dupont, but he just could not shake the feeling of mistrust and unease.

He ran a hand over his face and headed towards the *Rusty Anchor*. There, he could get a drink and maybe play a game of dice or two before heading back to his ship. Many of the men would find a place to stay on land when they went into port, but he always preferred to stay aboard his ship. Three men at a time were always on board in port, he insisted on it.

"If you will excuse me, I will only be a moment." Catherine said politely to her guests. The men left to play a game of cards and talk, while the women sat in the sitting room and discussed gowns and the latest gossip. Catherine needed a break; she did not care much about new gowns, or that Miss Whitby was soon to be engaged to Lord Ainsworth but was in fact seen just last night flirting with Mr. Bradley. Not that anyone could blame Miss Whitby. Lord Ainsworth was a perfect gentleman and would make a great match for her, but he was rather a little mouse of a man.

Catherine smuggled her Apple Charlotte into a cloth on her lap. It was wrapped up tightly, waiting for the perfect chance to get away for a moment. Allen would be thrilled when she gave it to him.

Allan was a young boy when he first came to the plantation. Her father was on his way home one day when one of the horses, pulling his carriage, spooked. The driver had fallen off the seat and was unable to calm the beast down. Allen, his head hardly even reaching the horse's nose, watched the whole event unfold. Without a moment's hesitation, he calmed the horse down with a single touch and humming a simple tune. Impressed, her father insisted the boy come back with him to work in the stables at the plantation. Allen had been there ever since.

"Allen?" Catherine called out quietly. The boy slept in the loft area above the stables. She walked over, stopping just below the ladder. "Allen? You awake? I brought you the Apple Charlotte."

Still no reply. Catherine climbed up the ladder, she would just leave the dessert up there for him. Careful not to drop it, she managed to climb up the ladder, though her skirts made it difficult. *It will be a miracle if I manage to get back down without breaking my neck,* she thought.

Catherine placed the dessert nicely by a pile of various items belonging to Allen. She had never been up in the loft before, soft straw was laid out with a pillow and blanket in one corner. In the other corner, there was a lamp, a pile of neatly folded clothes, a pair of extra shoes and a book. Catherine picked the book up to examine it, the head footman was teaching Allen to read. It was one of the books from her father's study, he must have loaned it to him. She looked around, she could see why Allen liked it so much in the loft. It was quiet and peaceful.

She spied the clothes again. On an impulse, she grabbed them and the shoes and quickly climbed down as best as she could without slipping. A sudden thought came to mind. The dress was such a hassle to climb in, she easily saw why men needed breeches instead of gowns to work in. It had also occurred to her, that if she was going to find a way to sneak out for a bit, that she could not very well walk out of the Plantation grounds without being spotted or stopped. If she dressed in boy clothes though, no one would glance in her direction. She ran back up to the large house and snuck up to her chambers to hide the clothes. Composing herself, she returned to her guests.

The next morning, she sat in the warm sun, taking in the sounds of the birds, the bustling sounds from the docks and the ocean. Her book sat open in her lap; she was completely lost in the story when she heard someone clear their throat. She looked up, blinking a couple times, she had not heard her father approach.

"My dear, I have been thinking a lot about the conversation we had the other day…and well." Sitting on the bench next to her, he grabbed for her hand and held it in his, looking down at it. "Catherine, last night, Lord Anderson, was quite taken with you. As you know, he recently purchased one of the larger Plantations." Catherine blanched, she knew exactly where this conversation was headed. The ladies the previous evening had even implied as much, they had suspected what she had dreaded.

"Catherine, he is a fine young man, I think you will be very happy." He tried to give his best, hopeful, smile. "When I return from my endeavor, we will hold your wedding here on the plantation." He gestured with his hand behind him. "Of course, you and your friends may start planning it as soon as you wish. I am sure you will have lots to go over. You will be so busy planning your wedding and then running your own grand estate that you will not even have time to dream of adventure. In fact, you will be living a new kind of adventure." He squeezed her hand.

Before he could wrap his arm around her in an embrace, she snatched her hand back, and ran off towards the stables. Her heart was thundering in her ears. She could not think straight, she needed a minute. How could he have done that? Her father had always told her he would let her choose who she wanted to marry.

Catherine ran into the stables, straight to Sunny, wrapped her arms around his neck, and sobbed. Why would he would promise her to someone so suddenly or to a man she only recently met? She would be living on the same island on another plantation, doing much the same as she did now. Nothing would change, she would be living the exact same life. Just sitting, talking, waiting. Once she married she would probably never get another chance to get out and see more of the world.

Her head snapped up. She would go through with the marriage if she must, but not before she saw what lay beyond the docks. Her father would be leaving the next day for a few months. That would give her plenty of time to leave the plantation in her disguise. She could buy passage to some of the lands and ports she had read about, live her life the way she dreamed and have a story of her own to tell. Then she would simply buy passage back, on another ship, come home…and plan her wedding to Lord Anderson.

Catherine and the head staff were silently lined up outside the entrance to the big house to bid farewell to Lord Benedict before he left on business. Catherine was a mixture of nerves, excitement, and sadness. She loved her father and did not wish to hurt him, she knew that when he found out she had left, he would be terribly worried. This was not the typical farewell. This was a farewell to life as they knew it. Her adventure and forthcoming marriage loomed over the parting.

Her father stepped out of the house. He spoke with staff, leaving little instructions to different maids and footmen. He placed a hand on Elijah's shoulder. "Take care, man. I trust you will have the entire house in order, much like you do every time I leave for a bit." Elijah had been a footman for many years under the Baron and had more than earned his right to be the butler. Over the years, they had become friends.

Lord Benedict looked toward Catherine, who stood opposite to the staff. "My dear, I am very proud of you. I am happy you came around about marrying Lord Anderson. You will have a happy marriage, I believe, and will never be far from me, should you ever need anything." He pulled Catherine into a big, fatherly embrace. Catherine desperately fought back tears.

"I love you, father. Be safe and write when you get the chance." She knew she would more than likely not see those letters, as she would be out on the rolling waters herself. The difficulty passed. It was not too late to change her mind, but she knew if she did, she would wonder all her life, what kind of adventure had she missed. Her father squeeze her one last time and smiled. Kissing her forehead, he turned and climbed into the waiting coach. As the carriage lurched forward, he waved and sat back in his seat. Catherine let out the breath she had not realized she had been holding. She turned and walked into the large house. The staff followed close behind her, quickly returning to their various duties.

The night before, she had tossed and turned, trying to decide what she would do and what her plan should be. The clothes she would wear were under her bed, tucked away safe from being discovered, or so she hoped.

She had not thought of anything else she would need, save a bit of money. After all, the ship would provide food and a cabin. She did not need to pack any gowns nor books; why read about an adventure when she was finally going to live one? She would wake before dawn and head to the docks. There, she would buy passage on a ship and be out of port before the staff even realized she was out of the house, let alone off the plantation grounds. She smiled to herself, she was confident that her plan would work.

Catherine had barely drifted off when another dream of crashing waves and screaming men scrambling about the deck of an enormous ship woke her. Light was barely peeking over the horizon through her window, warning her that this was her moment. She reached under her bed for the clothes she was borrowing from the stable boy. Slipping out of her soft nightgown, she pulled the large, baggy shirt over her head, then shuffled her legs into the very scratchy pants, that hugged her thighs, perhaps a bit too tight.

Accustomed to soft layers of fabric and clothing Catherine felt rather exposed and itchy. Tucking the shirt in, she glanced at her reflection in the mirror. The shirt was large, she had not realized that even though Allen was still a few years younger than herself, he was taller than her by a couple inches and his shoulders were broad. The baggy shirt hid her figure well enough; the pants did not quite do such a good job. She stared at herself for a moment. *It will have to do,* she thought.

Tying her hair back, she hid it under the hat, then pulled on the shoes. They were a bit too big. Grabbing her disregarded night gown from the floor, she tore a few strips of fabric from it and stuffed them in the shoes. It was not the most comfortable of outfits, to be sure, but at least now her feet would not be slipping out; she could move around freely and most importantly, she would not be recognized.

Taking another quick glance in the mirror, she grabbed the bag of coins off her dresser and stuffed them deep in her pocket. Lastly, she placed three notes on her dresser. One for Emma, one for Allen, and one for her father. She touched the folded parchment addressed to her father. "I love you," she whispered to the letter.

Catherine slightly opened the door to her chamber. The hallway was empty and silent. Slipping through the door, she edged her way down the hall and onto the stairs. There was no one on the stairs. She crept down and worked her way towards the front door.

"Emma, I will be setting the clocks this morning, John is

helping Gregory." Catherine froze.

"Alright, thank you, Edward." Catherine flattened herself against the wall, inches from freedom. She watched as Edward, one of the footmen, headed towards the large clock that sat just outside the door to her father's study. Emma walked into the main sitting room to open the curtains and fluff the pillows. Catherine exhaled, that was too close. She crept nearer to the door, slowly wrapping her sweaty hand around the handle. As quick and as silently as she could, she leapt outside, closing the door with a light click.

Catherine ran towards the front gate; if someone was to look out the windows, they might spot her and wonder why the stable boy was leaving. She could not risk any questions. The large gates screeched loudly as she passed through them.

Her legs carried her past the plantation grounds and towards the heart of the port. It was still too soon to assume she was safe from being spotted and recognized but she had made it this far. Now she had to find a ship to buy safe passage. As she got closer to the port, she slowed to a walk, savoring all the sights. Of course her father had been with her when she had visited the docks before, but now in disguise, it was an entirely different experience.

In the port men were everywhere, loading and unloading boxes, carrying goods and animals from all over. The smells assaulted her nose as she tried to focus. Perhaps she could ask one of the women at the stalls if they knew of a ship she could buy passage on. Glancing around, she walked towards one of the small stalls. The woman was putting out various fruits. "Excuse me, I was…" No, that would not do. Her voice was too high. She cleared her throat and deepened it. "Excuse me, would you happen to know of a ship that is taking on passengers?"

The women looked directly at Catherine, who swallowed

nervously, as if the woman could see right through her disguise. "Head down to the docks, ask to buy passage on The Alice. It is a passenger ship that is headed towards England. You'd better hurry, it will be sailing soon." The woman went back to setting up in her stall.

"Thank you, I am much obliged." Catherine said with the deepest voice she could manage. The Alice, she thought to herself. She would go to England and see a bit of where her mother and father were from. She hurried down to the docks, filled with excitement and nerves.

"Look out, lad!" A gruff voice said. Catherine stumbled, something hard bumped into her back. She turned to see a large, scowling man carrying a big box. "If you ain't goin' to help, I suggest you go find a place to sit…out of the way."

Catherine froze; the port was far busier than she had expected. Taking a step forward, she tried to find someone that looked as if they might know about The Alice. She spotted a tall man standing with a board and parchment, speaking to different men, ordering them to load boxes or to go on board the nearby ship. Perhaps he would know where she could find The Alice. She walked forward, a bit unsure of herself. What if he could tell she was not a boy?

"Hey, you! Boy!" A large hand grabbed Catherine's shoulder. "You must be one of the new sailors." The man grabbed Catherine's hand and turned it over. She was shocked.

"Not a single mark." He laughed and looked back at another man. "Come, you carry those there boxes on to that ship." He pointed to a group of boxes then to the ship that was behind the man with the board and parchment. Stunned, she found herself struggling under the weight of one of the wooden boxes. She marched her way towards the ship and practically dropped the box at the tall man's feet. "Excuse me, Sir, I…"

The man with the board cut her off. "I heard him tell you to carry the boxes." He gestured to the rather bossy and rude man behind her, that was now yelling at a young man that was quickly growing paler by the second. "You best do as you are told, lad, or you will find yourself in front of the Captain; that, you do not want. Get goin." The man said, hardly even taking a second glance at Catherine.

A man was coming up fast behind her, with a load in his arms that blocked his view. She quickly picked the box up again. If she did not hurry, he would run right into her and she did not fancy being yelled at again. Quickly, she rushed up the plank that joined the ship to the dock. Setting the box down, she looked around. An actual ship. She could hardly believe her eyes. It dawned on her: this was not *The Alice,* she was sure of it. There did not look to be any other passengers on board.

"Excuse me, is this *The Alice?* Where can I find T*he Alice?*" She said to a sailor, a bit more fanatically than she wanted.

"The Alice?" The sailor chuckled. "Sorry son, that ship sailed out already. This here is *The Trinity.*" The old sailor stomped his foot on the wooden planks.

"No, there must be a mistake, you see, I was supposed to buy passage on The Alice." Panic rose in her throat. This was all going so wrong, so suddenly. She had to find a way off this ship. She whirled around only to slam into a hard figure with dark eyes.

4

Lucas surveyed the scene. Men were bustling about loading cargo onto *The Trinity*. It was a familiar sight, if not a beautiful one; gruff men loading dirty boxes onto a ship, in the morning fog. It looked chaotic and yet there was a kind of grace to it. One exception being the small cabin boy that had just stumbled up to Alaric; nearly dropping the load that was unmistakably too heavy for him. Once on board, it all became clear. The lad had somehow found his way on board the wrong ship, not just any ship, but a privateer ship. Clearly, he had meant to board a passenger ship instead. Lucas laughed, the lad was in for a big surprise. They were ready to set sail. Even if he jumped ship and swam back to the docks, it would be of no use. There were no more passenger ships due to come in that day.

He walked over to the boy, ready to explain the situation and that he had just unwittingly signed himself onto a privateer ship. Suddenly the boy turned around, slamming right into him. Short, rounded shoulders, Lucas estimated him to be no more than fifteen.

"How old are you, lad?" Lucas asked.

"I...well...I," Catherine fumbled for words. It had not occurred to her to think of her age or a name for that matter.

She could not very well use her own.

"Spit it out, lad, we don't have all day. Your age!" Lucas demanded.

"Fourteen, Sir. I...I am fourteen." Catherine decided since she was wearing the clothes of a fourteen-year-old boy and it made her look far younger, she might as well say she was.

"Very well, and your name?" The man asked.

"I," Oh blast it, why had she not thought of a name? "Allen...Treadfast, Allen Treadfast, Sir." Catherine said, lifting her head a bit and sticking out her chin.

"Treadfast?" The corner of Lucas's lips twitched slightly. "Very well, Allen Treadfast," he said in a tone that made Catherine uneasy. "Welcome to *The Trinity*. I am Captain Lucas Harding and that there," he pointed to the tall man holding the board and parchment, "is Alaric, my first mate. By the looks of you and your state of confusion, I believe it is safe to say that you have never set foot on a ship before." Lucas looked the boy over, amusement in his dark eyes. "Follow Ol' Shorty around for a bit. He will teach you how things are done on board. Once you get the hang of it, we will find you a proper place."

Lucas gestured towards the older sailor that was working with the rigging. He chuckled, shook his head, and walked off. It was only then, that Catherine realized the ship was no longer anchored. In fact, the port was now growing farther and farther away. It would not be long before her home was but a speck on the horizon.

When they were a few hours from port, Lucas strode over to Alaric who was at the helm. "What do you make of the new recruits? Particularly the small lad?" Lucas gestured with a grin towards the boy who called himself Allen Treadfast. He had just fallen backwards onto a mess of ropes. The lad was definitely hiding. More than likely a runaway from one of the plantations, the boy's father probably owned or work on one of the many on the Island. He could not blame the boy, he would not want to live such a dull life either. The fact was he would have to find out who the boy really was and find a way to get word to his family, letting them know what happened so they would not think he kidnapped the lad. *While on board Allen is going to pull his weight, it will be good for him,* Lucas thought.

"The others seem to know a bit about sailing. Many of them have been on ships before and have at least done a hard day's work. I don't believe the lad, has done much of either. I heard what he told Ol' Shorty, 'bout being on the wrong ship and saying he was supposed to be on *The Alice*. What are you going to do about him?" Alaric asked, his hand steady on the wheel.

"I agree with you there, he definitely is not accustomed to working, let alone on a ship. But there is nothing to be done about it. We've a deadline to meet, we are merchants this time, remember?" Lucas smirked.

"Ah, it won't be too bad. Maybe we should slow down and enjoy this trip, if all goes well, we may not even have to see battle." Alaric shrugged.

"Well, with so many new recruits, you are probably right. Maybe that would be for the best, if we didn't see battle this trip." Lucas glanced back at Allen. He was not sure how the boy would take a battle. It was hard enough on a seasoned sailor to witness the destruction. He had seen grown men vomit or even faint from nerves, before they took a ship. "Plus, we need to think about our task the Governor assigned. We need to avoid enemy ships as much as possible. Not only can we not afford to be too late in delivering the parchment to Monsieur Dupont, we also cannot risk it getting into enemy hands." Lucas said, as he scanned the horizon.

Alaric nodded as they looked out over the deck of the ship. The sailors seemed to be getting along just fine. Lucas believed on keeping strict order, but he also allowed the men to have their fun. He did not believe in flogging and the crew had always respected him for that and he respected them in turn.

In the last several years as Captain, he had only ever made one man walk the plank, so to speak. The man caused trouble for him and the rest of the crew the moment they set sail; constantly stirring the men up and causing fights to break out. One night, after they had just taken a ship and half the crew was manning the prize ship, the sailor had tried to mutiny against Lucas. In the morning Lucas sailed the ship out to one of the tiny specks of an island and dropped the wretch there.

For the most part, it had been the same crew since he first became Captain of *The Trinity*. When they went into port, there would always be a few new men that would want to sign up. Usually, it was because they could not find work elsewhere, some wanted adventure. Most of them did not last, they would discover Privateering was not for them.

Lucas hopped down from the upper deck. He headed below and through the door to his cabin, straight to the long chest that fit snuggly against the far wall. He opened it, sifting through the large pieces of parchment until he found the one he was looking for. It had been a long time since he had sailed to France, he wanted to be sure of the best route to take and what ports would be safest.

He unrolled the map on top of the desk that sat in the back of the cabin, just in front of a small window. Studying the map, hands placed on either side of it, he held it down to keep it from rolling back up. The parchment was covered in marks that would have confused a non-sailor. Lucas studied it for some time; the different routes, where enemy ships would most likely be and what ports the merchants and passenger ships would stop at. He needed to speak to Cook and discuss how long provisions would last and which port would have the best food supplies. Before he spoke to Cook though, he wanted to meet with Doc.

Lucas knocked on the wall that led to Doc's quarters and surgery room. "Come in, come in, Captain," Doc waved him in not looking up from rummaging through his books that lay neatly stacked in a chest. "What can I help you with?"

"Well, I wanted to talk to you about the new recruits. One new lad in particular. He is very young and has obviously never worked so much as a day in his life, let alone been on a ship before, definitely not a privateer ship. I am a bit concerned. I believe he is the son of one of the plantation owners from the islands. He of course did not say as much. The lad claims to be an Allen Treadfast." Lucas said rubbing the back of his neck.

Other than being concerned about the boy's family possibly accusing Lucas of kidnapping him, he really did not know why he was so concerned for the boy's welfare. Him and Alaric had only been two years older than Allen when they found themselves on a ship for the first time. Of course, that had been different. They had each other and were used to hard labor and working out in any weather condition.

Doc looked up with a twinkle in his eyes. "You are a good Captain, try not to be too concerned. I have no doubt this lad will be like many before him. They find their way on the ships, and either find they have the salty, ocean water running through their veins and sailing becomes a part of them or they discover it's not for them and leave the ship at the next port." Doc paused. "If he did run away, it might have been for the best, I have heard some of those plantation owners can be ruthless and cruel. Perhaps his father was not that friendly towards him. If he were a good father, maybe the lad just needed to find himself."

"I should think you do not have to worry about the boy's father causing a ruckus, either." Doc added, as if reading the Captain's mind. He was right of course, they knew nothing of the boy's past or life. Being on Lucas's ship might be the best thing for the lad, at least that is what Lucas hoped.

"Thank you, Doc. You are probably right. Let's keep an eye on him. I would feel better if we learned more about him and who his folks are. I do not want any trouble, especially not when we are under direct orders from the Governor. If he says anything to you or you hear anything, let me know." Lucas sighed, feeling a bit better about the odd situation.

"You got it, Captain. I will see what I can find out." Doc turned back to his chest of books.

5

Catherine stood at the railing, watching her home fade away as they sailed on. She took a deep breath, is this not what she had wanted? To experience being on a real ship? To have a story to tell and see new places? She looked over at the old sailor she had spoken to earlier. *The Captain had said his name was Ol' Shorty, surely that was just what he was called on the ship and by the crew and not his real name, Catherine thought.* She looked around.

Sailors were everywhere, all focused on different tasks. Completely lost, she had not expected to work on the ship she would sail on. This was not what she had envisioned. It could not be helped now though; she might as well make the best of it and get busy. She looked over at the old sailor once more. He seemed kind enough when she spoke to him before. Catherine walked over to him.

"Excuse me, the Captain told me to come see you." She deepened her voice, she needed to do that if she expected this to work. What would happen if they found out that under these scratchy garments, she was a woman? Catherine grew pale. She would have to be careful and never let her guard down.

Ol' Shorty squinted up at her. He was about an inch or

two shorter than her. "Aye. Right then, see that there clump of ropes?" He pointed a gnarled, crooked finger at a large pile of ropes. "You untangle them, then once you are done, come see me again and I will give you your next job." Ol' Shorty smiled, showing a missing tooth. He slapped Catherine on the shoulder. The sudden impact sent Catherine stumbling backwards onto the mass of ropes. Chuckling he called out over his shoulder as he walked off, "Better get your sea legs there, laddie."

She looked around, several sailors were grinning and laughing. Her face burned. How had she gotten herself into this mess. She stood up, brushing herself off and set to the task of untangling the horrendous mass.

On the deck, most all the other sailors were doing their jobs with relative ease. She spotted the Captain and his first mate, Alaric, talking at the wheel. She felt her face flame again, had the Captain seen her fall? If he did see, she did not want him thinking she was not capable. This was far from the kind of passage she expected but she was here now and she could not let them see through her. She was determined to enjoy her adventure. Maybe once they got to the next port, she could find a passenger ship, though she doubted it. It had not worked too well for her the first time. For now, she had to hide her identity and enjoy herself. At least, this twist in her plans would certainly make for an exciting story.

The Captain made her feel uneasy, she got the feeling he did not believe her. She watched him step away from his friend and walk below deck. Now that he was out of sight, she felt as if she could breathe a bit easier.

Catherine busied herself with the rough and heavy ropes. The weight made it hard to untangle them and sort them out.

Occasionally, she looked up when a sailor shouted a command or when a sea bird squawked above. The salty breeze on her face cooled her. The swaying ship still felt odd to her; since she did not have her sea legs yet.

Catherine felt like she dealt with the ropes for hours, making very little progress with the mess at her feet. Soaked in sweat, her neck burned from the beating sun. Worse, her hands had become completely raw from the rough fibers. She ran her arm across her forehead, wiping away a bead of sweat that was slowly trickling down towards her eyes.

"Not bad, young Allen." Ol' Shorty chuckled as he walked up. "Let us take a look at those hands of yours." Catherine placed her small hand in his thick, rough one. "That'll do, kid. These here blisters will heal up and your hands will get used to the rough work. Bit o' time before they be lookin' like mine though." He said, letting out another chuckle. Catherine smiled despite herself. "Best go soak em' in the bucket of cool water for a bit," Ol' Shorty said, gesturing to a full bucket that sat beside her. Catherine slowly dipped her hands into the bucket, wincing when the cool water stung her raw, torn skin.

She soaked her hands for as long as she thought they needed, then stood up, and turned towards the edge of the ship. Peering over the railing, she watched as the water rolled and swirled as the ship passed through it. Catherine placed her hands on her back and stretched. To her horror, she realized her shirt was sticking to her from all the sweat. Her face flamed once more. She could not think of another time that she had been this mortified, so many times in a single day. She quickly folded her arms in front of her and whirled around, checking to see if anyone had noticed or if any of the men were watching her.

"You alright there, laddie?" Ol' Shorty asked, with a raised, bushy eyebrow.

"No, thank you, I...I just need a moment." Catherine said

with a squeak and rushed towards the hatch that led below deck. She ran down the hall and opened one of the doors. The room was filled with barrels, boxes, ropes and what looked to be extra sails. Catherine went in and closed the door behind her. Frantically looking around, she spied a pile of fabric folded behind some boxes. She had no idea if it was important, what it was used for or if it would even be missed but she had little choice at the moment. Tearing off a piece, she quickly wrapped her chest. She fixed her shirt and looked at herself as best she could. Letting out a very relieved sigh she decided it was safe to go back on deck and finish what she had been doing before anyone suspected her. She turned as the door swung open. Ol' Shorty stood in the doorway.

"I know what you are doing." He said simply, with a lopsided grin.

"You do?" Catherine asked, her heart dropping to her toes.

"Yes, I remember feeling the same way and having the same trouble as you are now, when I first stepped foot on board a rolling ship." He grimaced.

Catherine stared at the old sailor. Surely, he could not possibly be thinking what she thought he was. "I am sorry, I am not sure what you mean." She finally said.

"Ack, there is nothing to be ashamed of laddie, most new sailors find themselves with a wee bit o' seasickness." Ol' Shorty waved a hand in the air. Catherine felt as if she could breathe again, her pounding heart slowing. "Come, the trick is to stare straight at the horizon and wait until it passes." He explained, pointing straight ahead as he guided Catherine out of the door and into the corridor. "Do not worry though, I'll take ye to the doc and he can make you a tea to stop yer stomach from churning like the sea." They came to another door. "Doc, you in there? I got you yer first patient of the voyage." Ol' Shorty gently pounded a meaty fist on the door.

Doc opened the door and peered down at Catherine from above his spectacles. His silver hair making him look much older. "Do you indeed?" Looking Catherine over, he gestured for them to enter. "Come in, no need to block the companionway." He said with a welcoming gesture. "Shorty, you can get back up top, I believe I can take it from here, the boy doesn't look as if he could be too dangerous."

Shorty gestured as if he were tipping a hat to the Doc. "Aye," he said, walking out and closing the door behind him.

"Now that we got that old coot out of the way," Doc grinned. "What is it that is troubling you, lad?"

Catherine squirmed a little, "Err, it is just a bit of seasickness. Ol' Shorty told me that you might have a tea that can ease my stomach." She could not help but lick her lips, tea sounded wonderful to her parched throat. Her stomach grumbled, embarrassingly loud. Her hand flew to her middle.

Doc laughed, "Not to worry, I believe you just need a bit of food and drink and you will be just fine." He said, placing a gentle hand on Catherine's shoulder. "Lucky for you, I have tea and since we just left port, I was able to stock up on biscuits that I keep in here with me for occasions much like this."

Catherine watched as Doc made up a cup of tea and put several biscuits on a small, cracked plate. Her mouth watered.

Doc handed Catherine the plate and motioned for her to take a seat on a stool in the corner of the small room. "Thank you, Doc. This looks great." She spoke quietly, not daring to look up at the man, afraid he would see through her disguise.

"Not a problem, Young Allen." Doc replied, sitting in a chair in front of a small desk. "This is your first time aboard a ship? What made a young lad like yourself want to board a Privateer ship?" He asked simply, taking a sip of his own tea.

"A...a privateer ship? You mean this is actually a Privateer ship?" Catherine choked on her biscuit. She had known it was not a passenger ship, but she had thought perhaps it might be a merchant ship instead.

"Yes it is, this is *The Trinity*." He smiled. "I gather that you were not expecting to be on board this particular ship. What one was it you were meant to be on?"

She did not know how much she should say, but she figured sticking as close to the truth was best. "I was trying to buy passage on *The Alice*. One of the women tending the stalls had pointed me in the direction of where it was supposed to be anchored. Before I could find the correct ship, I was herded onto here instead. When I realized I was on the wrong ship, Ol' Shorty told me that The Alice had in fact already sailed." She explained, closing her eyes and thinking of how this all took a drastic turn. "If this is a Privateer ship, then it will be staying in these waters correct? So, as soon as we make port again, I can just find another ship to take me back to Barbados, right?" Catherine asked hopefully. She did not like the idea of her adventure ending so soon but she was not sure how long she wanted to stay on board a Privateer ship. She had read stories about them and was not entirely sure she was prepared to face what was to come.

"Sorry, but you boarded at a rather inopportune time. Yes, typically we would be staying in these very waters and I would say that you could easily find your way back home once we made port again. However, on this voyage we are headed to France on strict orders. There will be no turning back until the orders have been carried out." Doc stated sympathetically. He studied Catherine for a moment, the shock and disbelief clear on her face. "Do not fret, it should be a relatively uneventful voyage." Doc thought about asking more but from the look on Catherine's face, he thought it best to wait.

Catherine finished up her biscuits and tea. She thanked

the doc. He had been kind and made her feel a bit better about the situation. She headed back up on deck to find Ol' Shorty.

Lucas opened the door to his cabin to go back up top when Allen ran down the short companionway and into one of the extra supply cabins. He was about to go in and check when Ol' Shorty came down and waved the Captain off, explaining he would take care of the boy. Lucas nodded and left him to it, heading to the upper deck. Alaric was no longer at the wheel; he was speaking with one of the sailors. Lucas walked to the helm, "You may get back to your other duties, Eddie, I'll take it from here."

The sailor nodded, "Aye, Cap'n."

Lucas gripped the wheel; the wood was relatively smooth from years of wear. He felt the pull as the waves guided the ship. He listened to the crew as they worked, the sounds of the ocean and the sea birds echoed in his ears. Lucas could stand at the helm for hours, it helped him think, helped him focus.

He was seventeen the first time he ever stood behind the massive wheel of a ship. Him and Alaric had been sentenced to serve time on a Royal Navy ship for three years. The second year they served, the ship was approaching an enemy that they had been pursuing for weeks. Lucas was standing nearby as Captain Robert Harris shouted commands and the cannons exploded, rocking the ship. It was not the first battle Lucas had been in, but this battle had been different, they could not afford to lose this particular ship.

Suddenly the Captain was laying on the deck, bleeding from a wound on his side. The first mate took charge, shouting for men to carry the Captain below and giving orders to fire. Lucas, seeing that no one was manning the helm, leapt towards the wheel, a piece of splintered wood narrowly missing his head. As soon as his hands touched the helm, he felt completely in charge and knew that was exactly where he was meant to be. Him and Alaric served one more year aboard Captain Harris's ship. Then Lucas gained his own and was granted the Letter of Marque, with help from the Governor of the West Indies.

Lucas noticed Allen came back on deck and headed straight back to his duties. The lad certainly seemed to be trying to hold his own and was following orders as best he could.

A humming sound began to travel through the crew. Several sailors looked up as Lucas started stomping his foot in rhythm. The rest of the crew followed suit, many moved their feet or clapped their hands along to the beat. The crew often sung different shanties as they worked. The words carrying on the air seemed to invigorate the crew.

What will we do with a drunken Sailor?
What will we do with a drunken Sailor?
What will we do with a drunken Sailor?
Early in the morning!
Way hay and up she rises
Way hay and up she rises
Way hay and up she rises
Early in the morning!

Lucas sang along to the tune as the crew worked. Even young Allen was watching. No doubt he had not heard anything quite like it. As the shanty ended, Lucas called for Eddie to take the helm again. He needed to get back to his cabin and fill in his books. As Captain, he had to keep strict records of everything and everyone on board his ship. He also knew Cook would be serving his evening meal soon. Since they just left port and had stocked up on goods, it was sure to be a good one.

Lucas hired Cook not long after he became Captain. Cook walked right up to him in a tavern they had stopped at to recruit their crew and told him he would sign on as cook. Seeing as they did not have one as of yet, Lucas saw no harm in giving the man a try. Turned out to be one of the best decisions he had made. Cook had grown up in France and learned the trade from his mother who was the head cook for many years at one of the castles. Lucas sat down at his desk and set to work on marking the books.

There was a light knock at his door. Lucas looked up. "Come in." The door opened. Allen stood in the doorway, looking down at a tray with a jug on it and a plate of food.

"Come in," he said again. "You can set the tray on the desk, just there," he pointed to a spot on his desk. The boy still made no move. Lucas chuckled, "I am really not all that bad, laddie." The boy took a tentative step forward as if he were approaching a wild animal. Lucas watched as Allen set the tray down where he had indicated and looked up, his eyes wide as he looked around the room.

Lucas's lips turned up a bit, "Didn't expect this size of a room on a ship, aye?" he asked. Allen slightly shook his head. Lucas had been surprised the first time he walked into Captain Harris's cabin. He had to deliver a message and he could not believe how large the room was or how many books, maps, charts, and chests it contained.

He noticed Allen staring at the sextant on his desk. Lucas picked it up and turned it round in his hand. "It is called a sextant, sailors use it to help them navigate, it helps us to know if we are on course or which way we should be going. Care to take a look?" He handed it to Allen, who took it very gingerly in his hands. Lucas noted how small they were.

"I have read about these." Allen spoke quietly. "You look at the stars, moon or sun and the horizon with it, correct? That is how you find where you are going?" The lad looked up at Lucas, their eyes meeting briefly before the boy quickly looked down again.

Lucas grinned, he appreciated how interested the lad was in sailing and how much he knew about the sextant. For never being on a ship before, that was surprising. He wondered what else the lad knew about sailing. He looked down at the instrument in Allen's hand, "You are correct, that is more or less how it works. Where did you read about sailing?" He asked casually.

Allen shrugged, now looking at the map on his desk. "My father has lots of books, I read most of them. Several of them are about sailing." He said, engrossed with everything in the room. He gently set the instrument back down on the desk. Allen looked up; Lucas was studying him. "I need to get back up top." Allen hurried out of the room, clicking the door shut behind him.

For a minute Lucas saw a different side of the lad. He had said his father had lots of books and that he had read most of them, giving Lucas the impression that he did in fact come from a life of privilege. The corner of Lucas's lips turned up, the fact the boy was literate told Lucas that the boy's supposed last name was not a mere coincidence. Lucas looked over at his tray of food. His mouth watered. It was a roast, seasoned to perfection, surrounded by various vegetables and gravy. He took a swig of the ale from the tray.

Lucas looked out the window behind him, the sun was down, and the sea was steady. He kicked his boots off and climbed onto his bed. His men all slept in hammocks in the main sleeping quarters. He had a hammock he could string up in his cabin if need be, but he preferred the bed. He was asleep within minutes.

Lucas heard the canons firing, the clashing of swords, guns going off and the screams of men. He was trying desperately to see through the thick air of gunpowder and smoke. The fray. He had a sickening feeling, something was terribly wrong, he looked around. Alaric was fighting, unscathed. He scanned the fighting men, mentally checking off who was still standing. Sweat poured down his face and back, where was Allen? He heard a shout from behind him. He whirled around; the blood drained from his face. A figure was standing there, holding a flintlock to the boy's head. The boy looked terrified, exhausted, and helpless. There was a loud bang. Lucas's world went black.

He shot up with a jolt. Shaking from the dream, sweat poured down his body. Dreams of a marooned man seeking revenge on him, plagued his sleep. There was another bang, it registered that someone was at the door. He ran a hand over his face and swung his legs off the bed. "Come in." He grunted. He reached for his boots and slipped them on as the door opened. "What is it?" He asked.

"Ship on the Horizon Cap'n." The sailor said. "Alaric told me to fetch ye."

"Thank you, Benjamin. I'll be right up." Lucas said nodding to the young sailor whose scraggly long hair fell in his face. Benjamin turned and closed the door behind him as he left.

    Lucas stood up and grabbed his spy glass from his desk. He headed for the hatch and marched up on deck. Alaric was on the Quarterdeck, keeping a close eye on the ship on the horizon. "What have we got?" He asked as he approached his first mate. At the railing, Lucas raised the spy glass to his eye to get a better look.

7

Thomas shook the small cup then quickly tipped it over. The dice spilled out, rolling across the table, threatening to roll off completely. He laughed, his smile not reaching his eyes, "Looks like you lost again, mate." He said gathering up the coins he won.

"Another go?" The sailor asked, desperate to win his coins back.

"Nah, I have an important meeting to get to." Thomas stood, pocketing the coins. He sneered at the sailor who still sat at the table. He patted his pocket, the metal clinking together. He turned and marched out of the door of the *Rusty Anchor.*

Thomas waited in one of the many sitting rooms of the Governor's house. He snorted as he looked around at the fine rugs, furniture, and books that lined the room. Thomas noticed a long mirror in the corner of the large sitting room. He strode over to it. He looked himself up and down, turning to the side slightly. He smiled to himself, rubbing the stubble on his chin.

His blonde hair was tied back, a few loose strands falling along the side of his face. His attire certainly was not the finest, but, nor was it ripped or torn like many other sailors. His loose, white shirt hung low, showing part of the tattoo of a large compass with a map of the Caribbean waters under it, on his chest. A gold chain hung from his neck, many rings and bracelets adorned his fingers and wrists. In the mirror's reflection, Thomas spotted crystal glasses on a table that sat between two chairs, near the fireplace. He walked over to them and poured himself a glass. He took a long drink and sat the glass back down.

"I see you helped yourself," Thomas had not even heard the Governor walk in.

"Ah, I hope you do not mind." He said, nodding to the man before him.

"Not at all, what did you think of it? I just had it recently imported from France." The Governor said with a flourish, gesturing towards the drink. He ran his thumb and forefinger along his greying mustache.

"Not bad at all, though I must admit, I do prefer the taste of rum." He smirked.

"Come, let us talk in my study." The Governor walked out and headed down the hall. They entered a room, more shelves lined with various items, each probably worth more than Thomas saw in a single year. "Please, have a seat." The Governor sat on the other side of the desk. "Tell me, why have you asked to meet with me Mr. Banning?" He asked, folding his hands together on top of his desk.

"I have a ship and I have a crew, now I am in need of a Letter of Marque. I was hoping you would be able to help me obtain it." Thomas replied, leaning forward in the chair.

The Governor studied Thomas for a moment. "I tell you what. I have a man out on a voyage at the moment. He is to deliver a certain deed to a plantation to a man in France. If he is unable to carry out the task, then I will have you step in. Once you complete it, you will get your Letter of Marque. But only if he does not carry it out first." The Governor said bluntly.

Thomas clenched his jaw. He knew the Governor was using him and would continue to do so when it suited him. "Very well, I…" He was cut short by a knock on the door.

"Enter." The Governor demanded.

The Butler opened the door to the study. "There is a man at the door insisting on your presence, My Lord."

"If you will excuse me Mr. Banning, I shall be back in a moment." He said, then walked out of the room without a second glance. The butler closed the door behind them.

Thomas jumped up and quickly rummaged around on the Governor's desk, looking for any information he could find about the Captain or the ship the Governor had ordered to take the deed to France. He flipped a letter over. It was not finished yet, but it said all he needed to know. The man in France was a Monsieur Dupont and the Captain delivering the deed was Captain Harding on *The Trinity*. Thomas slammed his fist down before returning the letter to it's original position on the desk.

So, Lucas still had the Governor's favor, he thought, hate flushing his cheeks. Not for long, he would change that. He sat back in the chair and waited for the Governor to return.

"I do apologize for the interruption. A matter of business, you understand." The Governor commented as he reentered the study.

"But of course, no need to apologize." Thomas waved a hand in the air. "I thought about it, I will await your orders, Sir. Should this Captain not succeed, I will be ready to sail for France at once. I shall be patrolling the waters around here. If you should need me, I will not be hard to find." He assured the Governor.

"Splendid." The Governor rose from his seat. Thomas followed suit, taking his cue to leave.

"I look forward to hearing from you, Sir." He bowed and saw himself out. *The Governor certainly does not waste time,* he thought.

He headed back to the taverns to gather his crew. Thomas did not plan on waiting around in case Harding should fail. There was very little chance of that happening. If he wanted his Letter of Marque, Thomas was going to have to cause a little accident for *The Trinity*. He might be a couple days behind Harding but that would not matter. He had no doubt he could catch up. He looked forward to getting his revenge on his ex-Captain.

When Captain Lucas Harding marooned him on the tiny island, Thomas had to wait over a week before a ship finally spotted him, red and sick with exhaustion. There had been a little freshwater stream to drink from, but he had little shade and relatively no food. Luckily, he was able to catch a couple crabs that had washed up on driftwood from one of the larger islands. Harding had not taken too kindly to being mutinied upon. Thomas had underestimated Lucas's fighting abilities and the amount of loyalty he had earned from his crew. This time, Thomas would be careful to not make the same mistakes.

Thomas swung the tavern door open and scanned the tables. The whole building reeked of ale, rum, and the smell of men who had not bathed in weeks. There was a crash as a pint of ale went flying into a wall, followed by a sailor being tossed into a table. He shook his head and walked around the mess towards the man he named his first mate.

"Grady, round the crew up, prepare to sail. We leave as soon as everyone is on board." Thomas growled. He knew his crew would not be happy about sailing immediately. They had only arrived in Barbados the day before. Thomas moved his hand to his flintlock, daring his first mate to question his orders.

Grady swallowed hard, not taking his eyes off Thomas. "Yes, Capt'n, we will be ready to sail immediately." Grady attempted to aid Thomas in the mutiny on *The Trinity*. When it had not gone as planned, Grady was kicked off at the next port. Thomas knew that Grady would do just about anything Thomas asked of him.

"Good," He replied bluntly and walked out of the Tavern. He was itching to get his hands on Captain Harding and gain his Letter of Marque at any cost. Thomas boarded his ship and headed straight for his cabin, he would give his first mate a couple hours to get the crew together and on board. He needed to look at one of the maps, he had to try and stay one step ahead of Lucas to be able to catch him. He studied the map in front of him. Since Lucas was on orders from the Governor he would need to try and stay out of sight of enemy ships, which left only one or two routes and only a few ports.

8

Catherine watched the Captain and Alaric, they were talking and the Captain held his spy glass to his eyes. The Captain stood tall and confident, observing the ship they were approaching. His dark hair was pulled back and he stood with his legs apart slightly; many of the crew stood like that and she found herself doing the same. It seemed to help her balance though she figured she did not look as confident or as fierce as the Captain.

His white shirt billowed in the breeze, tightening briefly around the muscles that lined his arms. He turned to Alaric and spoke. Catherine was too far to hear them. Just then Alaric bellowed something about a flag. The crew seemed more at ease now, though most stayed at their stations. A few bustled about, raising a white flag. From what she had read, that meant they were not going to fight. She looked at the other ship, and noticed that they too were waving a white flag. Catherine slowly let out a breath.

"See lad, nothing to get worked up about, just a mere merchant ship." Ol' Shorty laughed.

The crew gathered a large plank as they approached the ship. They tossed ropes to the other ship to bring them closer and keep them joined as the Captain of the other ship and a few of the crew members crossed over to *The Trinity*. Captain Harding and Alaric walked steadily over to them. The Captains greeted one another then the Captain stepped aside and motioned to a man standing behind him. The man stepped forward; Catherine's heart leapt into her throat.

It was her father. Could he have heard of her escape already? The other Captain was now pointing to his ship and Captain Harding was nodding. She had no idea what they were saying but she could not risk getting any closer.

"Looks like we will be having guests tonight," Shorty grinned.

Excitement buzzed through the crew. Captain Harding, the other ship's Captain, and her father all strode across the deck and through the hatch. Catherine blew out another breath. If they stayed below, there would be little risk of her being discovered. She just had to avoid him at all costs. She busied herself with untangling the ropes, she still had not fully untangled them though she had made a lot more progress.

Alaric strode over to Benjamin, "Grab a few of the crew to help you, we are giving a couple boxes of our extra supplies to Captain Lester. They were preyed upon by a pirate ship yesterday. Most of their provisions and supplies are gone, they will also will need help repairing the rigging, they lost several crew members."

"Yes, sir," Benjamin shouted to a few of the shipmates to join him in transferring the supplies.

Alaric turned to Catherine, "Allen, Cook will need assistance in serving the meal to our guests. Captain Lester and Lord Benedict will be joining us tonight." Catherine paled.

"Sir, I have never served a meal before…I," she tried desperately to think of an excuse to not have to be in the same room as her father. She stammered, "Sir, I would not want to mess up or embarrass Captain Harding, maybe one of the other crew members should do it."

"Is that so? I am sure the Captain would be happy to hear you would not want to embarrass him. That being said, I suggest you do as you are told." Alaric arched an eyebrow and stared at Catherine. She swallowed hard. He was almost as intimidating as the Captain. "Simply bring in the meal and poor the wine when needed." The corner of his mouth turned up as he shot a glance at Shorty.

"Yes, Sir." Catherine whispered, not daring to look up.

"Best get yerself to Cook, in case he needs you now. It will be some time before he serves the meal but he might be glad of a hand before then." Shorty said as he walked off.

Catherine shook. Her father was sure to recognize her, then what? Not only would her father be furious, but she dreaded to think how Captain Harding would respond. She stepped through the hatch and into the galley.

"Cook, can I give you a hand with the meal? Alaric said you would be needing me to serve." She swallowed again, she looked at her shaking hands and tucked them into her pockets. She had to stop, or Cook would notice something was amiss.

"Aye, laddie, peel and chop these." Cook handed Catherine a knife and a bag full of potatoes. Back home, she had watched the cook and the other kitchen staff work. She would go down there just to have someone to talk to when her father was away. They had always been really kind to her, and they had taught her a few tricks. She carefully gripped the knife, and slowly began peeling. She caught Cook watching her, "You gonna have ta peel faster than that if we want 'em to be done in time." He pointed to the bag that sat next to her.

"Yes, Sir." Catherine whispered. It was a slow start, she peeled a couple more, by the fourth potato, she was peeling much quicker.

She paused, wiped an arm across her forehead and looked at her handy work. "Done!" She smiled up at Cook. The potatoes were peeled and chopped. "What next?"

"Chop the carrots and watch the gravy, don't let it burn." Cook replied, glancing up for only a second, his round cheeks pink from working over the makeshift oven in the galley.

Catherine chopped the carrots while watching the gravy, she was not entirely sure what she was watching for. She grabbed a small spoon and stirred it a bit. It smelled wonderful. Her stomach grumbled. She was not used to eating only twice a day. Back home they would eat throughout the day. If she were to get hungry, there was always biscuits in jars in the rooms or she would only need to ring the bell and the maids or footmen would bring her refreshments. Catherine watched as Cook sprinkled herbs and spices over the meat and vegetables.

"Start the biscuits." Cook pointed to what she guessed to be a bag of flour.

"Uh, biscuits?" Catherine had no idea how to make them or what she needed other than the flour that sat in front of her.

"Aye, biscuits, the water and salt are over there, mix them together and put them there." Cook pointed to the other two ingredients, then to a pan on the small table.

Catherine poured a bit of flour out, added salt and water. She tried mixing it together like she had seen the cook back home do, but it was far too runny. She added more flour and another pinch of salt. She stirred the batter with a wooden spoon, it started coming together and forming a dough. Catherine turned to see Cook watching her carefully.

"Aye, that'll do it." He approved. "Once the meal is finished, you will bring in the biscuits, cheese and more wine for them. Set the biscuits and cheese on the table and they will serve themselves." Catherine's eyebrows shot up. "We ain't like them fancy houses on the Islands. I will bring in the meat and vegetables. You pour the wine for the Capt'ns and the Lord." Cook explained.

"After I bring the food in and pour the wine, may I leave?" She asked hopefully.

"Sorry laddie, I will be cleanin' the galley, you need to stay and pour the wine when they should need more and wait in there in case Capt'n asks you for anything else." Cook shrugged. "Once they are finished with their meal, you clear the table and wait for further orders."

When the meal was ready, Catherine tried desperately to slow her pounding heart and her shaking hands. She was sure her father would recognize her. Firmly, she held the platter with cheese and biscuits as she followed Cook into the Captain's Cabin. His desk was against the wall and a large dining table sat in the middle of the room. Where they had pulled the dining table from, she could not imagine.

She carefully walked over to the table and sat the tray down. Turning quickly, she fled the cabin to grab the wine. The men were talking and laughing when she walked back in. Captain Harding nodded and signaled for her to pour his wine. She slowly walked over to him, not daring to look towards her father. Captain Harding flashed her a smile, thanking her for the food and drink.

Captain Lester was telling a story about a seagull that had followed them on an entire journey once. "He became like a part of the crew; he would even eat from our hands." He laughed. Catherine stepped over, filling Alaric's glass before moving towards Captain Lester's. She poured the wine, trying not to shake, for fear of spilling it and drawing attention to herself. Her father was laughing at Captain Lester's story, Alaric and Captain Harding were smiling politely.

She held her breath as she poured her father his wine.

"Thank you, boy," Her father spoke, causing her to jolt. He was not looking at her, instead, taking a long drink from his glass. She stepped back against the wall, wishing she could sink into it completely. No one seemed to be paying attention to her. She now had to wait until one of them needed more wine or until the Captain gave her further orders. The delicious food that lay on the table in front of her tempted her. The men that sat around the table, ate, drank, and talked jovially. She stayed alert incase anything was said about her or to her.

"What makes a plantation owner such as yourself travel on a merchant vessel, My Lord?" Captain Harding asked her father.

"Aw well, you see, I own a couple of merchant ships, that one out there being one of them," he stated. "For one thing, as much as I do not enjoy leaving my daughter for long periods of time, I do enjoy being out at sea and traveling. Though, that is not exactly what brought me on this particular venture. To be entirely honest," her father sat up and leaned forward on the table, resting his arms on it as he spoke. "I am in search of a partner for the plantation, one who will invest a bit in it." He took a drink before elaborating. "The first several years, my plantation yielded a goodly amount of crops. Unfortunately, these last couple of years it has not done so well. I have invested just about as much as I can to save the plantation."

Catherine felt as if the world was crashing in on her. Why had her father not told her? She put her hand on her middle, she blinked hard, desperately trying not to pass out. If she left though, she would be most likely discovered. She looked up to see if anyone had noticed her reaction. Her eyes locked with Captain Hardings, a flash of concern passing over his face.

"Allen, thank you, you may go and enjoy your own meal, we will call you if we need anything." He nodded to Catherine and smiled, then returned his gaze to his guests. Catherine turned and stepped out, closing the door behind her. She felt like screaming, like crying, like running back in that room and confronting her father. Demanding him to tell her how he could let this happen and why he had not told her. She wrapped her arms around her middle and stood at the closed door. Catherine wanted to know what else her father had to say but was thankful the Captain had excused her.

"I am sorry to hear it. If you cannot find someone to partner with you, what will you do?" Captain Harding asked.

"I am afraid, the Governor will seize the plantation. I would hate for that to happen. I know my daughter would be devastated. I am just thankful she will soon be wed, we have yet to announce it publicly but as soon as I return, I will be arranging for her to marry a Lord who recently became the owner of another plantation nearby." He replied, swirling the last of his drink in his glass before swallowing the rest.

Captain Harding's voice traveled loudly through the closed door. Catherine bit her lip, holding back the tears as best she could. That is why her father was having her marry Lord Anderson and so soon. It made sense. She closed her eyes, envisioning her home, her chamber, her father's study, the gardens and the stable, all the things she would miss terribly if they lost it.

From behind the door, a chair scraped against the floor. She stood up straight and inhaled, she thought of quickly going on deck but thought better of it. Cook had told her she was to clear the table. She better go back in and do it. She did not fancy the idea of facing the Captain if she disobeyed. Placing her hand on the handle, she opened it slowly, and stepped inside. Captain Harding caught her eye again briefly, before looking back at her father.

"At least you will not have to worry for your daughter. I am sure you will be able to find a partner to assist you with your plantation." Captain Harding raised his glass, the rest of the table followed. "To new adventures." He said, before bringing the glass to his lips, the rest of the men followed suit.

Catherine kept her head down as she gathered the plates and trays from the table. She quickly brought them to the galley. Cooked thanked her as she turned to head back to the Captain's cabin to clear the rest of the table. As she opened the door, she heard a tune begin on deck. The men started singing, she could hear what sounded like a violin and another instrument she could not name.

"Ah, a jolly tune, what do you say boys? Shall we go up and join the crew? Captain Lester asked, looking quite pleased.

"After you." Captain Harding and the others rose, he held his arm out indicating for them to exit the cabin.

Catherine stood against the wall, waiting for the men to leave before cleaning up.

9

Lucas noticed the boy begin to sway, he looked as if he would suddenly be sick. Perhaps being below decks for so long had brought on his sea sickness again. He had excused the boy, not wanting him to be sick in front of their guests. Alaric had already mentioned Allen's insecurities about serving their guests. He did not quite understand why the boy would be so worried, but he supposed he had his reasons. The rest of the crew enjoyed such events. It gave them a chance to take a break from their duties, play music, drink, and play dice.

As Lucas and the other men finished, Allen came back in, to Lucas's surprise and admiration. He suspected most young sailors would not have been able to pull themselves together to finish their duties. He saw many first-time sailors curled up or hanging themselves over the railing, ridding their stomachs of all their contents and not getting up for days. Lucas figured the boy's stomach would settle as soon as he got above deck and felt the breeze.

He felt sorry for Lord Benedict and was glad when Captain Lester suggested they go above deck and enjoy the entertainment from the crew. He had to admit, being a partner for a large plantation like Lord Benedict's was a mighty good offer. He was surprised he had not found a taker yet. Lord Benedict seemed like a decent fella; any man would be lucky to be his partner.

On the quarter deck, the men were having a good time, laughing and dancing a jig as the music played. Eddie played violin, he brought the instrument on board with him the day he signed on as part of the crew. Lucas found a comfortable seat against the wall next to the hatch. A lantern shined above him. He sat down on a barrel, tapping his hand against his leg to the rhythm that played around him. One of the crew members walked over to him and handed him a jug of ale.

"Cheers, Mate." Lucas grinned, smacking his cup against the sailor's. He looked around; a group of men, three from his ship and four from Captain Lester's, were engrossed in a game of dice. The men were cheering each other on and slapping one another on their backs, sloshing their drinks. One man stumbled as he was dancing along to the music, causing his drink to fly in the air. The sailor tripped, landing on his back. The men around him howled with laughter. Lucas shook his head, chuckling.

Alaric was leaning against the railing, talking with a man from the other ship. He spotted Allen sitting next to Ol' Shorty and a couple others. Ol' Shorty looked as if he was telling the young man a grand story. Lucas snorted, he could only imagine what exaggerated tale Shorty was telling the boy. Ol' Shorty stood up, waving his arms around frantically in the air before sitting down with a plop.

"Mighty fine night, wouldn't you agree?" Lord Benedict stood next to Lucas, watching the activity around them.

"Aye, it is." Lucas nodded. "Where is it you will be headed to from here?"

"Oh, I would like to make it to England. I am a bit behind schedule. I have exhausted all my resources in the West

Indies, so must try further from the Islands. I mentioned earlier that the Governor would seize my property if I can not get the plantation back to what it used to be and pay off my debts. The truth is, I do not have much time, I know there is a man the Governor has promised the plantation to. If I cannot find a partner in time, this man of his will get the deed to my property."

Lucas gave the Baron's shoulder a brief squeeze. "I wish you the best of luck, Mate. The Governor is a tough man." He thought about mentioning that he was under orders from said Governor, but thought twice of it.

"Ah but my daughter, she would love to be here, seeing this right now." He gestured to all the excitement on board the ship. "You know," he shrugged, "she asked to come along. I could not let her, of course. She does not know of the situation with the plantation. I believe a ship is far too dangerous for a female, particularly long voyages. She longs for adventure, she will be eighteen soon, and is growing restless." He smiled. "She is a lot like her mother."

Lucas could relate, he was much the same way at a younger age. "Well, you cannot blame the lass. Boys, waiting to become men, are often times just like that. That is the reason Alaric and I ended up here." Lucas looked up at the sky then back to the crew. He drained his cup and stood up, stretching. "I will see you first thing tomorrow to make sure you are set to sail." Lucas turned and opened the hatch, looking back over his shoulder at the Baron. "Enjoy the rest of your night." He said with a quick nod before ducking under the deck.

Lucas laid in bed, tired, but sleep evaded him. Something was bothering him but he did not know what. He felt uneasy about the parchment he was to deliver and after all the Baron had divulged, he felt even more uncertain about the Governor's order. The Governor was hiding something.

Clearly there was someone he wanted for the Plantation for one reason or another. Lord Benedict was obviously doing all he could.

Lucas sat up and swung his feet off his bed. Not bothering to pull his boots on he headed for the hatch. By the sound of it everyone, except the men on duty, were asleep. He strode on deck, pausing as the cool sea air hit his face. He rubbed his hand along his stubbled jaw. Gray, one of the new recruits high in the rigging, was keeping a close eye out for storms and approaching ships. The small waves hit against the hull of the *The Trinity*. There was a large splash, he turned but did not see what hit the water. By the sound of the splash and the force behind it, it was a whale, breeching the surface. He had seen whales leap from the ocean depths before, it was quite the sight, and certainly not one you are to forget in a hurry.

He spotted a figure with slender shoulders leaning up against the railing. He walked over to the boy. "Couldn't sleep either? Or is the sea sloshing in your stomach again?" The boy jumped at the sound of his voice but did not turn around. Lucas stepped up to the railing beside the lad.

"Did you see the whale?" Allen spoke quietly.

"Aye, I did not see him but I heard the splash as I walked up on deck. Quite a sight, eh?" Lucas leaned over and rested his forearms on the railing.

"Yes, it was. I have never seen anything like it before. I did not realize such large creatures were capable of leaping from the water like that. I had heard dolphins often follow ships and I have seen them once or twice from my window back home." His voice sounded far off but he now spoke a bit louder.

Lucas stared at the water, at night it looked almost black. "I have had dolphins follow the ship on occasion. It is not often I get a chance to see a whale leap out though. Usually, we see them simply swimming along, letting the sun warm their backs."

"They are so massive, have they ever attacked a ship?" Allen asked.

Lucas laughed. "Nah, I have heard tales of the Sperm whales being not too friendly towards ships, they can be mighty protective of their waters, but it is not something sailors need to generally worry about." He said, casting a sideways glance at the boy.

"Will Captain Lester's ship be sailing on in the morning? Where do they plan to go?" Allen asked. "Aye, they are on a schedule as well. They are headed to England. They have goods to deliver. Well what is left of them, the pirates took quite a bit, according to the Captain. They will be bringing goods back to the islands and the Baron is in search of a partner for his plantation."

He felt Allen tense next to him. Allen was staring straight at the water. Something was clearly bothering the boy. "You mentioned your father owns several books. I have a chest in my cabin filled with all kinds. If you want, tomorrow you can look, you are welcome to borrow any you wish. A few of the sailors on the ship enjoy a good book every now and then. Just be sure if you take one out to put it in the logbook. It is sitting in the chest as well." He thought maybe it would cheer the lad up if he had something to occupy his mind when he was not on duty.

Allen looked up at Lucas then, his eyes shining and his lips moved as if he were trying to speak. Lucas chuckled. "You are welcome." Lucas looked back at the rolling black water. The stars and moon's reflections were visible on the the glassy surface. Lucas looked up at the night sky, staring at the lights that broke up the blackness. "Carina," he said simply.

Allen turned to him. "I'm sorry, what?" His brow furrowed.

"Carina, it is a constellation. Many ships use it in these parts to help them navigate. It is part of the constellation Argo, named after the great ship. Carina means "keel" as in part of a ship." He paused. "Knowing your stars is important for sailing." Lucas pointed at the constellation. He put his hand down and stood up. "I'll show you the chest of books tomorrow, lad. Try and get some rest." Lucas turned to leave.

"Thank you, Captain." Allen whispered. Lucas looked over his shoulder; the lad was busy staring up at the night sky.

In his cabin, Lucas moved to his desk though he was not entirely sure what he was looking for. Spotting the parchment, he carefully slid the ribbon off. Laying the letter flat on the table, he realized it was not a letter at all, but a deed, a deed to a plantation. Lucas clenched his jaw, he quickly scanned the document, looking for the name he prayed very much was not on it.

Lord Henry Benedict. Lucas slammed his fist onto the deed. He had felt sorry for Lord Benedict. He had enjoyed his company and dining with him. The Governor's actions towards the Baron were unjust and it angered him that the Governor was willing destroy a man's livelihood for his own benefit. It was made far worse by the fact that Lucas was the one that was to carry out the task of delivering the deed to Lord Benedict's plantation to the Governor's man in France.

Lucas fumed; he needed a way of getting out of delivering the deed. Of course, then the Governor would take away his Letter of Marque and simply have someone else deliver it. It was simple, do the task for the Governor or lose his Letter of Marque.

Lucas walked to the water basin on a small cabinet and splashed a bit of the cool liquid on his face. He leaned over and placed both his hands on either side of the basin. He had to deliver it whether he thought it right or not, he just prayed that the Baron was able to find a partner in time. Even once he delivered the deed to Monsieur Dupont, it did not mean the man could take possession of the property. If the Baron found a partner in time and was able to get word back to the Governor, the deed to the Frenchman would be void and the Baron would still own his Plantation. Back in Barbados, the Governor had told Lucas, "Know that, while one man on the island might be displeased by my man receiving the parchment, it must be done and will not make a difference to anyone on the outside."

Lucas looked at himself in the mirror that hung above the cabinet. His hair was falling every which way and his blue eyes were angry. He shook his head and reached for a cloth, patting his face and neck dry. He took off his shirt, tossing it aside and headed for his bed. Feeling more exhausted than before and hoped now he would be able to rest.

The next morning, Lucas awoke to footsteps moving on deck. He rubbed the sleep from his eyes and got up. He went to the trunk and pulled on a fresh white shirt, that hung loose on his chest. He pulled his boots on and headed for the hatch.

It was time to say farewell to Captain Lester and the Baron. Lucas clenched his jaw again and stepped onto the quarterdeck. He walked over to where Alaric stood.

"Looks as if you didn't get a wink of sleep." He raised an eyebrow and grinned. "Did the bed bugs bite?" Alaric stepped back in time to avoid a smack on the head from his friend.

Lucas stepped up to Captain Lester and the Baron. "It was a pleasure meeting you men. I wish you the best on your voyage. Try not to run into anymore pirates." He gave a lopsided smile. "And I hope you find a willing partner to assist you."

"I thank you. Safe journey's to you. I hope we will have the chance to dine together again. Until next time." The Baron said before walking across the plank to board the other ship.

"A good day to you, Captain." Captain Lester gave a slight bow to Lucas and Alaric who returned the gesture.

The crew separated the ships and unfurled the sails. The wind caught them with a loud crack and the ship jolted forward. Lucas scanned the deck, he had promised Allen he would show him the chest of books. He did not see him anywhere on deck. He turned to Alaric, "Where is the lad?"

Alaric simply pointed up with a huge grin, his eyes shining with a mixture of amusement and pride. "He heard the new recruits daring each other to climb the highest on the rigging, only one or two of them actually have climbed it thus far. The boy overheard and stepped forward. He asked if he could have a go. I gave him the ok, just before you came on deck. For such a spindly lad, he isn't doin' too terribly." Alaric shrugged. "The boy pulls his weight and does what he is told."

Alaric crossed his arms over his chest as they watched Allen climb high up in the rigging. As Allen reached the top, the crew erupted in howls and cheers. Allen waved down at them. Lucas swallowed hard, his hands balled into fists. He did not want to dampen the lad's spirit; it took a lot to face the fear of climbing the rigging. Not all sailors could do it. But seeing him way up there made Lucas's stomach tie in knots. He could not explain why, it was entirely normal for the new recruits to be dared to make the climb.

With the lad it was different though, he supposed it had to do with his young age and the fact that he was half the size of the rest of the crew. He would never make the fall if he slipped from that height. Allen began to make his descent.

"Have Allen see me in my cabin when he gets down,"

Lucas said gruffly.

Alaric grinned, "Aye Capt'n," he replied with sarcasm. "Don't you worry, I'll not tell the crew that I was the one who made the climb before you." He let out a loud laugh as Lucas scowled at him. Alaric walked up to meet the boy at the bottom, no doubt going to congratulate the lad before sending him to Lucas.

Lucas stepped through the hatch. He walked over to the small window and peered out. There was a knock at the door. "Enter." He called out without turning around.

The door opened slowly. Lucas did not look over at the boy; he was still afraid he would say something he should not about the lad climbing the rigging. Lucas walked over to the chest of books and clicked the small latch that held it shut, then lifted the lid. He gestured with his head for the lad to come over.

"Go ahead, see if there is anything in there that catches your interest." He stood at the trunk; his arms folded across his broad chest.

Allen hesitated only a moment, then crouched down in front of where the books lay. Allen slowly and carefully began riffling through them. He would take one out, read the spine then set it aside. Lucas could tell the lad was enjoying the feel of books in his hands again.

Lucas crouched down beside the chest. He shuffled a few books around before he found the one he was looking for. He handed one to Allen. The binding was worn, and it had a bit of wear and tear on it. It was a dark brown and had been one of Lucas's favorites. He noticed the boy's eyes light up "Oh, the…". Allen glanced at Lucas, his face turning crimson.

Lucas grinned, "*The Adventures of Nicholas Treadfast,* are a favorite of mine as well." He would have laughed at the lad's reaction if he had not looked so terrified. "I had known

Treadfast was certainly not your actual last name. What about Allen? That is not really your name either, is it?" The boy shook his head slowly, staring down and the books. Lucas nodded, a grin still playing on his lips. "Are you going to tell me your real name now?"

Allen looked up at him, "I will tell you, I promise that." Allen paused, swallowing hard. "I just cannot tell you at the moment. Once the voyage is over and we are back in Barbados, I will be off the ship and I will tell you then. You have my word." Allen spoke low, almost a whisper. Lucas could tell the lad meant every word and decided to leave it at that. He would not press for his name, but he did want a little more information about him.

"I will hold you to it. Tell me though, you wear those clothes but clearly you are from a higher class. Your home is in Barbados, as you have said so yourself. What made you wish to buy passage on *The Alice?* I know you did not intend to end up on a Privateer ship." Lucas patiently waited for him to answer. Allen was looking at the book again, running his small hands over the cover.

"I love my home; it is beautiful and…safe. I was rarely allowed to even leave the gates though, and if I did, it was only for a short time and usually it was to go dine at one of the estates." Allen paused, looking up at Lucas again. "I mentioned before how I could see the ocean from my windows. I used to watch the ships coming and going, wondering what it would be like to be on one." He paused again looking around the cabin. "One day I found the opportunity. I found my way to the docks and well, the rest you know." He shrugged.

"I cannot fault you for wanting a wee bit of adventure, lad." Lucas chuckled and shook his head. "I do not wish to explain to your parents that you fell from the rigging on my ship though, so promise me, no more climbing." Lucas stood up. "Did you decide on a book to borrow?"

Allen grinned up at him. "I think we both know which book I will choose." He said as he clutched the worn, brown one to his chest.

"Captain Nicholas Treadfast it is then." He reached his hand out to help the young sailor up. The lad grabbed his hand as his face slowly grew scarlet again.

Allen quickly let go, brushing his hand against his breeches. He cleared his throat and looked at the floor. "Thank you again, Captain, for lending me the book." Before Lucas could reply, the lad was out the hatch, heading on deck to continue his duties, still holding the book in his hands.

Lucas closed the chest and headed for the hatch. He needed a bit of fresh air himself. He enjoyed talking with Allen and had even looked forward to showing him the books, but there was something different about Allen. He could not place it.

Allen was not at all like the other men that boarded ships, granted he was younger than most, even young Benjamin was seventeen already. He also knew Allen came from a gentle born family but that still did not explain it. He shrugged it off and headed to the helm to join Alaric.

10

Catherine gripped the book in her hands tightly. She was shaking from having her hand in the Captain's and revealing more than she intended. It felt good to finally speak about it, at least some of what had been plaguing her mind. The Captain was pleasant, he made her feel as if she could confess anything to him, though her true name and the fact that she was actually a woman was still going to have to wait.

The Captain was standing at the helm, his shirt slightly opened at the top, with his dark hair pulled back. He was gripping the wheel and talking with Alaric. Fear bubbled up at the thought of how angry he would be when he discovered her lies.

When he placed the Treadfast book in front of her, she had been overwhelmed with joy but then had realized why he had handed it to her. Her heart had stopped before she saw his eyes sparkling with humor. At that moment, she had not wavered in fear of retribution but rather in the fact that she had been completely taken in by the Captain's eyes. She had never noticed before how much like the sea they were.

"You best go put that there book of the Capt'n's in your hammock below decks before it falls inta the sea. He will not thank ye for that, laddie. You hurry and put it away, then come back here and finish your tasks." Ol' Shorty waved Catherine away, dismissing her before turning back to what he had been doing.

Catherine quickly raced through the hatch and into the room that held the swaying hammocks. She scrunched her nose as the smell hit her. It was damp and hot; the stench of the sweaty, unwashed bodies was enough to make her eyes water. Some of the men that had been on duty the night before were sound asleep, their snores echoing against the walls. One man looked near to falling out of his hammock, his arm and a leg were hanging off, close to dragging on the floor. His other arm was draped over his large chest, he was about as round as one of the barrels that held the grog. Catherine quietly placed the book in her hammock.

She was almost near the hatch to go back up on deck when Doc poked his head out of his cabin, stopping Catherine in her tracks. "I wonder, Allen, would you mind bringing me a fresh bucket of water?" He asked, looking at her over his spectacles.

"Oh, of course, I will bring it to you right away, Doc."

"That a boy, lad." He shared her smile before going back into his surgery.

Catherine felt more confident as the days went by. She now knew where most everything was and was catching onto the different terms used on the ship. When it was time for her evening meal she ate heartily, getting used to the ale and grog. The first time she tasted the ale, she had choked, spraying ale on the men that sat across from her. The table erupted with jokes and laughter. She enjoyed the friendly banter between the crew members and had jumped at the chance to climb the rigging.

When she heard them daring each other to climb the rigging, she knew she had to give it a try. The nervousness was replaced by the thrill of being so high up and being able to see across the vast ocean. As she climbed, her arms and legs grew tired and stiff. She was getting stronger by the day though. Still not nearly as strong as the rest of the crew. By the time the day was over, she was so exhausted that she no longer smelled the stale air or heard the snoring crew members. Despite her aching body, she even looked forward to her daily duties, the sea air and the feel of the ship cutting across the waters.

Catherine gathered the water in a wooden bucket that looked as if it would snap from the strain of carrying such a load. Carrying the wobbly bucket with two hands, she carefully stepped up the stairs, trying hard not to slosh the water. She heard a laugh and looked up,

"Come now sailor, put your back into and get yourself moving." Benjamin bellowed, grinning down at Catherine.

"If you aren't going to help me then quit standing there gaping." Benjamin laughed even harder. "You know, if you don't close that big mouth of yours the flies will get in." Catherine blushed, though she felt pride for standing up to the sailor.

He was always cracking jokes and teasing her and the others as often as he found the chance. Quickly, he swooped the bucket up with one hand, still grinning, but now closed mouthed. She would never have dared to speak like that on the plantation. Emma would have been horrified.

At the top of the stairs, Benjamin handed her the bucket again. "You aren't so bad, kid." He ruffled the old hat that Catherine wore to conceal her hair. She quickly adjusted it. Benjamin was a good whole foot taller than her, he was slim, with muscular arms. His shaggy brown hair hung loose, not tied back like the Captain's or Alaric's. Benjamin leapt out through the hatch, letting in a burst of sunlight. Catherine stumbled along to Doc's cabin. She set the water on the ground and knocked.

Doc answered the door, "Ah perfect, thank you. I don't suppose you know how to stitch a torn sail do you?" Doc asked.

"I am sure I can. I have never stitched a sail, but I have worked on other fabric." Catherine avoided saying she sat in a quiet room working on her needle point for absolutely no reason other than it was what women of her station were supposed to do. All that practicing would finally pay off.

"Wonderful!" The Doc exclaimed. "Let me get you what you will need to repair it. The sail is waiting on deck for you to patch, the men carried it up already." He reached into a box and pulled out a thick needle, thread, and patch. "That should do it," he said.

The hatch swung open and a large, solid figure collided with her. Catherine stumbled backwards almost dropping the needle and thread. She rubbed her forehead with her hand.

She heard a groan, followed by "Bloody hell."

She looked up and her eyes widened. "Oh, Captain! I am so sorry, are you alright? I did not hear you coming towards the hatch, I had been just about to open it. I am to patch the sail…" She stammered, completely mortified.

The Captain rubbed his chin. He raised his other hand to silence her rambling. "It is alright, it was not your fault." He managed to say. "Though I think you've gone and broke my jaw." To her surprise he let out a low laugh that sounded more like a rumble.

"I can assure you, while it may hurt, the wee lad did not indeed break your jaw. You probably did more harm to him than he did to you." Doc poked and prodded the Captain's jaw then patted him on the cheek before turning to Catherine to examine his patient. He tilted her head up and felt around.

"You will have a small bump but no worse for the wear. Tis surprising since you knocked into one of the hardest objects on deck." He grinned and pointed a thumb over his shoulder at the Captain. "I reckon his head is harder than the mast." Catherine and Doc both burst out laughing. The Captain scowled at them.

"Don't you two have tasks you should be doing?" The Captain said gruffly.

Catherine stopped laughing but could not manage to wipe the smile from her face. "Yes, Captain." She shot a glance at Doc, who winked at her. She walked past both men, glancing briefly at the Captain. She noticed his lips twitched slightly.

Catherine sat herself down and got as comfortable as she could in front of the massive sail. She tried threading the needle through the thick canvas. It was far tougher to punch the needle through the material than it was to do her needle point through the thin and delicate fabric back home. It did not take long before she got the hang of it though. She was focused on sewing the patch on properly and had not noticed how dark and breezy it had become.

"Allen, I want you down below. You are to stay there until told otherwise. You will be doing as Doc and Benjamin say and helping them if they should need it." The Captain was standing above her. His jaw was clenched and his eyes were as grey as the sky. Catherine stood and looked around. The sky was growing darker by the minute, the boat was swaying more than usual, and none of the crew was smiling.

She looked back at the Captain; terror written across her face. "A storm?" She swallowed the lump forming in her throat and wrapped her arms around herself. This was her one true fear of being aboard a ship. It was what her father had feared and what her mother had never recovered from.

"It will be alright; I only allow the most seasoned of sailors on deck during the worst of it. You are to stay below and help where you are needed." The Captain's gaze was serious and did not leave hers until she nodded.

"Aye Captain." She was worried for the entire ship. He had turned to leave but she put her hand on his arm. "Please take care of yourself." Her voice quavered.

Lucas's brow furrowed. "It will be fine, just a wee storm." She watched him head for the helm. She swallowed her fear and walked down through the hatch, leaving the more seasoned sailors on deck to brave the quickly building storm. The ship was now swaying and bucking, the roaring, angry ocean pounding against it's hull. The sky had been near black by the time she had headed below decks.

"How long do you suppose the storm will last?" She asked Doc when she had found him.

He shrugged, "No telling, they can last for mere minutes to several hours." He was helping Benjamin and a few other sailors get ropes and plugs ready in case of leaks or holes that might spring forth in the hull. Catherine heard a rumbling and a pounding from on deck. The storm was now entirely upon them. Shivering, Catherine grabbed onto the ropes, readying them, following the others sailors' lead. There was faint shouting from above deck.

"Allen, help me with the leak, I'll show you how it's done, see here," he pointed to a hole where water was now rushing in. "If it looks more like a hole it can be plugged, with one of these." He held up a piece of round wood and a large club. He shoved the wood into the hole, causing the water to spray in all directions. She wiped her face with her sleeve, and watched as Benjamin hit the wedge, pounding it a few more times before water stopped spraying and the wedge held tight.

"Nothing to it," he smiled at Catherine. "If the water rushes in from a long crack, that is when we use the ropes to plug them." Catherine nodded, grateful for the distraction. Had any of the sailors been washed off the deck and into the dark waters? Would the Captain be able to steer the ship through the storm? She had little doubt about his ability to control his ship, but if a wave hit it or the mast snapped, then what?

Catherine felt water suddenly rushing against her leg. Remembering what Benjamin had showed her, she grabbed a wedge and the club. Benjamin had made it look simple, but the water poured in with more force than she had thought. The piece in her hand slipped out of her grasp. The hull had a few inches of water filling it, it usually had a few puddles in spots from small leaks but the rising water that was bursting through new holes and cracks was making it harder to find the wedge she had dropped. She felt around in the salty water and her fingers brushed against it.

Before it slipped away, she grabbed it and shoved the wood in the side of the hull with far more strength this time. She felt part of the wood splinter off and dig painfully deep in her hand. Wincing, she swung the club against the wedge. She slammed it again, this time the water ceased to spray out. She turned; the other sailors were busy threading a pitch-soaked rope in another leak that had formed. She looked at her hand. It was turning an angry red; the dark outline of a thick, long shard of wood, was deep under the skin. It had dug in the inside of her hand just below her fingers, where her blisters had only recently finished healing.

"Doc! Doc! It's Eddie! A wave threw him against the railing, his head is cut bad!" A sailor, Gordy if Catherine remembered right, was rushing in down the stairs, dragging an unconscious Eddie along beside him. Gordy's arm was around his waist, the other holding Eddie's arm around his shoulders to try and keep him upright. If it were not for the slow rise and fall of his chest, she would have thought the sailor dead. His pale face and the front of his shirt were covered in blood.

Doc rushed over to the sailors that had just come down. They slowly lowered Eddie onto a small wooden crate so he would not be resting in the water.

"How is the Captain and the rest of the crew holding up?" Doc asked, as he worked on his patient. It felt like they had been in the brutal clutches of the storm for over an hour already.

"Alright, a couple of us have a few minor cuts and bruises, but nothing bad. Captain has to be tiring, the wheel is pulling mighty hard. The waves are some of the highest I have seen." Gordy looked back at Eddie, "Will he be alright?"

"Aye, the cut was not as deep as you originally thought, most of the blood was coming from the nose, it is slowing now." Doc said, dabbing a wet cloth against the cut on Eddie's forehead. "He will be unconscious for a bit and will have a mighty fierce headache when he wakes, but he will do."

"I best get back up there." Gordy turned, heading back up the stairs.

Catherine stood rooted to the spot. Seeing Eddie so pale, so silent and still, had frightened her even more. He just laid there, his head turned to the side, eyes closed. She found it hard to reconcile his current sate with the one he was in a few days before. His smile wide, foot stomping along to the tune he played on his violin.

Gordy's words echoed in her mind, "the Captain has to be tiring…" What if he could not keep a firm grip on the helm? What if he became too exhausted to hold on any longer? Instinctively, Catherine spun around and rushed up the stairs. She heard Benjamin's desperate yells, begging her to stop, that it was too dangerous. She had to do something. She could not stay down there, plugging holes when they needed more help on deck.

The hatch flew open, the slippery, wet deck made her grab hold of the opening as she gained her footing. The ship was pitching and rolling beneath her. She held a hand above her eyes, squinting against the wind and heavy rain that almost stung as it hit her. One of the sails seemed to be moving far more than the others, the lower corner of it whipping around with a blur. The rigging was barely holding it. Catherine saw that one of the belaying pins had almost completely come out. She tried running to it, the hounding rain and wind made it near impossible to do more than a slow walk.

The Captain's voice was barely audible in the storm. He was probably telling her to go back down below, but she could not do that. She had to do what she could to help. It would be far more dangerous if the sail was destroyed and near impossible to maneuver out of the storm. It was already difficult enough.

Catherine managed to reach the belaying pin that was lose and threatening to break free. She grabbed for it as it swung out, she held tight as it pulled and whipped her arms. The Captain yelled again, she turned her head just enough to see him through the storm that raged about them.

"Keep it!" The Captain bellowed. It was hard to hear over the thundering noises around them. She was not sure if she had heard him right, the look on his face was a mixture of fear and anger.

Catherine turned back, desperately trying to hold on and to put the pin back in. It was yanking her hands and arms. The sliver of wood was still in her hand, she was trying not think of how terrible it would look or feel after. Ignoring the increasingly searing pain and steady flow of blood; she had to get the pin back in.

The Captain shouted again, even over the roaring of the storm she could hear the desperation in his voice, "Allen!" He yelled.

Catherine looked out at the raging sea, fearful as the ship suddenly tilted, a wave crashing over her. She held on, not just so she would not lose her grip on the belaying pin but so she would not be tossed into the ocean's depths. The ship tilted back, she felt herself slide on the fresh sea water that ran over the wooden planks. It was too late, her hands slipped from the metal. The wind grabbed hold of the pin, throwing it back at her with furry. She felt a bursting pain in her head as she fell to the hard deck, seeing nothing but black and feeling the water rush over her helpless form.

11

Lucas saw the water rise. The wave swept over Eddie, knocking him to the ground and throwing him against the railing. At first he feared his friend had been thrown out to sea. As the water on the deck ran off, Lucas spotted Eddie, laying there, blood flowing from his head. He yelled for Gordy, who was nearby, to take him to Doc. Lucas felt the pull from the wheel, his shoulders, back and arms were tight. Despite the drenching rain and waves, his muscles felt as if he were on fire. He had extraordinarily little control over the large brig. He stood with his legs spread steadily apart, keeping his balance as the ship bucked and tilted.

From the corner of his eye, he caught movement coming from the hatch. Gordy had already come back up from taking Eddie below. Who would be coming out? Most unseasoned sailors were too frightened to come above deck during their first storms and did not mind when he ordered them to stay below, though most of them would never admit it openly. It might be Benjamin. If something had gone wrong, or Eddie had taken a turn for the worse, Benjamin would be the one to come alert him or Alaric. Though Benjamin was only seventeen, he had proved himself time and again and had earned his and Alaric's respect.

The figure stepped from the opening of the hatch, Lucas felt the blood run from his face. Of all the sailors below, he had not expected Allen. What was the lad thinking? He had seen the terror on Allen's face when the boy had realized they were headed into a storm. What would possibly make the boy come up now?

He called to Allen, he yelled louder. If the lad heard him, he made no move to show it. A gust of wind hit the ship and Lucas focused on the helm, he had to right the brig. He knew they had already been thrown off course, but he had to stay as true to it as he could. They could not afford to lose more than a few days.

Lucas looked back at Allen; the boy's small figure was being pelted by the hounding rain. He was headed for the belaying pins. They were loose but Lucas could not tell through the storm if a rope had snapped, come loose, or if it had to do with the pins. He looked for Ol' Shorty or Alaric, someone to get the boy below deck. They were struggling with rigging further up the deck and were too far to shout commands to through the raging wind.

The waves roared, causing the brig to moan in protest as it heaved the ship over the water. Allen had a hold of a belaying pin. He knew the lad would not be able to hold on and he was far too close to the railing. If a wave hit, he would be thrown from the deck and into the black waters below. He tried again, competing with the thundering wind and waves.

"Leave it!" Lucas screamed, praying the young sailor could hear him.

He saw Allen turn to him, blood running down his arm. A wave came up, heading for the small figure. Rage and fear consumed him. Why did Allen disobey? This mistake could cost the boy his life. Lucas gripped the wheel harder, helpless as the scene unfolded in front of him. If he let go of the wheel he would be risking his entire crew. *The Trinity* could be hit by a wave that could flip and destroy the entire ship.

He watched as the belaying pin flew back and hit Allen hard across the head. The boy's limp and bloody body fell to the deck. Lucas felt himself sway, he saw Alaric, his eyes wide.

Alaric rushed to the lad. Lucas held his breath, a blow to the head like that could have killed him. Alaric bent down next to him, he glanced up at Lucas and nodded. Relief flooded through him and he blew out a long breath. He looked about the ship's deck, searching for the other crew members that were braving the storm with him. They were all there, he just prayed there would be no more incidents before they reached the end of the storm.

Alaric picked Allen up, his limp arms falling to the side. He knew Doc would care for the boy. Lucas had no idea why the boy's arm was bleeding, he assumed the rope must have cut through his soft hands. They now were slightly tougher than they were when he first joined the crew but still nowhere near tough enough to hold up against wet rope ripping through the wind.

Several hours later, as the storm ended, Lucas felt as if his hands had been welded to the helm. He had managed to get his crew through safely. He slowly peeled them off, straightening and bending his fingers. His whole body ached and was as stiff as the wood planks that made up the ship. He stretched and twisted to the side. His clothes were soaked through. He wanted to check on Eddie and Allen and make sure all was well.

First, he needed to change or he would find himself a patient of Doc's, fighting a fever. The crew was just as exhausted and hungry as he was, he knew Cook was probably already working on a broth to strengthen the men up. They would need to head to a nearby island to make proper repairs and let the men rest for a few hours before continuing. He needed to double check their coordinates as well. Chances were, the storm blew them a ways off course.

He opened the hatch to his cabin and went straight to his chest. Quickly, he tore off the soaked shirt that clung to his tired muscles. Digging around for a new shirt and pants, he eventually found some in the deep chest and pulled them on. Dressed and drier, he strode straight to Doc's. When he knocked on the solid door, it opened a crack.

"Shhh our young sailor is resting." There was a slight twinkle in Doc's eyes.

"Him and Eddie are both doing well then?" He asked nervously. Doc was not acting quite himself, though he seemed pleased.

"Oh aye, Eddie regained consciousness quicker than I had expected. He is resting in his hammock. A slight headache and a scratch on the side of his head but not bad. It looked far worse than it really was." Doc smiled, crossing his arms across his chest, rocking back on his heels

"And Allen, how's the lad?" Lucas asked, his eyebrow raised.

"Oh, just fine, resting as well." He paused, looking a bit more serious. "Needed a bandage on the forehead, just where the hair begins and had a rather bad splinter that tore through the hand. All in all though, doing mighty fine and is a brave patient. I expect her to be up and about within a day or two." Doc grinned, his eyes twinkling.

"That's great news, the belaying pin hit…" Lucas's face fell. "Her?" He blinked a couple times, running a hand over his face. He could not have possibly heard Doc correctly. "What do you mean, her?" His voice was low and serious.

Doc held up his hands, looking not as pleased, but still

held a small hint of a smile. "Capt'n she is resting, she is doing just fine but she did take a fierce blow to the head and her hand will be very sore for a few days." Doc was trying to reason with the Captain and attempt to calm him a bit, but the look on the Captain's face was as stormy as the sea the night before.

Lucas clenched his jaw, "Let me in, Doc." He blew out a breath, he knew he was tired, angry, and shocked. He did not mean to take it out on his friend. "Please." He softened a bit.

Doc relented. Lucas slowly walked in the room. A white sheet had been hung up to give the injured sailor some privacy. Lucas, hand trembling, moved aside the divider. He had been expecting to see Allen's friendly face when he came to see the Doc, instead he now came face to face with a young woman.

Her blonde hair spilled over her shoulders, her eyes were filled with a mixture of fear and something he could not quite describe. He knew he must look a fool, standing there, staring like a young buck. He scratched his chin, looking away for a moment to clear his mind. He looked back at the girl that had managed to board his ship, work as hard as the rest of his crew and now sat there, staring back at him. She bit her lip, waiting for him to say something.

How had he been so blind? One eyebrow raised, "I suppose I cannot very well call you Allen anymore." He could not believe she had fooled his entire crew and him.

The girl blushed and looked down at her hands. She was resting in the hammock Doc kept strung up in case anyone became ill or injured. He noticed she looked quite a bit older than the fourteen years she had claimed.

"My real name is Catherine." She glanced up and he noted her eyes had flecks of gold in them, he had never noticed that before either. There was a bandage on her forehead and on her hand. Even though it pained her, she looked as if she was perfectly content and even glowing.

Lucas tapped the side of his leg with his fingers, unsure of how to respond. "Welcome aboard *The Trinity*, Miss Catherine." He bowed slightly.

"Thank you, Captain." She was looking at her hands, a pink hue in her cheeks.

"Come Captain, let us allow the lass to rest." The Doc smiled at Catherine, placing a hand on the Captain's back. Lucas turned, he had all but forgotten about the Doc.

"Of course." Lucas cleared his throat. "When Doc says you can get up and move around again, you will be moved into my cabin, you will be safe in there and will not be having to sleep amongst the men." He turned to leave.

Catherine leapt up angrily. The movement made her head feel as if it would burst, she swayed and closed her eyes against the pain. She felt strong arms suddenly wrap around her. Her eyes fluttered open, locking onto fierce grey ones. Lucas clenched his jaw and sat her on the hammock.

He heard Doc shuffle behind them, "Catherine, unfortunately I have to quite agree with the Captain. Now that the crew knows you are a young woman, it would be best if you stayed in the Captain's cabin. Of course, you are welcome to come keep me company and I am sure Cook would not object to you helping him still as well." Doc smiled down at her. Catherine returned his smile before looking back at the Captain. Her eyes were guarded.

Lucas scowled, not entirely sure how he felt about her helping out on the ship anymore. He trusted most of his crew and knew they would not harm her but there were a few other new recruits he did not know well enough to feel sure they would keep their eyes or hands to themselves. His hands balled into fists at the thought. "You are to be accompanied by Doc, Cook, Ol' Shorty, Alaric or myself at all times. I trust the crew will behave but I will not take any risks." He stared at Catherine for a moment before turning and leaving.

    Lucas headed straight for his cabin, shocked over the woman that now rested in Doc's surgery. Walking over to the trunk that held the maps, he kicked it open. Flipping through them, he found the one he needed. He looked on the map, searching for where he suspected they might be. If he was correct, there was an island not too far from them. Tapping his finger on the location a couple times, before rolling it up and throwing it back in the trunk. He grabbed his sextant and headed to the deck to give the orders to anchor at the island once they reached it.

    As he walked on deck, many sailors stopped and stared at him, most of them wearing smirks and grins. He knew the crew was aware of what had transpired. He stepped up to the railing, doing his best to ignore his crew.

    "Alright scoundrels, get back to it." Alaric yelled, grinning at the crew before leaning up against the railing next to his friend. His shout was quickly echoed by Benjamin, earning him cuff on the head by one of the older sailors.

    "She's a bonny thing, wouldn't you agree, Luke?" Alaric was leaning back against the railing, his feet were leisurely draped over one another. Lucas could feel his friend staring at him, searching his face for any trace of interest in the little chit below decks. He did not miss the smile in his voice. Lucas continued to work with his sextant, pretending he did not hear his first mate's remark. "She'd make a mighty fine wife someday, don't you think?" Alaric was picking at his old vest absently.

    Lucas groaned, "How would I know?" He did indeed think she was possibly one of the most beautiful woman he had seen in a long while and he was sure she would make a good wife but he would never admit it to Alaric. Especially when his friend was trying to rile him into confessing it.

"Well, if you are not at all interested and are not willing to find out what kind of a woman she is," Alaric paused dramatically and pushed himself off the railing. He stepped forward, staring at the hatch that led to where the very woman sat. "I suppose I might as well get to know her better." He turned to glance at Lucas, winking and flashing a smile at him.

Lucas swung around, facing his friend. "You bloody will not." Alaric roared with laughter. Lucas shook his head, turning back to the blue waters, he did not know exactly how he felt about Catherine, he was still getting over the shock of all of it.

"Not to worry, your lass is safe from me." Alaric teased, then turned serious. "What are you planning on doing with her?"

Lucas lowered the sextant, he had found his coordinates long ago, he had only been using it as a distraction from Alaric's persistent teasing. He turned and ran his hand over the back of his neck. "I will pay for passage for her on a passenger ship at the next port to take her back. I cannot have her on board the ship, she would become a distraction to the men. Not to mention her family must be looking for her. It was bad enough when we thought her a younger runaway boy." He waved a hand in the air exasperated. "If it gets out that she was aboard The Trinity, her reputation will be ruined. Her family is much more likely to claim I kidnapped her as well, if they find out. We cannot risk any of it, as much for her sake as ours." He blew out a breath. "I trust most of the crew but there are still some recruits we do not know well. Doc already knows but, she will need to be accompanied by one of us, at all times." He stood up straighter and without looking at his friend. "She will be staying in my cabin; I will not have her sleeping in the same room as the rest of men." Lucas felt the grin that spread across Alaric's face.

"Of course, Captain." He let out a low chuckle. "I do have to say though, I do not think she will take kindly to being dropped off at the next port. I think the men will do just fine, they will be respectful, well, as respectful as they can manage." He watched Lucas, "She did well, very well as part of the crew, they have enjoyed having her on board, I realize it was a bit different before, but she did her work. She never complained, even when her hands were covered in blisters. Not many well brought up young ladies are capable of such things. There must be a reason why such a lady would run away in the first place. Before dropping her off and sending her back, I think it would be wise to find out the answers first." Alaric put a hand on Lucas's shoulder. "Get some rest. I will have Benjamin bring you some broth, I already had some."

Lucas nodded. "Thinking of her as a young boy aboard my ship was bad enough, but a young woman…she could have died last night. I gave her strict orders to stay below, she disobeyed and it almost cost her her life. I cannot have her on my ship knowing she might do something foolish again." He shook his head, "I can't imagine what caused her to do what she did."

Lucas thanked his friend and let him know to steer the ship to the small island so the crew could rest and they could properly repair the damaged hull. He headed for his cabin, he needed to think.

There was a knock at the hatch. Benjamin did not wait for him to answer, he walked in carrying a jug of grog and a steaming bowl of broth. He set it on the desk that Lucas sat at.

"Her name is Catherine, huh? She's my age, did you know that?" He asked, grinning, raising his eyebrows, and pointing a thumb at his chest. "You and Alaric are busy, so are Doc and Cook, it's up to me. I will keep an eye on her, two eyes in fact." His grin broadened. "I will protect her from those scalawags out there. Leave it to me, Capt'n," Benjamin crossed his arms over his chest that he was trying his best to puff up; it was a humorous attempt.

Lucas nearly choked on the grog. "Thank you, Benjamin, for your gallant offer. I am sure you will do your best." He paused, leaning back in his chair. "I am sure two eyes won't be necessary, just the one should be sufficient." He tried to hold back his laughter.

"Right. Of course Capt'n." Benjamin puffed his chest out more. "I will go see if she would like some more broth." He reached for the hatch and stumbled through it.

Lucas looked down at his own broth, shaking his head and letting a low chuckle out. He picked the bowl up, not bothering with the spoon. Draining the bowl in a second, the liquid hit his stomach, warming him and relaxing his body. He rolled his shoulders. His muscles were beginning to loosen up now that he sat down and had gotten some food and grog in him. It would not be long before they reached the island. He leaned back in the chair and closed his eyes.

12

Thomas looked through his spy glass. He could not see any sails in sight. There had been a terrible storm and if he judged the distance right, *The Trinity* was likely caught in the middle of it. The corner of his mouth turned up in a smile. Likely Captain Harding's ship had taken some damage. They would either need to anchor at a nearby island or would have been blown off course a bit.

This gave Thomas the opportunity he needed to close the distance between them. He knew very well that Captain Harding would make repairs and get back on course as quickly as possible, he would not linger. Thomas hoped to be able to catch him at the next port. He put the spy glass down and went to go back to his cabin, one of the crew member's words stopped him.

"Aye, I heard the lady is a Missus Benedict, the daughter of one of the rich men on the Island. O' course them at the big house are trying to keep it all quiet like so as not to ruin the Lady's reputation and all. They said a stable lad's clothes were missing from the big house and it's suspected she dressed as a lad and ran away. At them docks a lad that spoke a bit funny was going to board a passenger ship but the ship had already left port. There were only a couple other ships there at the time that lad could have stowed away on."

The sailor sneered and grinned a half toothless grin. He spat on the deck. "Imagine, a lone Lady being on a ship, I just wished it be our ship she was aboard." He laughed, shoving his fellow crewman.

"Sailor," Thomas bellowed. He did not know most of the men that were on his ship, let alone all their names. It did not bother him, he did not care to get to know his crew, some would likely be killed in a battle or would sign onto a different crew when this voyage was done. Many of the men had just signed on with him, only a few of the men from *The Trinity* that had tried to help him mutiny against Captain Harding were still with him now. The only crew members that mattered were the ones that he knew would do his bidding no matter what. "What is it you are discussing? What is this about a Ms. Benedict running away?" The name rang a bell.

The sailor stared at Thomas for a moment, the men around them had all but stopped working. The sailor swallowed hard, "A Missus Benedict, she is the daughter of a Baron I think they says. Her father owns a plantation on the island. There was talk at the taverns Capt'n. They says she stowed away or was kidnapped on a ship in port at the time." He looked nervously at the Captain who was staring menacingly down at him.

Lord Benedict, the Baron whose plantation deed he was after. The very same one Lucas Harding had possession of at this moment. He could hardly believe what he was hearing. "You said there were only a couple ships in port that she could have been on, what ships were those?" He thought he knew, but he wanted to hear what the sailor had heard. Thomas had little patience and was growing tired. He waved a hand in the air, glaring at the rest of the crew. They quickly scrambled back to their duties.

"A ship named The Jenny and another called The Trinity, Capt'n." Thomas nodded to the sailor and dismissed him with a wave of his hand. The man scurried off. He could not believe his good fortune. He guessed which ship the girl ended up on and planned to use this new turn of events to his advantage. He grinned and headed to his cabin; he had a kidnapping to plan.

In his clean cabin, he nodded in approval. He had told the cabin boy to clean up the room for him. The lad had done a decent job. Grabbing the bottle of rum that was on his desk, he pulled the cork out with his teeth, spitting it on the ground. Taking a swig, he kicked off his boots and sat at the old chair in front of his desk. The chair creaked as he put his full weight in it, he lifted his feet, and rested them on the desk.

Kidnapping and bargaining, it would be simpler then he had originally thought. He may not even need to fight. Not that he did not enjoy a good battle, in fact he often looked forward to them, but he was not about to underestimate Lucas Harding again. He knew that the Captain was a skilled fighter and his crew worked well together. The ship was better equipped than his, it was also a bit bigger though. Thomas hoped that this would give him more maneuverability and he might be able weaken Lucas's ship enough if it did come to a battle.

With the girl possibly being on Harding's ship, Thomas now had the needed leverage. He would do what he had to. He could not hold back, if he failed, the Governor would find out and that would be the end of him. It would end with a noose around his neck and swinging from the gallows like the common pirate he was often accused of being.

There was still a ways to go before they reached the next port. He closed his eyes, folding his hands together over his chest. He was sinking comfortably into the chair and relaxing when a commotion on deck reached his ears. Listening, he put his hand on the pistol that was still hanging from his side.

There was a loud bang at the hatch and a sailor barged into his cabin. Thomas sprang to his feet, raising the flintlock at the sailor's chest.

The sailor raised his hands and waved them frantically, "Capt'n please, there is a fire! On board the ship, Capt'n." He eyed the pistol in the Thomas's hand.

Thomas lowered his pistol and put it back in the worn belt that hung along his waist. "Where did it start?" He asked, quickly pulling on his boots; a fire could cause the cannons to fire themselves. A small fire could cause an entire ship to sink. He raced towards the hatch. "Wet the sails down, make sure the sand and water barrels are being used."

The sailor followed quickly behind him. "Yes Capt'n, the men are wetting the sails as we speak and they are already using the barrels, Sir." Most crews were well trained and drilled on how to stop a fire on a ship. Even with a seasoned crew of rough sailors, a ship still was at high risk of even the smallest of flames in the wrong place.

Thomas unwrapped the cloth tied around his neck. He held it to his nose as the smoke drifted through the entire ship, filling it with it's choking fumes. The cloth reeked of sweat and salty sea water. The men were rushing around, coughing, and gagging on the thick grey smoke. The cabin on fire held supplies, ropes, sails, and various containers.

As the flames licked the tar-soaked ropes, black smoke threaded its way through the cabin, causing the sailors to cover their burning eyes. Thomas watched the sailors desperately trying to put the fire out. They lifted another sand filled barrel, dumping the load on the orange flames that were clinging to the walls and containers.

Thomas yelled for them to move faster, "Get those flames out or you will all burn with this ship." His anger rising with every second, he backed out of the room, unable to breathe any longer. He stumbled onto the quarter deck. Whoever set this fire would pay. He knew it was very likely an accident, but it could have cost him everything, including his life. Thomas suspected that the crew was getting the fire under control and it would be out soon. He waited at the helm for his crew to come up. Someone, Grady he suspected, had tied a rope to the helm to keep the ship on course, while the entire crew worked to put the fire out. He pulled the line loose and gripped the helm.

Men slowly began coming on deck, faces and clothes black from the smoke, still coughing and choking. Several were holding their hands and arms or limping from where the fire burned them. They did not have much in the way of a surgeon on board. The men would have to tend their own wounds, but only after he was through with them. Thomas indicated for Grady to take the wheel when he came through the hatch. Thomas walked over to the railing that sat in front of the wheel and looked over the deck at the men. He eyed the group, it looked as if they were all present.

"Who set the fire?" He bellowed.

The crew squirmed, looking at the shipmate that stood next to them. He heard a few murmurs, but no one spoke up. They were terrified, he could see it in their eyes. They knew that a fire on board could have cost the entire ship and crew their lives. The punishment for being careless and setting a fire on board was several lashes. Anger rising, he smashed his fist into the railing. "Cowards! Who set the fire? I can whip each an every one of you until you speak up."

A man with long, dark hair pushed through the crowd. He walked straight, strong, staring right back at Thomas unafraid. His shirt hung loosely about his broad shoulders. In a confident, strong voice he announced. "I did, Captain. I was smoking my pipe and failed to remember to cap it. An ember fell out, catching the cabin alight."

Thomas fumed, this man did not seem like the typical sailor that would join just any crew or ship. His words were clear and he spoke with a richness that indicated he was not the average pirate or sailor that inhabited the taverns, waiting to join the next ship that came along. He also did not seem the type to be careless with a pipe on board a vessel. "What is your name, sailor?" Thomas's fingers were turning white from gripping the railing so hard.

"Ethan Clarke, Captain." The man said lifting his head a bit higher, his eyes narrowing.

Thomas was growing impatient with the man's impertinence; he was clearly challenging him. He wanted more than anything to have the man's shirt stripped from him and to show him he was the captain of the ship and was to be obeyed. He deserved to feel the cat o' nine tails on his back. Thomas clenched his jaw. This man was no coward and there was more to this situation than it appeared.

Ethan was clearly covering up for one of his shipmates. Why, Thomas had no idea, but whatever the reason, he would be punished. Thomas motioned to one of his men that had come with him from *The Trinity*. "Go fetch the whip." Ethan had not even flinched. Thomas looked at the rest of the crew, "Back to work, or you can join your friend and be strung up against the grate as well." He yelled, watching to see if any of the men showed even the slightest hint of defiance.

"You there, fetch a rope and tie his arms up to the grate." The big man's face broke out in a grin, showing a silver tooth. The sailor had a long braid that hung down along his back. He walked over to Ethan who peeled his shirt from his damp chest. Ethan tossed it aside and simply allowed himself to be strung up by the burly sailor.

Thomas grabbed the whip, cracking the cords through

the air, watching to see if Ethan made any sign of distress. Ethan was looking straight, his jaw clenched, his bare back glistening with sweat from the hot sun. His arms were tied up above his head, causing his muscles in his shoulders to bulge out.

A sickening slap echoed across the ship as the knotted cords struck against flesh. Still Ethan made no move, the whip came down several more times. Thomas waited for any sign of weakness, it angered him that the man was proving to be so resilient. He took no enjoyment from punishing a person if they gave no indication of feeling misery or pain. Twenty-five lashes was the penalty, but Thomas would not slow his hand until he saw the sailor weaken.

As blood began to seep from the wounds in his back, and his skin was an angry red, the man's head slunk forward slightly. Sweat beaded down Ethan's face and dripped onto the deck. Thomas's lips curled. He let the whip come down one last time. He had not been keeping track of the lashes, but he knew it was far more than the typical amount.

"Take him below, let him sleep in the brig with the rats." Thomas wiped an arm across his forehead and tossed the whip back to the big sailor. The crew had stopped working to watch the flogging. One of the men rushed to the edge of the ship, emptying the contents of his stomach into the water below. Thomas had seen men faint at the sight of floggings. He turned and walked in the direction of his cabin. He needed a drink and did not wish to stay under the hot sun any longer.

"Grady, see me in my cabin." He shouted over his shoulder. Two of the sailors were still dragging the exhausted and beaten sailor into the brig.

Thomas looked to Grady as the man ducked into the cabin. "When did Ethan Clarke sign on? What do you know of him?" He spat the sailor's name out with disgust.

Grady was looking out at the water though the small window in the cabin as the ship easily sliced through the curling waves. His arms crossed, resting against his chest. "Not much," he shrugged. "His clothes are a bit dirtier and torn now but when he signed on you could see they was new and o' good quality. His speech ain't that of the regulars at the ports. I'd wager he had an education, and a fair one at that." Grady glanced at Thomas. "He came in the tavern askin' about joining a crew. Some men pointed him to me, saying we be taking men on. I asked him if he had experience working ships, he says he did and that he had a fair bit o' knowledge about them." Grady explained. "Don't know what ships he sailed on before. All he said was that he was looking to sign on with a crew."

Thomas shook his head, he did not trust this Ethan Clarke. He would need to keep a close eye on him. He would also need to keep a closer check on the rest of the crew, to see if Ethan had gained any followers. Thomas did not know how many of his other crew members he could count on. Most of them only wanted their pay and did not care what they had to do to get it. It was a good thing he had Ethan locked in the fowl smelling brig, he had little time to worry about the man. He had bigger things he needed to focus on. Whatever trouble Ethan was going to cause with him was going to have to wait. After he took care of Harding, he would deal with the cretan below decks and dispose of him on some island like he had been stranded on.

"Capt'n, many of the men have burns," Grady said this, turning his arm over to show a patch of blistered red skin. "They will need to take care of them before they can continue with their duties." He did not dare look at Thomas while he spoke.

"Very well, have those that need to go below. Go with

them and make sure no one goes near that brig." Thomas commanded, taking a swig of rum.

13

Catherine's head was splitting. Her eyes felt as if they would pop out at any second. Doc had given her a few sips of whiskey. It burned a path down her throat, pooling in her stomach. Doc had said the whiskey helped with the pain. She had just started to feel better when Doc had answered the door. She had been terrified of what the Captain would do or say. Doc had been so understanding.

She remembered waking up, feeling dizzy, and like she would lose all the contents in her stomach. Doc had put his hand on her back and had given her a drink of grog. He told her how he had wrapped her head and cleaned up her hand. She explained how the shard of wood had dug into her palm. She did not remember much about going on deck during the storm. As she came round a bit more, she realized her hair was falling down. She had looked up at Doc with horror and shock. He simply smiled and said, "you sure fooled the crew, lass." He had laughed and asked if she had any pain anywhere else.

The Captain's response was far different. She was not sure if it would have just been easier if he had acted with the anger she had expected. Instead he had walked in and pulled back the curtain, stopping dead. His eyes roamed her body, making her feel as if she did not have a stitch of clothing on. She tried her best not to squirm under his stunned gaze. He had just stood there, his mouth opened slightly before snapping shut again. She would have laughed at the situation had she not been so afraid of what his reaction would be.

When the Captain had told her she would be accompanied by one of his chosen men or himself at all times, that she would not be doing the work on the ship anymore she was furious. Catherine was enjoying the work and was getting rather good at most the tasks. For once in her life, she felt accomplished and proud of her abilities. She was mortified at the fact he was going to have her stay in his cabin. What would the crew begin to think?

Angrily, Catherine had stood up, meaning to confront the Captain about his plans and tell him just what she thought about them. Instead, she had been blinded by pain and dizziness, and willed herself not to dare collapse in front of the Captain. Instead, a pair of strong arms had coiled around her and lifted her onto the hammock as if she weighed no more than a child. She felt herself melt into the warmth of the body holding her. The dizziness subsided as she was set down. When she had realized it had been the Captain holding her, she had felt sure both the Captain and the Doc could hear the pounding of her heart.

"How's our patient doing, Doc?" Benjamin walked in with another bowl of steaming broth. He sat it down on the table next to Catherine's hammock. He leaned up against the wall, his arms crossed over his chest. He grinned at Catherine. "Looks like you have a bit more color, now. You must be feeling better."

Catherine smiled and nodded, "My head is feeling a bit better now, my hand though," she lifted her bandaged hand, "it is now throbbing something fierce, but at least I will now have a story to tell." She laughed, she had just been thinking of what kind of reactions she would get from her friends back home. She was sure some of the ladies would faint. Especially Lady Glenville, she was always making a scene at the parties and balls. She never went anywhere without her smelling salts. Catherine was sure she held the record for causing the plump, old women to have her fits.

"I imagine you will, we all will. You are the lass that fooled an entire privateer ship into believing you were a lad. Holding the disguise for several days, working, eating and sleeping like one of the men." Benjamin chuckled, waving his hand in the air dramatically. "Not to mention, braving a storm that was one of the fiercest we have seen."

He glanced at Doc, sitting at his small desk, flipping through one of his books. "What made you leap on deck in the storm in the first place? One minute you were standing there, looking pale at the sight of Eddie, next thing I saw you were running up the stairs. I tried calling after you to come back." Benjamin looked curiously at Catherine who now had pink cheeks.

"I just thought, maybe somehow I could help." Catherine shrugged twisting her hands. "Eddie was hurt, so they were one man short on deck and well, when Gordy said the Captain was tiring, I could not just stand there anymore and do nothing," She loudly let the words tumble out. "I was afraid for the Captain, afraid for the crew. I saw the belaying pin and the sail, I knew that it would only make it that much harder on him to steer the ship if the sail was loose or torn." Catherine slowly lifted her gaze to Doc then Benjamin.

Doc had a knowing look on his face, "That was very brave of you, lass and thoughtful. The Captain has been through many battles and storms, he is a strong and smart man, you needn't have any fear for him."

Benjamin shook his head, "and here I was, thinking I had a chance." He placed a hand over his chest, feigning heartbreak. Benjamin chuckled and winked at Catherine, ducking out of the hatch before Doc could scold him for his teasing.

"We best get some rest, Lass. I am sure Captain is sailing us to an island to make proper repairs and you will not want to miss it. The islands around here have many beauties." Doc walked over, checking her head and hand. Catherine gladly leaned back in the hammock, she had now begun to think of them as rather comfortable. Though she certainly had not thought so the first time she had slept in her's in the sleeping quarters. She nearly fell out several times that night.

The ship rocked and bucked; wave after wave pounded the crew. She could hear their screams as they were swept from the deck. She looked to the helm where the Captain stood, he was soaked through, steering the ship through the wind and rain for hours. He would not be able to go much longer, no man could. She saw the wave come over him. The foaming water pulled him loose from the helm and dragged him down. Catherine ran, she tried to scream but not a sound would come out. She could not let him be taken by the enraged sea. She reached the railing ready to throw a rope to him. The wind was too strong, the rope too short, it would not reach him. They locked eyes as his disappeared under the blackness. Catherine sobbed, she could not save the crew and could not save her Captain.

"Catherine, you are alright. Catherine, wake up." A deep husky voice reached her ears. She blinked a couple times, clearing the blurry sleep from her eyes.

"Oh, Captain, I am sorry. I am awake." She looked around, avoiding his face "Where is Doc?"

"He is on deck, readying to go ashore, we reached a small island. The men need to rest and we need to make repairs.

Are you alright? Does your head hurt?" He gestured to the bandage. "Would you like me to fetch Doc?"

"Oh no, it is alright, I am quite fine. Thank you." She quickly wiped a single tear from her cheek, hoping he had not noticed. She realized she was far more upset about the dream then she had thought. "We are anchored then? Doc said the islands around here are quite a sight." She began to stand slowly, afraid of getting dizzy again. Captain quickly reached his hand out again, gently grabbing hold of her elbow. "I think I've got it, thank you." He let go, letting his hand drop to his side, still looking a bit cautious. Catherine could still feel the heat on her arm from where his hand had been.

"Aye, alright then, after you." The Captain gestured towards the hatch, his eyes not leaving her.

Catherine carefully stepped out of the room and up through the hatch. The bright sun blinded her as she emerged. Squinting, she placed her bandaged hand just above her eyes, adjusting to the light. The Captain cleared his throat behind her. Catherine hurried forward on the deck, she looked out over the island.

Her breath caught; she had never seen anything quite so beautiful. The lush green trees and bushes sat behind the white beach. Flowers bloomed all around in bright reds, oranges, yellows and purples. Birds fluttered about, chirping and singing as they danced between the leaves.

"What do you think?" She could hear the smile in the Captain's voice.

"I've never seen anything like it. It is beautiful." At a loss for words, she glanced up at the Captain who was now standing beside her, watching her. She quickly looked back at the island. Men were loading crates and supplies onto small boats.

"Go ahead and climb down into one of the skiffs, then we will go ashore. There is something I would like to show you." The Captain winked causing Catherine's breath to hitch. Speechless, she nodded in reply. The Captain gripped her elbow as she slowly stepped onto the ladder and worked her way down the hull of the ship. When she neared the bottom, one of the sailors helped her into the wobbly boat. The Captain stepped into the skiff, causing it to bob with his weight. Catherine reached out, grabbing his arm for support as she sat down. The sailor picked up the oars and rowed them quickly to the shore. The waves gently lapped against the small boat.

The Captain hopped out as they reached the beach, his boots splashing in the water. He reached his hand out. Catherine hesitated only a moment. She placed her hand in his and did not dare look up at him for fear he would see how much he affected her. "Come, you do not mind walking a bit through the trees, do you? There is a trail, not a well-worn one but it will do." He asked as she slipped her hand from his.

"Not at all, I would love to see more of the island." She looked around, amazed at all the colors and just how soft and white the sand was. It felt strange to be on solid ground, she was used to the sway and roll of the ship.

"Alright, right this way." Beaming down at her, he gestured for her to follow him. As they entered the thick jungle, he kept glancing back making sure she was following close behind.

The jungle was lush, filled with flitting birds of various sizes and colors. Lizards and insects scurried about the trees and the ground. Soft sand made up the narrow path that led the way. Catherine was careful not to trip over the roots and branches that stuck out along the trail.

"I take it you have been to this island before?" Catherine asked curiously.

"Aye, a few times. In truth, even if we did not need to repair the ship, we more than likely would have made the stop." The Captain spoke, glancing over his shoulder.

"Where are we going?" Catherine trusted the Captain entirely, but this was the first time they had been completely alone, even on the ship, there was always someone close by.

"Do not fret. I promise you; you will love what I have to show you. Come, we are close."

They continued on, stumbling over the roots. Massive palm trees dotted the island. They followed the trail as it twisted through the towering trees and large rocks. At the end of the trail, roared a waterfall raining down into a shimmering pool of water that was almost completely clear. She had read about waterfalls on the islands but had never seen one. As it poured the water out from the top of the rocks, mist and droplets suspended in the air for a moment before landing on the landscape around it.

The Captain grinned down at her, "I will stand over here," he gestured to a small boulder next to them. "I'll make sure no one comes, you enjoy yourself, go on in." He chuckled, "Not to worry, I will not peek, I give you my word."

Catherine looked in shock from the refreshing looking pond and back to the Captain. He actually expected her to bathe with him standing right there? Color rising, she glanced back at the water, it did look wonderful and her and her clothes needed a good wash. Perhaps she could leave the long, baggy shirt on and just take the breeches off. She did not fancy the idea of the scratchy material getting wet.

The Captain was sitting on the grey rock, his back to the pond. His knife was out chipping away at a fallen coconut. "Alright, I'll do it, but you better not break your word. If I catch you peeking, you'll be sorry." She tried to sound stern, but Catherine did not have a clue what she would do if she did catch him peeking. A low chuckle emanated from him and his shoulders shook slightly.

The jungle around the pond created a green wall, the only entrance was behind her and she knew the Captain would not let anyone near. She quickly undid her clinging breeches and dropped them to the ground. She touched her foot to the water, surprised at its warmth. She stepped fully into the glistening pool. She waded in further, holding down the white shirt so it would not float up.

Catherine sighed, she had forgotten how nice a bath felt. She also had tried to ignore how she had begun to smell of sweat and dried salt water and just how dirty she was after days working in the beating sun. Her skin had been as white as the sandy beach, now it was tinted from the sun. Back home, women were not allowed to be in the sun for too long, it was said that it was not good for their complexions. Yet, another rule that Catherine had now long since broken.

She swam around the pool, and approached the waterfall slowly. Standing up, she placed her hand in the falling water, causing a stream of drops to land on her face. Closing her eyes, she walked directly under it, and let the warm water fall around her.

Catherine dove back into the pond. Surprised at how deep it was, she could see the bottom but could not touch it, even with her toes outstretched. Feeling completely at ease and refreshed, she let out a giggle. Shocked at the sound of her voice, she had almost forgotten about the Captain sitting on the rock.

His back was still to her and he looked to be drinking from the coconut he had been working on. His shoulders were broad, stretching the shirt tight across his solid back. She almost felt bad, she was enjoying herself in the water and he was sitting in the hot sun on a rock, waiting for her to finish. She swam a bit closer but stayed in the deep middle.

"Are you wanting to come in? You could probably use a

good bathe yourself." She suggested, trying to keep her voice even. If she stayed in the middle, he would not be able to see her well, she thought.

"I do not think that would be a good idea." He said, his voice a bit deeper than usual. "When you are finished, we will head back. I am sure Cook has already begun preparing the evening meal. I think you are going to be surprised at what he will be serving." He did not turn to look at her.

Catherine swam to the edge of the pond and stepped out of the reviving water. The Captain's back straightened. Quickly, she grabbed the breeches she had disregarded a moment ago. She disliked the idea of putting the rough and dirty fabric back on but she had little choice. She pulled them on, her white shirt now looked almost new again. Twisting her hair, the drops falling off it like the waterfall. Closing her eyes, she ran her fingers through it, enjoying the feel of her now clean hair.

Catherine opened her eyes and froze. The Captain had soundlessly gotten up from his place on the boulder. He took a step closer to her, his eyes roaming her face and hair. She saw his hand move, coming up slightly before dropping back down to rest against his side.

He cleared his throat, "If you are ready, we can head on back to the beach." His eyes had not left hers; they were filled with something Catherine could not explain.

Her stomach flipped. "I am all set, Captain."

The Captain nodded and turned towards the trail, his boots hardly making a sound on the sand and vegetation. Catherine followed close behind, shaking from being so close to him. She had seen how he glanced at her lips, how his hand had moved to her for a moment.

They slowly worked their way back to the beach; in a few hours the sun would be going down. Catherine was curious as to what Cook was fixing up. The Captain had made it sound interesting and different from their usual meals of oranges, biscuits, dried beans, salted meat, and the occasional pickled vegetable. A small bird with a black body and a vibrant red head bounced from branch to branch, distracting her, causing her foot to slip on a root. She squealed, trying to catch her fall. Involuntarily, she closed her eyes tightly and put her hands out to brace herself. Instead of falling right onto the hard ground, she fell into a solid chest. The Captain's arms wrapped around her waist. He gently pulled her foot free of its entanglement. Her breath hitched, his hands were placed on either side of her hips and their chests were near to touching.

"Your ankle alright? Can you put weight on it?" He asked in a husky whisper.

"Aye, Captain." Catherine slowly nodded, glancing from his lips to his eyes. Part of her felt that if she spoke like her shipmates, then it would help to hide the emotion in her voice and slow the beating of her racing heart.

They heard a shot ring out, followed by a shout. The sounds came from further down the beach from where the men waited. The Captain turned, pulling his flintlock from his belt, one arm still on her, keeping her positioned behind him. They listened for a minute, several cheerful whoops and hollers reached them. The Captain's shoulders relaxed, and he put his pistol back in his belt. He released Catherine, looking back at her. "Ack, it is just the crew, they probably shot a wild pig or some other animal."

As they neared the beach, the smell of smoke and roasting meat met them. Catherine inhaled deeply. It smelled wonderful. They broke through the edge of the jungle and onto the soft, sandy beach. The Captain released her hand that he had kept hold of since she had tripped and they heard the shot.

"Can I do anything to assist with the meal?" Catherine's gaze traveled from the several small fires and back to the Captain.

"I should think they have it well in hand, the crew typically enjoys roasting the pigs and iguanas." He was watching the activity on the beach, his legs still spread apart as if he were aboard his ship, his arms crossed over his chest. "Find yourself a spot on the beach close by, the meal should be ready soon and I am sure Eddie will bring out his violin." He looked at her. "I hope you enjoyed the waterfall today and the walk was not too tiring for you."

"I did, very much, thank you for taking me." She looked down at the sand. "I enjoyed the walk as well, it was refreshing and the island is beautiful." Catherine looked back to the crew, no one was paying them any mind. The men had settled down around the different fires and were passing jugs of drink around.

"I am glad to hear it." The Captain nodded and walked towards the fire that had a pig roasting on a large stick, one of the sailors was slowly turning it.

Catherine looked to see if she could find Doc or Ol' Shorty. She spotted them and walked over to their spot by the fire. She looked at the strange meat that was cooking over the dancing flames. "What is it exactly?" Catherine asked pointing towards the charred mass.

"Iguana, one of those big lizards you see runnin' round. They are all over the islands and make a fare meal." Ol' Shorty explained.

So the Captain had been right; she just had not believed him. Catherine had to admit, the smell was making her mouth water. She had never thought of eating a lizard before and the idea was not entirely appealing. However, as hungry as she was from the swim and walk, she had no doubt she would enjoy the meal.

Alaric pulled the cooked iguana off the fire, placed it on a crate, and quickly cut the meat up. Cook came over, bringing a steaming pot of beans and a few biscuits. They began tearing at the food. The pig was still roasting and from what she had gathered, would be for a while still. Doc handed her a coconut, "Here Miss Catherine, there is already a hole punched in the top."

She sat her plate on another crate. She took the rough, round fruit in her hands. It smelled sweet, she had tried the milk that was inside a coconut once or twice before. She remembered how delicious it had been then. Now though, it was far better, she had gotten used to the rum and grog but still did not think it tasted too well. The coconut milk did far more to quench her thirst. Catherine sat down and dug in.

14

Lucas watched Catherine from his place at a fire further down the beach. The men around him talked, joked, and ate. Lucas took a bite of meat and biscuit, washing it down with a swig of grog. The light made Catherine look as if she was glowing, the breeze blew strands of her golden hair around. She was smiling at her shipmates, listening to them tell stories of their times at sea. Ol' Shorty had told Lucas that she was very curious about the ships and the waters, and always asked to hear more of their stories.

Lucas watched her eyes light up at something one of the men around her said. He had seen her eyes light up much the same earlier when he took her to the waterfall. He knew she would love it and she probably had never seen anything like it. Sitting on that rock took every bit of self-control he possessed to try and focus on the coconut and not the sound of her splashing and swimming in the water. He had nearly lost his composure when she had asked if he wanted to go in the pond, let alone when he heard her step out.

As he watched her, he saw just how happy and at ease she was with the crew. Lucas had been concerned earlier when he went down to wake her up and take her ashore. He had walked into Doc's surgery to find her having a nightmare. She had let out a little sob and he would have wagered the clothes on his back that she had said his name. When she woke, he did not miss the tear she had wiped away and tried to hide. He was not sure if it had been the dream or if her injuries were causing her pain. In that minute he was torn between wrapping her up in his arms or running and grabbing Doc.

"She's quite a lady, ain't she, Capt'n?" Lucas looked away from the girl that had been plaguing his thoughts to face the plump and rosy cheeked cook.

"Aye, that she is." Lucas blew out a breath, he had been caught staring at her like a cad and saw no use in denying it.

"You know, I have never had much help in the galley. I have thrown all the other sailors out soon as theys try ta' help. That girl though, she catches on quick and knows what she's doin' in there. She told me that the cook at her father's estate used to let her go in their great, big kitchen and help on occasion." Cook said, watching Lucas who was now staring into the fire, slowly chewing another piece of meat. "If it was up to me, Capt'n, I'd let her stay on a bit longer. I know it could be dangerous, but she can stick close and the crew and I's, well we won't let no harm come to her. I could really use her in the galley for the remainder of the voyage if that is what she is wanting." Cook picked up a small stick he saw on the ground and tossed it into the fire. It spit out sparks and wrapped its red flames around the twig, eagerly devouring it.

Lucas glanced back over towards Catherine. Ol' Shorty and Doc sitting on either side of her. Just then she looked over to him, their eyes met for a moment as she gave him a soft smile. Lucas sat down in the sand; he threw a small bone in the fire that he had worked all the meat off of.

"I am not sure it is a good idea, Cook. Her reputation is already in peril and we know nothing of her family. Not to mention we need to focus on the task at hand and do what we need to under the Governor's orders." Even as Lucas spoke the words, he knew he did not agree with them. He dreaded what he had to do under the Governor's command and was trying to devise a plan so that the Baron could keep his land. What the Governor was doing to the man was not right or honorable for that matter. Plus, from the little Catherine had divulged about her home, it seemed that she had been well looked after by a caring father and the household. He rubbed the back of his neck, he could not think of her staying on board, in fact he needed to try and keep his mind completely clear of the woman. Lucas had been worried about his crew not keeping their eyes and hands off of her, but it had instead proven to be a far more difficult challenge for him.

"Oui, I hear ya Capt'n." Cook answered. "Well, you cannot very well drop her off at the next port. It is not a very big one and not too savory. You would have to wait until we reached France. Then decide which would be safer for her, a passenger ship that could be set upon with no means of protection," he waved a hand and scoffed. "Or have the girl sail back on our ship where, yes, we may be set upon, but we have a way to protect the lady." Lucas glared at Cook. He knew the Frenchman was right and looking at it from that perspective left him little option. He rubbed a hand over his face and reached for the flask of whiskey that was being passed around.

Eddie sat himself on a crate and picked his violin up and played a tune most of the sailors knew. Many sang along, still eating and relaxing. Others got up and began dancing to the beat. Alaric moved closer to Catherine around the other fire. He was standing in front of her, his arm outstretched. Catherine stood up, placing her hand in the crook of his arm. Alaric led her to the middle where others were stomping around on the sand. Lucas clenched his jaw; he could not quite explain why it bothered him so much, but he did not care to see Catherine smiling up at his friend or to see him twirling her around.

As the song ended, the two faced one another. Alaric gave an exaggerated bow, followed by a perfectly formed curtsy by Catherine. She laughed, Alaric headed to the fire, grabbing a drink from one of the other sailors. Catherine walked along the beach, letting the small waves bump against her bare feet. Lucas had noticed she had long since disregarded her thin, worn shoes by the fire. Catherine sat down, staring out at the sea. Lucas knew she was enjoying herself but had to be exhausted from the last few days and their relentless events, not to mention, her injuries had to be draining her. He stood up and walked quietly over to her.

"You must be exhausted. You are free to return to the ship at any time, just say the word. You will not be bothered, the bed is made up in my cabin." She could not hide the brief look of shock, and her yawn. "Not to worry, I had one of the men set up my hammock in the opposite side of the cabin. You have nothing to fear." He sat down next to her. In the moonlight he could see the pink shade of her cheeks which now matched the color of her lips. Lucas looked out at the water; a dolphin leapt in the distance. He heard Catherine gasp. He tried to ignore the way it made his chest tighten.

"I cannot get over the beauty of the sea or the life that resides in it. When I am on the ship, I feel as if I am a part of all of it." She blushed even more, "I know it probably sounds silly."

"Not at all, you clearly have adventure and sailing in your blood." He knew exactly how she felt and knew many of Catherine's crew mates felt likewise.

Catherine yawned again, placing the back of her hand against her mouth. "I suppose I am ready to retire." Now that the crew knew she was a woman, she caught herself talking the way she was properly brought up with a mix of how she had gotten used to talking with her shipmates.

"Very well, I will have one of the sailors row you out to the ship, I will follow in a bit." He knew she would need her privacy for a little while and to be able to relax alone before he came in. Lucas stood up and walked over to a group of men, he signaled for one of them standing to take Catherine to the ship and come directly back to the beach. There were currently no sailors on board, he knew she would be in no harm and planned to follow in a bit. Doc would probably not be far behind them either, he was usually the first to find his hammock.

Lucas watched Catherine climbed the rope ladder to the deck of the ship. He took a swig of the rum. He sat on a crate, his foot moving along to the sound of Eddie's violin. He sang along as Eddie started up a new tune. A song about the fish and the weather of the sea.

Most of the iguana meat had been picked off, as well as the biscuits. The pig would finish roasting that night. They would enjoy it on the ship the next couple of days while they traveled to the port. The crew would likely bring along several coconuts and iguanas. There were cages on board that they could keep the lizards in until they were ready to be cooked, this way the meat would remain fresh. Lucas had also told the men to fetch plenty of water from the pool they had visited earlier. Water spoiled quickly in the wooden barrels below decks. It would be nice to change them out and have clean water again for a few days.

Standing and stretching, he walked over to one of the skiffs. He got in, picking up the oar and paddling over to *The Trinity*. It was not as big as a Man o' War of course, nor was she one of the smaller ships in the waters. She was strong, solid, fast, and easy to maneuver. He climbed up the side of his ship, the ladder swaying. The tied off skiff would be fine. The men would raise it up the next morning before sailing off and the rest of the crew on the beach had skiffs they could use to get back.

Lucas carefully opened the hatch to his cabin. He did not want to wake her if she was already asleep. She was curled up on his bed, facing the wall. He stepped into the cabin, closing the hatch behind him. Quietly he took his boots off and walked over to the water basin. He splashed a bit of the water on his face before wiping it off with a cloth. He thought about taking his shirt off like he usually did but thought twice about it.

Then he turned, watching the woman in his bed sleep peacefully. The blanket was draped over her legs, she shivered a bit. The nights on the ship could get chilly. Lucas walked over to the bed and gently pulled the blanket up and over her shoulders. She seemed to dig deeper into the mattress. Her hair draped across the pillow and he gently brushed his fingers against the yellow waves. He pulled his hand back, clenching it at his side and went to where his hammock was strung up in the corner. Laying on his back, his arms rested on his chest, his feet crossed over one another. Cathcrine's steady, soft breathing filled his ears. He worked his jaw, knowing he would not get much sleep while the lass slept peacefully in his bed just a few feet away.

15

"Cook, I will be quick, I just need to get another bucket of water to finish washing these in." Catherine gestured to the plates, trays, and cups.

"Oui," Cook nodded, focusing on the vegetables he was cutting up.

Catherine quickly made her way down to where the barrels of water and grog were kept. She popped one open and began filling the bucket. A sense of unease filled her and something felt a bit off. She quickly closed the barrel and turned to head back up the stairs to Cook.

A sailor was standing against the wall. She had not seen him when she came down or heard him if he had followed her into the dark room. Catherine's feet sloshed in the bit of water that was on the floor. Focusing on the hatch, she walked towards it, trying to ignore her nerves. The sailor had not taken his eyes off her or made a move. He was one of the new recruits. She had not spoken to him before and was not even sure if she knew his name. She neared the stairs and the man stepped in front of her.

She swallowed hard, "I need to get back to Cook, he is expecting me." The sailor's blonde hair was pulled back. He wore a dark shirt and a brown, worn vest over it. Leering, his eyes slowly roamed her body. The Captain's words echoed in her mind. His warnings of how he did not know the new recruits as well and to always stay with one of the men he trusted more.

Catherine tried stepping around the sailor, but he grabbed her arm and slapped a hand against her mouth so she could not scream. The bucket slipped from her grasp and water splashed up, soaking her legs. Trying to free herself, his grip was too strong and beginning to hurt her arm. She bit down, hard, on his hand. As soon as her mouth was free, she let out a scream, it echoed through the wooden, damp room. She prayed someone heard her cry.

The next scream was cut short by a vicious slap across the face. She tasted blood. She kicked at the man but it did little good, he had pinned her against the wall. His hand gripped her thin white shirt, ripping it nearly clean off. In that brief moment, she was thankful for the wrap around her chest. She closed her eyes, she knew she could not pry the sailor off of her. Sobbing, she felt the weight that pressed against her lift and the grip on her arm release. There was a growl and a loud crack. Opening her eyes she saw the Captain, his eyes darker than ever, his jaw clenched tight. His fist coming down on the sailor's face, blood spurted from the broken nose. Lucas grabbed the man by the shirt, forcing him to stand as he struck him again.

"Lucas. Lucas, that is enough." Alaric was standing there. "I will take him below; you take care of the lass." Alaric put a hand on the Captain's shoulder. The Captain let go of the man's shirt, dropping him to the wet floor. His broad chest heaved as he turned to Catherine. The look on his face went from pure rage to concern and anguish. Hesitating for only a moment he reached out a hand and Catherine rushed to him. He wrapped his arms around her, holding her close.

Despite what had just happened, she had never felt safer then she did in that instant. He kissed the top of her head and the tears flowed down her cheeks, she let out another sob. A quick step back, he took his shirt off in one fluid motion and slipped it over her torn one. Picking her up, he carried her up the stairs to his cabin. She laid her cheek against his chest and closed her eyes, trying to wipe away the images of the man grabbing her.

In his cabin, he laid her in his bed and covered her up with the blankets. The Captain walked over to the hatch in his cabin and opened it, hollering for Doc. Doc immediately came in, carrying a tray of cloth and various other items. She winced as he dabbed whiskey on the lip that had now grown to twice its normal size. There were scratch marks on her chest, just above the wrap. Catherine noticed him hesitate before cleaning them as well, causing her to flinch again. The Captain stood nearby, his hands balled into fists.

The Captain walked over to her and sat in the chair he had put next to the bed. He placed her hand in his. "Catherine, I am terribly sorry. I should have kept a closer eye on you as well as the crew."

"No you couldn't have. It was not your fault or anyone else's accept that man's." She tried to smile at him but her mouth would not let her. She closed her eyes and the Captain held onto her hand.

The next several days passed without any troubles. Catherine took turns between assisting Doc, Cook, and going up on deck. Ever more vigilant, she made sure she was never out of sight of the Captain or one of the other men he told her to stay with.

Under Cook's watchful eye, she could now manage several parts of the meals without assistance. The first time she had tried to make eggs for the Captain's breakfast she had turned them to rubber. Cook had been going over the galley's inventory and was not able to help her. She had brought the meal to the Captain who she knew was probably getting very hungry. He politely tasted the scrambled mess on his tray, having to use a knife to cut a piece off. Choking, his eyes had watered at the taste. Despite her embarrassment they had laughed. From then on, she had to at least have Cook approve her dish before she served it.

During the evening meal, her and the Captain ate in his cabin together. He insisted that she not eat with the rest of the men since some of them tended to get further into their cups. The first time they ate in almost complete silence, not entirely knowing what to speak about. She asked various questions about the ports he had travelled to, which ones he liked the most and which ones he did not enjoy. How many ships he had taken and how he had become a privateer. He had obligingly answered all her questions, occasionally asking his own. She looked forward to their evening meals, he had seen so many places and met so many people. Catherine could not wait to see France. It would be the biggest city she had ever been to.

That evening, she entered the cabin holding their tray filled with salted meat, the last of the fruit and a few potatoes with a bit of rather flat biscuits. They were running low on supplies. The Captain had mentioned that Madeira would be their next stop before finally reaching France. It was much like the islands in the West Indies. She sat the tray on his desk, next to a small, old pendant. There was some kind of design on it. She touched it gently with her finger, "What is this?" she asked curiously.

"It was my Mother's, that is a Celtic knot."

"Are they back in Ireland?" Catherine sat down, ready to start her meal. The Captain followed suit.

He shook his head a bit as he sliced at the meat on his tray. "No. My parents passed on about a year after Alaric and I joined the Royal Navy."

"Oh, I am sorry." She took a small bite of her food. "My own mother passed when I was born, I never knew her." Catherine looked back up. "What about Alaric's folks?"

"He was an orphan. We grew up in a small village, he had lived with an aunt for the first couple years of his life, but she got ill and did not make it through the next harsh winter. My family took him in. Probably a big mistake on their part," he grinned. "We got into far too much trouble together. The village had had enough, when we got older, we were sent to join the Royal Navy. My Da believed it would be good for us, we would learn a new skill, become more disciplined. I am not entirely sure how well it worked."

Catherine giggled, "Do you think you will ever go back to Ireland?"

"Aye, not for a while though, I am sure." He took another bite of food.

"Alaric mentioned you two got into a bit of mischief. He actually told me to ask you about a time when you and him were supposed to take some items to a nearby town."

Lucas laughed and to Catherine's surprise turned a bit pink.

"Aye, well," He shifted in his seat. "There was this one time. It was probably what caused my folks and the rest of the village to decide it was time for us to leave to get some proper discipline." He sat forward a bit more, stabbing a slice of meat with his knife.

"We were charged with taking a wagon full of livestock and crops to a larger town a couple days ride away. We had accompanied my Da or other villagers a few times, so we knew the route well. It was not that difficult; we were to simply trade the wagon of goods for the other provisions our village needed. It was a simple dirt road that led the way, easy to follow." He shrugged.

"We would set up camp along the way, it got cold at night so we made a decent fire to sleep close to. It was the first time we had done the trip alone; without supervision. We were feeling much older and proud of ourselves. Well, we arrived at the town, we were to stay in a specific inn. We knew it well and had stayed there the times we had been to the town in the past. We went there first to get our room and to eat before trading the goods.

As it happened, the inn was full and they did not have any rooms available. So, we left and decided to find another inn. We walked down the muddy streets trying to find a place, we rounded a corner and a woman was standing outside. She caught sight of us and immediately urged us inside, saying we looked cold, tired and near to starving." Lucas chuckled and shook his head.

"We were cold, tired and hungry, to be sure but we were not doing too bad and had gone longer without food and rest before. We followed her in the building and were about to ask if the place was an inn and if it had rooms available when another younger lass came walking down the stairs." Lucas shifted again in his seat and scratched his chin. "She was, ah, clearly not of good morals. We of course being barely fourteen could not keep our eyes from her. She led us over to a table and served us a hot bowl of stew. We devoured it, completely forgetting about our wagon of supplies outside. The lass then poured us some whiskey, at the time we had only ever tasted it once or twice." Lucas was speaking through a smile now. "We did not want to appear like the young lads we were, so we quickly drank the entire cup as well."

Lucas sat back in his chair and looked at Catherine. "The

rest of the evening was a blur, we woke the next day, as green as grass and our eyes feeling as if they'd pop from our skulls. We ran outside, finally remembering why we were even in the blasted town only to see that not only were the crops and livestock gone but our horse and wagon were no longer parked outside either." He shook his head again. "We arrived back in our village days later, heads hanging low. This time we really were exhausted and near starving. We recounted the story to my folks; I had feared by the look on my mother's face she would swoon. When my father had eventually finished roaring with laughter, he took us out back and gave us a whippin' for losing so much of the village's crops and livestock, not to mention the wagon and horse. It was not until later that we learned just what kind of establishment the place had been and that it was most definitely not an inn." They both laughed as they finished their meal.

"You and Alaric certainly were wicked boys." She giggled.

He grinned and nodded. "Aye, Lass, that we were."

"I think I will go back up on deck for a bit before it gets dark." She stood up, taking the trays.

"Tomorrow I except to hear about all the terrible and rebellious things you did as a child." He winked, raising his cup to take another drink. Catherine flushed and felt her belly do another flip. She tore her eyes away from his addictive smile and walked through the hatch. She could not get enough of how the Captain spoke and the stories he told. He openly answered any question.

She stopped at Cook's galley and dropped the trays off. As she stepped onto the quarterdeck, the cool breeze hit her face. She could almost taste the air, it was sweet with a touch of salt from the mist that sprayed up from the sea. She walked over to the railing, wanting to watch the sunset. Each evening the sky lit up with oranges and pinks. Leaning against the railing, she was mesmerized by the foamy waves that passed by the ship.

"For most of us on board it does not get old, lass." Ol' Shorty stepped up beside her, watching the waves and the colorful horizon. "The sway of the ship passing over the water, the sound of the sails snapping, even the grog and salted meat ain't so bad once you've lived off of it for so long."

"How long have you been sailing?" Catherine asked, glancing down.

"Oh too many years to say. I have far more voyages under this leathered skin than the rest of the lads on this ship." He tapped the railing.

Catherine let out a small chuckle, "I completely forgot," She laughed again, looking at O'l Shorty. "In a couple days it will be my birthday. Back home my father and the entire household would be planning a lavish party. There would be desserts and dishes of every kind, there would be dancing and new gowns. I would be having to go to fittings, discussing place settings and the menu. The guest list and seating chart, and to think out here, I have been enjoying myself so much with people I only just met, without hardly any luxuries, that I had completely forgotten about my birthday."

Ol' Shorty looked at her, his eyes twinkling, "We are all happy you are here with us, little lady." He sniffed and looked away quickly. Her heart was happy, she was doing what she had always dreamt about doing, having an adventure. It was certainly far different an adventure than she had expected but she had come so far, learned so much and changed more than she had imagined.

The Captain took the helm, she marveled at his intimidating, sturdy appearance when he was commanding his ship. Watching him a few moments, she headed through the hatch and down towards his cabin. Stretching when she got in the room, she headed over to the chest that held the books. Trying to decide which one she wanted to settle down and read before she fell asleep for the night, Catherine shuffled through the variety of books.

A book about a whaling ship caught her interest. Ever since she had seen them earlier in the voyage Catherine had found herself fascinated with the giants that lived in the oceans.

They had spotted whales in the distance and she hoped they would see them a bit closer. She waited at the railing for a good while, no sign of the massive animals. Turning her back to the railing, only briefly to see if she could see them in the distance on the other side of the ship. There was a rumbling and a splash as the water moved over the body of a very large humpback. Slowly, she turned around to see the tail covered in small rock like bumps coming up and rising from the waves.

As the tail rose higher, along side the ship, the Captain told her to take a step back. Frozen, she was mesmerized by the magnificent display in front of her. The tail came down quickly, meeting the waves again. It caused the water to spray up, splashing onto the deck of the ship and covering her in water. She spat and wiped the water from her face with her soaked sleeve. A roar of laugher had erupted from the crew and the Captain.

Catherine sat at the desk, getting comfortable to begin reading. There were many drawers that lined both sides of the Captain's desk. The Captain's chair was a bit bigger and reminded her of the large chair her father had in his study back home, though not nearly as soft. Curiosity got the better of her and she pulled open a drawer, seeing not much but logbooks. She slid it closed, opening the one below it.

A parchment tied with a red ribbon sat in the drawer. In a very un-lady like fashion, Catherine slid the ribbon delicately off and unrolled it. Quickly, she scanned the document, her color drained and she felt as if she would be sick. Her father's name was on the parchment. Realizing what it was, Catherine's mouth went dry and she was dizzy. Placing a hand on her stomach, she tried to control her nerves. She paced the room, not knowing what to do next or wanting to believe what she held in hand.

The Captain was under the Governor's orders. She had heard her father tell the Captain about the Governor's plans to take the plantation from him. All that time the Captain sat, listening, pretending to care and all along he had the deed in his desk on the ship. Anger rose in her throat. How could the Captain do this? How could he allow the Governor to simply give her father's land away? How could he partake in any of it? She wrapped her arms around her middle.

The hatch opened and the Captain ducked in. He stopped dead in his tracks at the sight of Catherine glaring at him, tears spilling down her cheeks. He looked panicked. The Captain took a step forward, reaching a hand out to her.

She shook her head, "Don't come any closer!" She yelled. "You knew! All along you knew! Why didn't you give my father the deed right then? You dined with him, in this very room." She choked, sucking a deep breath in, trying desperately to control her raging emotions. She could not remember a time she had ever felt so scared, angry, hurt, or betrayed.

"Your father? Catherine what on earth are you talking about?" He shook his head, his brow furrowed. "Who is your father, Catherine?"

"The Baron, Lord Benedict, the owner of one of the largest sugar plantations in Barbados. The same man that you allowed on your ship, the same man that you feigned pity for when he told you his fears of losing his estate." Catherine shook in helpless rage.

"The Baron is your father?" He staggered back as if he had been slapped. "Why the bloody hell didn't you say anything?"

"No, you do not get to question why I did what I did. Not until you first explain how you could possibly carry out this order from the Governor. How can you give my father's land away? You heard him that night, it is not his fault, and he is doing all he can." She sobbed.

"Catherine, look at me. I promise you, I had no idea the deed was to your father's plantation until I had gone back to my cabin that night and opened the document. I also had no idea he was your father. I had guessed you came from a well-off family and probably a plantation owner's daughter but I did not know for sure or which man was your father." He looked at her apologetically, his eyes flashing with fury.

"As for you, you should not have been going through my desk without permission." He sighed and rubbed a hand over his face, briefly closing his eyes. "Catherine, I never told you about the deed because I did not know who your father was. Most of the crew does not even know that I carry a deed. They only know we are under orders from the Governor, nothing more. I gave the Governor my word I would not say a thing." He explained.

Catherine just kept shaking her head. "When you realized that night it was my father's, why did you not just give him the deed back and explain to him what happened?" Anger overtook her. She did not understand how she felt, she could tell the Captain had not known but he was still the man that had not done a thing to change it.

"I couldn't." He let a long breath out. "It is not merely that simple. If I do not get the deed to Monsieur Dupont on time, the Governor will simply find someone else to carry out the task. Catherine, you have learned a great deal about sailing, but you still do not know how all of it works." The Captain took a step closer to her. "I would lose my Letter of Marque. Without it, I cannot sail this ship. I would be branded a traitor, imprisoned or hanged. Do you think they would pardon Alaric? The rest of my crew?" He paused. "No, they wouldn't, not even Benjamin would be spared."

Catherine stared at him, her mouth hung open. He was right, she did not know any of it, how any of it worked or why. "So, you and your crew lose your ship and quite possibly your lives or my father loses everything he has." She looked at the ground, she felt helpless. She felt angry at the Governor, angry at the Captain for having no choice but to carry out the task and not coming up with a way to change things. Surely there was something he could do, there had to be. She looked up into the Captain's eyes, normally a bright blue or sometimes grey, now they were dark, troubled.

"I am sorry Catherine, truly. I will do what I can. I will try and think of a way it can work, but I cannot promise you I will succeed." He turned to the hatch and opened it. With a quick glance over his shoulder at her, she had not moved or said another word. He walked out, clicking the door closed behind him.

Cathcrine walked slowly to the bed and fell into it. Tears soaked the pillow, which still smelled like the man she had began to have feelings for. She cursed herself for not being stronger. How could any of this have even happened? Catherine desperately tried to come up with a solution, but her mind was exhausted, she had cried harder than she had in years. She drifted off into a restless sleep. Dreams of a large estate, sugar cane fields, and a tall, handsome man standing there, his eyes matching the waves.

She woke the next morning with a start. Men were bustling about on deck. Shouts and commands could be heard.

"Pull in the sails, lads. Let's get ready to anchor." More shuffling could be heard. Catherine sat up. She rubbed her face with her hands, she was still exhausted from the night before, she felt tangled and confused. Getting up, she walked over to the water basin and poured the cool liquid over her puffy face.

There was a knock at the hatch. "Miss Catherine? You awake? We are going ashore soon. We have reached Port." It was Ol' Shorty. Where was the Captain? Was he furious that she had read the deed or angry at how she had questioned him?

"Yes, I will be right up. Thank you." She answered as cheerfully as she could. As upset and frustrated as she was, she was still excited to see a new city and a new port.

16

Lucas had not slept very well the night before, tossing and turning in the spare hammock in Doc's cabin. He wanted to give Catherine some space and he had needed time to think. Lucas felt his chest tighten when he had walked in and saw the tears streaming down her face. He could not have known of her connection with all of it and had been completely taken aback.

Lucas walked to the railing, resting his hands on it. Perhaps seeing the port and getting off the ship a while would do him and Catherine good. He had been up most the night trying to figure out a solution. Finally in the wee hours of the morning a conclusion arose to his mind but was not entirely sure how he felt about it or if it was a good idea.

As *The Trinity* bobbed in the water near the docks. Lucas gave the order to ready the barrels and crates to be unloaded. They needed to trade for more goods to make it to France. Nothing stayed fresh for long on a damp ship. Lucas turned to see Benjamin excitedly looking out at the port with boyish anticipation.

Benjamin had been with his crew for about three years now. He was the youngest, but that had not stopped him from trying. He had also proven he was a natural born sailor, and he had seen and done more than most lads his age. Lucas walked over to him and gave him a pat on the shoulder, "Are you ready to go ashore, lad?" He asked, just as Alaric approached.

"Aye, Capt'n. Alaric gave me a few coins and told me to be back on the ship in a couple hours." Benjamin grinned.

It was not a particularly large port but it was a well-traveled and busy one. It was clear the lad was excited to explore it by himself a bit. "Well, I suppose you best get yourself onshore then." Lucas tried hiding his smile as Benjamin rushed over to the plank and scrambled down as fast as he could.

"Have you spoken to the lass this morning?" Alaric asked, watching Benjamin.

"No," Lucas shrugged. "I will take her ashore and show her around a bit. Mayhap she will feel better after stretching her legs and getting some fresh air." After the confrontation Lucas went to Alaric the night before and had told him everything. Lucas's original plan of putting Catherine on a passenger ship was now definitely out of the question. If Lucas had been being honest with himself, he knew he would never have put her on one when it came down to it.

"You care for her, don't you?" Alaric looked his friend over.

Lucas swallowing hard, "I suppose I do, but I think many of the crew care for her."

"That is not what I mean and you know it." Alaric raised his eyebrows.

Lucas sighed, "We will be in France in a couple days. Once I have done what is needed, we will be on our way to Barbados where I will deposit the lass back at her estate with her father."

Alaric nudged Lucas with his elbow, "Here she comes now. I will leave you to it." He walked up to Catherine and kissed her hand. "Enjoy your time at Port, Miss Catherine."

Lucas's stomach knotted as he watched Catherine flash Alaric a smile. He looked down at the deck before raising his head back up. Lucas's eyes caught hold of Catherine's. She stuck her chin out a bit and walked over to him. "Captain."

"Good morning, Catherine. Would you mind accompanying me ashore?" He held out his arm.

"That sounds wonderful, thank you." She turned and walked towards the plank that connected to the dock, ignoring his arm. Lucas's lips twitched, he could not help but admire her strength and stubbornness. Following her down the plank and onto the busy dock, men were rushing around, shouting and pushing through crowds. Lucas stood close to her, he held back a grin when she stiffened next to him. He knew she was still angry and confused, he planned to change that. No matter how head strong she was, he was determined to break down the wall she had built up.

"Best stay close, I would not want you to get lost in the rush." He whispered in her ear so she could hear him over the noise. The last few days he had been wondering just what she would look like, all dressed up in one of the fancy gowns. Now, he was thankful she was in the disguise of a young lad, she had even tucked her hair back up in the hat. He knew very well that there were men in the ports that would not hesitate to try and take advantage of a young woman, especially one as bonny as her.

"Come, I will take you over to the shops and stalls. They carry various goods from all over." He placed his hand on her back, again feeling her flinch, but she made no move to step away from him. Lucas led her a ways away from the busy docks, not without a bit of shoving and cursing on his part as well as the sailors around them.

"How long will we stay in port?" Catherine asked.

"Just the night, we will leave at first light in the morning." Lucas answered, keeping a close eye on their surroundings. They came to the main street that held fruits, animals, supplies, gowns, jewelry, and an array of many other items. It was not far from the main docks, but it was a bit less busy and slightly less dangerous.

They walked along, slowly looking at the stalls and shops. Catherine picked up a large shell. "Did you know, if you hold the opening up to your ear, you can hear the ocean?"

Catherine looked at him skeptically, then covered an ear with her hand and held the shell up to the other ear. She listened carefully for a moment, a smile began playing on her lips. Giggling, she set the shell back down carefully. "You were right." She exclaimed, "I had no idea shells did that." Catherine beamed up at him, then looked back down at the items on the shelves.

They continued to walk, enjoying the sounds of the port and seeing something other than just blue ocean. Small bushes and vines spread along the stone wall, lined with tall, full trees. As they walked down the street towards a tavern he remembered, they passed a man with a woman pressed against a wooden building. She giggled, grabbing the man closer to her.

Lucas glanced at Catherine to see if she had noticed the indelicate display. It was after all to be expected in most ports. Though it no longer shocked him, Catherine had probably never witnessed that kind of behavior. Catherine was positively scarlet and was looking in the opposite direction. "Try not to pay too close attention to the actions of the people in port. They are, well…" He tried to think of the proper word.

"Much like the women that stole your's and Alaric's goods those years ago." She said simply, looking up at him.

Perhaps she was more perceptive that he had realized.

"Well, yes, I suppose they are." He looked straight ahead, hoping to find the tavern soon.

After a while winding through the narrow streets, they found the place "Welcome to *The Shipwreck*." He waved an arm up at the swinging sign that hung above the door. It had a picture of an old, half sunken ship carved into it.

Lucas grabbed the handle and opened the door. The smell of delicious food hit him and his stomach answered. He walked them to a table that sat in a far corner. The place was cleaner and far better than the taverns closer to the docks. A woman came over, batting her eyes at Lucas and standing much too close, her skirts brushing against his sleeve.

He cleared his throat. "An ale for my friend and I and tonight's special, please." He looked at the woman and smiled politely as he tried shifting further away in the small chair. All around them, men were gambling, talking, laughing, and drinking. A few men were holding onto women that clearly worked at the place. The women would lean against them or sat on their laps, talking and kissing. Lucas tried to draw Catherine's attention back to him. Catherine however, seemed completely fascinated.

"I dreamt of adventure, from the time that I could talk. Now here I am, in a tavern, miles from my home, with a Captain sitting across from me." She blushed at the last statement.

"Is it all that you hoped it would be?" He asked. The woman brought their ale and a steaming dish of meat and vegetable pie. Lucas took a bite of the delicious and fresh fare and was pleased when Catherine took a small bite and smiled in approval.

"It has been far better than I ever expected." She favored him with another smile. "Completely different than what I had imagined, but certainly better." She took another bite of her food.

"Adventure wasn't the only reason I left, though." She hesitated. "Before I left, Lord Anderson asked for my hand." She looked down at her plate, pushing the food around. "My father accepted. I was so distraught that I knew I could not wait any longer. I would never get another chance to leave and see the world on a ship, if I did not leave right away." She let out a soft breath, not looking at the Captain who had all but stopped eating. "I gathered my things and left the next morning after my father had gone."

"I see. You are not pleased with the match then?" He asked, searching her face. It had not occurred to him that she might be engaged. Thinking back on it though, he did remember the Baron mentioning that his daughter was to be married. Despite himself and what she had just told him, he was happy that she did not care for this Lord Anderson.

"No, my father had always told me I would be able to choose who I married, but he did not keep his word. When a good match came along, he agreed to it, without even asking me." She whispered.

Unsure of what to say next, he watched her for a moment before taking another bite of food. He was hungry but had lost his appetite. They continued to eat in relative silence since the boisterous tavern made it hard for them to hear one another.

Lucas took the last bite of his meat pie, running it through the remaining bit of gravy that pooled on the plate. He wiped his mouth with the napkin. Catherine took one last sip of her ale and stood when Lucas did. He dropped a couple coins on the table as they turned to leave. He was pleased she stayed close to him as they walked out of the crowded and noisy tavern. They were not two steps out of the door when a man pushed himself off the wall.

"Well, well, well, if it ain't the notorious Captain Harding.

Ain't it a grand coincidence we are both here at the same port?" Lucas could not believe who stood in front of him. His shirt hung open, revealing the large tattoo on his chest. The man's smile never reaching his eyes. Lucas tensed and stepped closer to Catherine. "You know, I never did think I would ever see you again. I suppose there was a time I never thought I would see anyone, ever again." He sneered at Lucas, who never took his eyes off the pirate. "You see," the man shifted his eyes to Catherine. "This here Captain of yours, didn't take too kindly to me and had me marooned on an island, with nothing. It was a miracle a ship passed by when it did and took pity on me." His gaze raked over her body, Lucas's eyes hardened. Did he know? Catherine shivered next to him.

"What is it you want, Thomas?" Lucas spoke firmly.

"Oh, nothing. Just wanted to say hi to my old Captain." He tilted his head at them and walked off down between a couple of buildings.

"Let's get you back to the ship. I have a few things I need to get. I will make sure there are men on board to look after you." Lucas said, his hand resting on her back again as he steered her in the direction of the docks. Seeing the worry on her face, he tried to reassure her. "It will be alright, there is nothing to fret about. I will not be long and that man you met will not try and board the ship."

Back on the ship, Lucas made sure Catherine was safe with Doc and Cook. He knew Ol' Shorty was somewhere on the ship as well, and it would not be long before Alaric was back on board either. He had to make sure Benjamin made it back to the ship and had not gotten himself into any kind of trouble.

Leaving Catherine in the galley with Cook, she set herself to peeling potatoes. Cook probably did not need the help, as most of the crew would be eating in one of the taverns. But, Lucas knew Cook welcomed the company and he would do anything to protect the lass, especially after what had happened. Lucas felt sorry for the red-faced cook, he blamed himself for Catherine's injuries and the incident with the sailor. It had not been his fault but Cook had expressed to Lucas, that he had indeed allowed Catherine to fetch water on her own, therefore should assume responsibility.

Lucas walked past the various stalls and shops, looking at and picking up several trinkets. Ol' Shorty had told him it would be Catherine's birthday any day now. Lucas came across a stall that had many bracelets, watches and brooches. He remembered Catherine's interest in his mother's pendant. He scanned the items looking for a specific design.

"Canna help ya?" The attendant said lazily.

"Thank you, yes, I'd like this brooch, please." Lucas pointed to a brooch with vines and small flowers engraved into it in the shape of a knot. In the middle was a small sapphire. The attendant cocked an eyebrow at him. Lucas placed a few coins on the desk. She grinned a toothless grin, her wrinkly skin crinkling at the corners of her eyes. She handed him the brooch, quickly stowing the coins away safely in some hidden place in her gown. Lucas thanked her and continued further down the street.

Knowing Thomas was in port and Catherine was on board the ship, he did not feel entirely comfortable leaving her too long but wanted to make today special. Despite how much she told Shorty she loved being at sea and on board *The Trinity*, there had to be a part of her that was missing her father and her friends.

It was not long before he found a shop where several different styles of gowns were displayed. They may be in France in a couple days and Catherine would probably enjoy having a proper gown to wear in the new city. He walked in the shop, hesitating a moment. A plump woman came forward, "And how can I help you, young man?" She looked Lucas up and down with an appreciative smile.

Lucas shuffled his feet, "I am looking to purchase a gown and…well…all that goes with it." Lucas cleared his throat, feeling a bit foolish. Perhaps he should come back with Catherine.

"Ah, not to worry, just tell me a bit about your lady friend and I will find you the finest of gowns and garments we have that might suit her." The woman assured him, leading him to a book that was filled with gowns of all colors and styles. Lucas rubbed the back of his neck.

It took a while but finally they had decided on what the seamstress had assured Lucas would be the most modern and appropriate of gowns. Lucas left with a large box under his arm and the brooch in his pocket. He patted it, making sure it was still safely tucked away.

"Where is Catherine?" Lucas walked into the galley, expecting to see her.

"She is in your cabin, Ol' Shorty is standing outside the door. She said she wanted to rest a bit and read." Cook grinned when he saw the box. He opened his mouth but quickly shut it when he saw the glare Lucas was giving him. Cook chuckled and turned back to his work.

Lucas went straight to his cabin. His chest tightened at the thought of giving her the gifts. He did not know how she would react. He reached the hatch and nodded at Shorty, who grinned and winked in return. Lucas knocked on the door, cracking it open a bit. "Catherine?" He waited for a response.

"Come in Captain, I was just reading a bit." She sat up in his chair and smiled.

Lucas cleared his throat and placed the box on the table.

In the window behind her, the stars were becoming brighter as the sky darkened. "I was told it was your birthday. I, uh, wanted to get you a gift." He nodded to the box.

Catherine's eyes were wide with surprise. She glowed in the lantern light. She looked from him to the gift. "I, I don't know what to say, Captain."

"Go on, open it." he nodded at the white box, tied with a blue ribbon.

Pulling the ribbon gently, it unlaced. She lifted the lid and moved aside the thin paper. "Oh, it is lovely." She stood up and pulled the dress out, holding it up to herself. Lucas could not tear his eyes from the sight. She twirled around with it, causing the bottom trim of the dress to flare up. The color of the dress reminded Lucas of the sunsets Catherine often went up on deck to watch. "Captain, it's beautiful. Thank you." She walked over to him and wrapped her arms around his neck.

Lucas pulled her in tighter, his hands spread across her back. He could feel every curve, and reluctantly let go of her. "I nearly forgot," He reached into his pocket and pulled out the brooch. "Just one last thing I saw. I thought you might like it." He placed the gift in her hand.

With a small gasp, she ran her fingers over the design. She looked up at him and his breath caught. A tear escaped and slid down her cheek. He gently wiped it away, not taking his eyes from her. He bent down and placed his lips to hers, pausing, waiting to see if she would pull away from him. When she did not make a move, he deepened the kiss, pulling her closer to him, crushing her body against his.

17

Thomas had his men spread out through the small city. It had not taken him long to find Lucas. He followed him, hiding behind the different shops and booths. He suspected that the sailor with him was the Baron's rebellious daughter but was not completely sure until he spoke to them at the tavern. He noticed how Lucas stepped closer to her, willing to protect her from him.

At first glance the girl did look simply like a very young sailor. On closer inspection, there was no mistaking her curves, slightly hidden in the baggy shirt or the look of fear that flicked through her eyes. He watched them go into the building. He was not going to let the Captain know of his presence at first, but he could not resist seeing Harding's stunned expression. Thomas had not missed how quickly the Captain had taken the girl back to the ship or how Harding bought a trinket and purchased a gown.

He shook his head; he could not believe how soft the fierce Captain had become. It was clear the man had fallen for the wench. He wondered if the girl knew he had the deed and was simply trying to get him to hand it over to her.

Thomas was biding his time; he knew the Captain was likely to leave his ship the next morning. He would want to make sure they had all the supplies they needed, and all was in order to make it to France as soon as possible. Especially now that he knew Thomas was in the same port. He would not hide in his cabin with the girl, he would be watching over his crew, instead. Once Lucas left his ship, Thomas would have his opportunity.

There was nothing he could do at the moment; he would have to stay alert and make sure Harding did not try anything that would ruin his plan. He hung close to a tavern that had a perfect view of *The Trinity*. Taking a long drink from his tankard, he sat back in an old, wooden chair. The activity from the tavern filtered outside. He listened to the ruckus as he kept his eye on his prize.

The next morning Thomas was awoken by a hard kick to his boot, "Captain, git up, the docks are gettin' busy. I'm bettin' Harding will be makin' his way off that ship soon." Grady said, rubbing a hand over his tired face.

Thomas stood up and spit at Grady's feet, "Kick me again and you will no longer have a foot to kick with." He snarled at his first mate.

Thomas stretched and twisted, his back cracking. He had spent all night in the old chair. He rubbed the back of his stiff neck. On Harding's ship, a few men were walking about the deck, testing the riggings and checking the sails.

As he had suspected, *The Trinity* was clearly not wasting any time. They would be setting sail as soon as the supplies were all loaded and the crew was accounted for. If his plan went correctly, they would be short one particular crew member.

The next several minutes passed achingly slowly, he needed Lucas to leave his ship if he had any chance of carrying out this kidnapping. He looked around, he saw his men were all where they were supposed to be, awaiting his signal.

Thomas watched the crew on board working efficiently.

More men were filling the deck, the sound of wood scraping over the planks drifted to Thomas's ear. The men began putting supplies in position and taking already loaded goods below. Several men stepped down the plank and onto the docks. He watched them move over to a few casks and barrels. He recognized a couple of the crew members, though he could not remember their names except for the one everyone called Ol' Shorty. Thomas stepped closer to the wall of the tavern.

Finally, the blasted Captain emerged from below deck. He ducked not wanting to be noticed. Lucas was speaking with his first mate.

He disliked Alaric, almost as much as he disliked Harding. He had been right there with Lucas, ready to defend his Captain, and did not so much as blink when they had marooned him. Thomas kept an eye on them, waiting. He saw Lucas go below decks again.

He took a step forward, glancing at Grady who stood nearby, and shrugged in response. A few minutes later the Captain came back up, but he was not alone. Lucas shoved the man forward, taking him to the plank that led to the dock. Thomas chuckled, so another man met with the disapproval of the mighty Captain. He wondered what the man could have done.

Harding took the sailor a ways from the docks, he must be taking him to the authorities that were in charge of the port. Thomas could not let him out of his sight, he nodded for one of his men to follow. He spat on the ground again, twisting his lips, he had not anticipated this. He would have to wait until his man came back. He punched the wall next to him, he needed this to work.

Impatient, he was about to send another man after them

when he spotted Lucas winding his way back through the now busy and loud docks. Harding confident as he strode through the crowds. It irked Thomas, he would wipe the smile from the man's face soon enough. Thomas checked to make sure his men were still in their positions and ready to carry out the plan, his ship was already waiting for them.

They all looked ready for a fight; they were itching for some excitement. It had been a long voyage. Normally Thomas and his crew would be out pillaging smaller ships, whether they be enemy ships, passenger ships or merchants. He did not care much what they were or who they worked for, as long as he got what he wanted out of it.

The crew from *The Trinity* were loading the remainder of their cargo back on board. Alaric stood on deck, marking the records, and keeping track of crew, barrels, and cases. Lucas stood against the corner of a nearby building, watching over the proceedings of his crew. Lucas shouted something at one of the sailors that caused a ripple of laughter to travel through the men.

Thomas nodded to a couple of his men, they ducked behind the taverns and other buildings. Thomas led them to the back of the building Harding stood against. He motioned for three of the men to continue forward. There was a thunk, Thomas grinned as he watched Captain Harding falter and stumble backwards. Thomas's men quickly dragged the unconscious Captain into the alley. They bound his hands and legs, stuffing a dirty, old rag in his mouth in case he woke. As the men lifted him, Lucas let out a groan but did not move.

They hurried around the buildings, careful not to be seen. The ship was anchored further down the docks a bit. "Get him below and locked up, as quick as you can. Hurry!" Thomas commanded. "Make sure that lock is secured, I cannot risk him escaping." Thomas turned to the rest of the crew that stood on the deck, ready to set sail.

"Way anchor," He shouted. "Make it quick, we need to get a bit of distance between us, we cannot be near the ports when we meet with The Trinity." Thomas gripped the wheel at the helm, turning it as the sails clapped in the wind. The men shouted as they yanked on the rigging, tying it down. Thomas did not dare look behind him. It would not be long before the messenger he hired delivered the note to Alaric and the rest of Captain Harding's crew.

Thomas took a deep breath, blowing it out slowly. He had finally caught and locked up the fearsome Captain Harding. A smile tugged at his lips as he stared straight ahead. He would give it a couple hours before he went below to talk to his new prisoner.

His plan was working, the next part would be more challenging however, he would be facing *The Trinity's* crew once again. His only hope was that they would not engage in battle to protect the girl on board their ship. Clearly the Captain had feelings for her, the crew would not want to jeopardize her wellbeing. There was a squawk from above, he looked up, watching the sea bird fly alongside the sails of his ship. The wind was on their side, they were making good speed. The port was beginning to fade from the horizon. In the note to Alaric, he gave coordinates on where to meet. If they wanted their Captain alive and back on *The Trinity,* they would need to do exactly as he said.

"Grady, take the helm. I am going to see if our esteemed prisoner is awake." Thomas motioned for his first mate as he stepped away from it. He strode to the hatch that led to the brig. He scrunched his nose as he descended the stairs, it smelled of rot, waste, and rats. He stepped off the last rung with a splash into the stale water that pooled in places belowdecks.

Rats squealed and raced about, some Captains kept a cat on their ships to keep the vermin down, but Thomas did not care if they ran free in the cells, biting at the prisoners. He kicked at one that got to close to his boot, it let out a loud screech and ran off.

"Still alive, I see." He looked over at Ethan. He still had not found anything else out about him yet.

Ethan stood against the wall in his cell. One leg propped up against it, his hands lazily tying knots in a string. "Looks like it. Does that disappoint you?"

"Not particularly, whether you live or die is no concern of mine." Thomas shrugged, looking over to Lucas who sat in one of the few dry spots of his cell with his arms draped over his knees.

"Oh good, you are awake. I was concerned my men hit you a bit too hard. You dropped to the ground like a fainting woman." Thomas snickered as he wrapped his hands round the bars of the cell. "I always said you would pay for what you did to me. You will lose everything; you will rot in a prison with your dear shipmates. I will be the one to deliver the deed to Monsieur Dupont and the Governor, he will grant me what I wish." A grin spread across his face. "Of course, all this will have to wait. I would first like a taste of the Baron's lovely daughter. She was with you at the Tavern, don't think her little disguise fooled me." Thomas laughed as the color drained from Captain Harding's face. The Captain sprang to his feet and grabbed the same bars Thomas held.

"You will keep your bloody hands off her." Lucas's eyes blazed.

Thomas let out another laugh and shrugged, "You going to stop me?" He let go of the cell and spread his arms out wide. "Not this time Harding."

"Where the hell did you get that?" Ethan stepped forward,

his face hard and serious. "Answer me!" He bellowed, the noise caused the rats to squeak and scatter.

Thomas took a step back. Harding was looking from Thomas to Ethan. "I have no idea what you are talking about." He said, waving a hand in the air, turning to leave.

"The bracelet, where did you get it?" Ethan's voice was cold and steady.

"Oh, these?" Thomas ran a finger over the bracelets on his wrists. "I get them here and there." He stared at Ethan curiously. "A bit of a hobby, you could say." He spun a silver one around. "Which one has struck your fancy? Perhaps you also knew the friend that I got it from." He eyed Ethan carefully.

Ethan looked as if he was about to spring from the cell and strangle him right where he stood. Thomas chuckling, walked from the brig and back into the bright light of the afternoon sun. Ethan recognized one of the bracelets and the woman who had worn it before him, obviously meant a lot to the man. *A wife or lover perhaps,* Thomas thought. It was the first time anyone had asked him about them with such anger, he would of course get the occasional query, usually when he gambled.

Thomas was curious to know which of the women Ethan Clarke had known and how well he had known her. Most of the jewels and bracelets he had acquired rather unceremoniously. A few of them he had gambled for himself, where the men before him got the jewels and bracelets from, he did not know or care.

Thomas set foot on the quarterdeck and almost collided with a sailor. "What is your name? I saw Harding take you off his ship." Thomas puffed up, tilting his head back slightly, looking down at the man.

"Jonathan." The sailor replied curtly, irritated at the exchange.

"Follow me to my cabin, I will share a bit of wine with you that the Governor of the West Indies gave me." He waved the man on to follow him. He already did not care for the sailor much, but if he was going to get any information, he would need to show a bit more patience than he felt.

Thomas slowly poured a bit of the rich wine into a small cup and handed it to Jonathan, who was eyeing him closely. "Cheers, mate." Thomas raised his cup then took a sip, carefully watching to see the man's reaction. There was something about the man, he was sure they had never met, yet he looked almost familiar. "Aye, not bad. Different from our usual fair I'd say. The Governor gave it to me as a gift." Jonathan cocked his eyebrow.

"You have dealings with the Governor as well, do you?" Jonathan swirled the wine around in his cup, studying Thomas closely.

"Aye, I met with him just before I left on this voyage." In all truthfulness it had been his only meeting he had had with the Governor, but Jonathan did not need to be privy to that information.

"So tell me about Harding and this voyage he was sent on." He waved a hand in the air and set his cup on the small desk as he walked around to stand near the chair.

Jonathan shrugged. "Not much to tell. He was headed to France under orders from your very same Governor. None of the crew, 'cept Alaric, his first mate knows anything about the orders he is under and it never really mattered to me so long as I get my pay." He scoffed, "Course now I won't be seeing a penny of it cause of the whore he's got on board."

Thomas looked at Jonathan a bit closer, "Tell me about her. I heard she is the daughter of a rich Baron. The word in the ports is she ran away. Any truth to it?"

"Aye, she is Lord Benedict's daughter. She happened on

board, same day I was hired on as part of the crew. We didn't know she was a lass till she got thrashed in the storm." His face contorted. "The wench is the reason I lost my pay and got booted from the ship. If she had kept her mouth shut and had given me what I had wanted, the Capt'n and I wouldn't have a problem." Jonathan drained the last bit of wine in his cup. His face scrunched at the taste. "Why did your man bring me on board? You got the Capt'n." He gave Thomas a questioning look.

It was Thomas's turn to shrug. "I will need all the men I can get to face *The Trinity*. Will you stand with me? I will pay you what Harding had promised you when you signed on with his crew." Thomas stared hard at the man.

"Aye, count me in." Jonathan sniffed and held his hand out to Thomas.

Thomas smirked as he watched the man walk from his cabin. Things were going better than he planned. Not only did he get the prized Captain, but he also managed to convince one of his men to join his crew instead.

He kicked his boots off and headed for his desk. He sat down hard, making the chair creak under him. Thomas looked at the map on his desk. In a day or two he should be meeting with *The Trinity* to exchange a Captain for a deed and his chance to take everything from Lucas Harding.

18

"Alright, Mate. Let's get ready to set sail." Alaric motioned to Benjamin. "Care to take the helm for a wee bit?" He gave the lad a nudge.

"Of course!" Benjamin exclaimed, turning to yell to the crew to way anchor. "Where is Captain?" He furrowed his brow.

Alaric chuckled. "Probably back down in his cabin with the lovely lass." He gave the boy a wink, who in turn flushed.

"Mister Alaric?" A thin, pale man rushed to the edge of the dock. "Excuse me lads, where might I find Mister Alaric? I believe this is *The Trinity,* aye?" The man's face looked as wrinkled as his shirt, a greying beard growing on his worn face.

"Aye, what is it? I am Alaric." Alaric walked to the edge of the ship but did not walk down the plank. He curiously looked the old sailor over.

"I am supposed to deliver this here letter to you before you set off." The man looked at the men behind Alaric. He slowly stepped up the plank, handing Alaric the letter, before rushing back onto the dock.

"Who gave you this?" Alaric asked, waving the letter in front of him, looking severe.

The man shrugged. "Some sailor, bouts your age, I reckon. Says I was to give you the letter." He tipped his torn hat at Alaric and rushed off, fading into the crowd of the docks.

Alaric stood there a moment, staring curiously after the man. He shrugged and turned to Benjamin, "Well lad, what are you waiting for? Give the order to sail and get herself to the helm." He started to unfold the letter when Catherine emerged from the hatch.

She spotted him. "Are we leaving?" She had a hand over her eyes, shading them from the bright sunlight. "Where is Lucas? That is, where is the Captain?" She looked at the deck and blushed.

"You mean to say he wasn't in his cabin?" Alaric shifted and looked about the deck for signs of Lucas.

Catherine shook her head. "He isn't with Doc or Cook either. I just came from speaking with them."

Benjamin who was watching them from the helm awaited further orders. Alaric held up his hand and shook his head briefly. Benjamin shouted for the crew to hold their positions. Alaric unfolded the letter, his jaw dropping slightly. He looked up at Catherine, adjusting his stance.

"What is it?" Catherine nodded towards the letter he held limply in his hands.

"It appears Lucas was taken." He scratched the back of his head, unsure of what to make of this information.

"What do you mean, taken? By whom?" Catherine stepped closer trying to look at the letter in the first mate's hands.

He handed it to her. "Catherine, when you were in port with Lucas, did he speak with anyone or did he mention anything to you?"

"No, I don't recall," Catherine looked about the port then suddenly back at Alaric. "Yes, there was a man. The Captain took me to a Tavern. When we were leaving, this man stopped us. Lucas seemed very unhappy. They clearly knew one another, though I cannot remember what the Captain had called him."

"It's alright," Alaric assured her, though he still looked fierce and worried. "What can you remember about the man's appearance? Anything stand out?" Alaric asked.

"He was about the same height as the Captain, with blonde hair and what looked to be a large tattoo of his chest." Catherine thought about it, looking at the deck of the ship once more. "The markings on his chest looked like a compass or a map of some kind."

"That Thomas Banning, I'll wager." Ol' Shorty spat. He had been standing nearby, listening. "What are the chances of running into the scoundrel all the way up here?"

"Aye," Alaric acknowledged the older sailor. "What did he say to Lucas?" He glanced from Shorty to Catherine.

"Something about how the Captain had marooned him. It was strange, the way he spoke and watched me. It was almost as if he knew who I was." Catherine wrapped her arms around herself.

Alaric rested a hand on her shoulder. "Don't worry: we will get Lucas back. As for knowing who you are, it is possible. He knows about the deed so there is no telling where he is getting his information or how much he does actually know." Alaric reached for the letter again that Catherine held. "He gave coordinates on where to meet him. He says he will exchange the Captain for the deed. He clearly spoke with the Governor or knows a member of the Governor's household." He looked to Ol' Shorty and Eddie. "Come, let's go speak in the Cabin. Catherine, why don't you join us as well." He looked over to Benjamin who held his spot at the helm. "Give the order to sail out. I will come up in a bit."

Alaric filled the men in on the Governor's orders and all he knew about the situation. The cabin suddenly felt empty, despite the three other men in the room. Alaric marched over to the chest that held the maps, he flipped it open and rifled through them, eventually finding the one he needed. Pulling it out, he walked back over to the desk, unrolling the map on top of the ledger.

"Right, we are here," he pointed to Madeira. He pulled the note from his pocket and laid it too on the table. He glanced from the paper to the map, running his finger along the map, until he found the spot he was looking for. There did not seem to be anything other than open ocean.

"Why so far out? Would he not like to make the trade sooner and closer?" Catherine asked, confused.

"No lass, he knows the Capt'n and Alaric have ties still with the British Royal Navy. Seeing as how we are not far from some very important and large ports, Thomas probably feared we'd bring the navy down upon him." Ol' Shorty explained.

"Well, why shouldn't we bring the Royal Navy down upon his ship?" Catherine placed her hands on the desk. She was worried and confused. The day before had been something she was sure she could have only conjured up in a dream. Everything had been so wonderful. Now suddenly it all felt wrong and terrible.

"He would see the ships coming from far off. He would likely kill Lucas in his anger. We cannot risk it. We need to play his game, after we have our Captain back, then he can decide what we do with Banning." Alaric stood up straighter and crossed his arms across his chest.

"And what of the deed? If we give him that, my father will lose his land for sure." Catherine choked back the lump that was forming in her throat.

"You leave it to us. We have been in scrapes before. We will get Lucas back safely and Banning will not get his hands on the deed either." The look on his face reassured her.

The men discussed various plans and strategies, moving two small ship figures on the map, visualizing different moves that might give *The Trinity* an advantage if it came to a battle. Catherine walked over to the side of the desk with many drawers and pulled one open that contained the deed. Taking out the rolled-up parchment, she examined it.

That was all it was, a simple piece of parchment, like any other, yet this one could take away everything she cherished. Another piece of parchment with similar writing on it caught her eye.

Catherine let out a laugh of surprise, "He was copying the deed. He was making another. This is it; this is how we can get the Capt'n back, still keep my father's land, and hopefully avoid battle." She looked at the men who were silently staring at her.

"I do not understand. How does another deed save your father's land? Yes, it would get the Capt'n back, that is, if Thomas stays true to his word, but I do not see how this would work in your father's favor." Eddie said doubtfully.

"The deed we make will not be signed, by my father or anyone else. Thomas will not know the difference; I am sure of it and clearly the Capt'n believed Monsieur Dupont would not either. He might have even thought to sign fake names. At any rate, it could at least buy us more time." She felt certain her plans would work.

Alaric laughed. "I do believe you have a knack for privateering, lass. You have become more cunning." His grinned broadened. "I say you are in need of a bit of a higher rank, cabin boy doesn't really suit you anymore."

He walked over to a shelf that held an oddly shaped black

hat. Alaric picked the hat up, and went back over to Catherine. He took her old, beat up hat off her and placed the larger one on. "There, I think that suits you far better." The men around him were grinning, the mood lightening a bit. Alaric nodded to the parchments in her hands, "I suppose you best start copying that deed, Captain Catherine Benedict. I best go check on Benjamin and make sure he isn't going to run us aground."

Catherine sat at the desk, concentrating on copying the deed. Despite believing the plan would work, she was still nervous and uncertain. She could not help but wonder what horrid things Lucas might be enduring on Thomas's ship. Catherine also worried about battle.

The men seemed to believe that Thomas would not likely stay true to his word, and a battle of sorts might be inevitable. She feared for the safety of the crew and for Lucas. She pulled out the brooch that was tucked away snugly in her pocket and held it tight in her hand.

Catherine stood; she needed a bit of air. She worried that her father would not find a business partner and, in the end, they would lose the plantation anyway. She placed the treasured gift back in her pocket and made her way to the quarterdeck.

The fresh air felt wonderful. She closed her eyes, soaking in the warm sunlight. Catherine walked to the railing, adjusting the new hat on her head. The gesture from Alaric meant a lot to her. Wearing the Captain's hat given her the confidence she desperately needed. Benjamin stood near the railing, buckets of water at his feet.

"What are the buckets for?" She asked.

"Wetting down the sails, Captain." He looked up at her. "You always wet down sails if you are preparing to possibly engage in battle. It helps them from catching alight." He gestured at the water and the sails that were laying near him.

"Oh, I see." Benjamin did not seem nearly as cheerful as usual. "Are you worried about the Captain?" She felt her nerves begin to waver again.

"Nah, the Capt'n can take care of himself and I have no doubt Alaric will get him back. I heard you are the one that came up with the plan." He gestured to her. "You are lucky you were able to even be in the cabin when they were talking." He looked back down at the sail he was patching.

"Here let me." Catherine took the thread and needle from him. They sat down and continued to work. Catherine was suddenly feeling even more self-conscious in the big hat. "Well, you are lucky you got to man the helm. I have yet to be given that opportunity." She gave him a small knock with her elbow.

Benjamin chuckled. "I suppose, when you put it like that." He pushed another needle and thread through a sail. "Alaric said your father was the Baron that dined on the ship a few weeks ago. I had not realized. He also said the deed the Governor tasked the Capt'n with delivering is the deed to your plantation." He shook his head and scoffed. "What are the odds, not to mention Thomas kidnapping the Capt'n for the same deed. Here I thought this would be a fun and easy voyage." He stopped stitching the sail and looked up at Catherine. "You really have accomplished a lot. My first real voyage on *The Trinity* was much harder on me than it was on you, I admit."

Catherine watched Benjamin for a bit. "What do you mean?"

"Well, my first ever trip on here," he patted the deck. "I was only ten. Alaric found me in London, him and the Capt'n were there on business. I was in the streets, starving and sick with fever. Alaric took me aboard, they healed me. I begged him to keep me on the ship, but he said I was too young. He found a family to take care of me while he was at sea. The family I stayed with were kind, but I was never very close with them. They take in a few kids here and there that need help. Alaric would always visit when he could. When I turned fifteen, he told me he would allow me to join the crew."

Benjamin smiled. "It was not easy, we had not been at sea long when we had to intercept an enemy ship. It was one of the worst battles, we lost several men. I will never forget it, the screams, grown men crying." He focused harder on the sail. "It got easier though and much better." He looked at Catherine. "I would never change a thing, I love this ship, it is my home, and Alaric, he is the closest thing to a father I have ever had."

Catherine placed a hand on his forearm. "I had no idea. I thought you were all just really close and I had no idea about your past. I am sorry." She was so used to seeing the happy Benjamin that was always joking with the others, she had never seen this side of him before.

"Nah, don't be sorry, Miss Catherine. In truth, I have enjoyed every moment." He adjusted stretching his long legs out and tying off the stitches in the sail.

"Well, I best go see if Cook needs any help." Catherine stood, brushing sand off her breeches. "Benjamin, thank you for telling me." Turning, she walked across the deck and opened the hatch that led to the galley.

19

Lucas watched as Thomas climbed through the narrow hatch. He shook his head and turned, back to the only dry spot in his cell. He glanced over at Ethan, the man looked as if he were in pain. Lucas had been surprised at Ethan's outburst, he had obviously recognized one of the bracelets and Thomas knew he had as well. Thomas had worn them when he was part of his crew, he still had the chain necklace as well. He had never questioned where he had acquired the jewels or why he wore them before this moment. Lucas sat back down, draping his arms over his knees. He had known Thomas was reckless and a troublemaker but he had far underestimated his vicious nature. There was more hate and deception in him than Lucas had originally thought. Locked in the stinking and moldy brig, he knew Thomas did not have the deed, only him. Chances were, Thomas was planning on trading Lucas for the deed, and if that were the case then there was no doubt a battle would ensue. He just prayed that Catherine remained belowdecks and safe from any harm. He trusted Alaric would come up with a plan and do what needed to be done. In the meantime, he would wait for the opportunity he needed.

"You alright?" Lucas asked Ethan, who still stood with his hands on the bars.

He slowly glanced over at Lucas. "Aye." He answered, looking towards the hatch.

"Why'd he put you down here?" He asked, noticing the bloodstains on the man's shirt. Lucas shuffled his feet a bit to keep the rats away. He knew if he sat still for too long, they would not hesitate to take a nip.

"A fire broke out on board the ship, one of the younger and new recruits accidentally set it. He had forgotten to cap his pipe. When we went on deck the poor lad was shaking, sweat dripping off him like he had just been dunked in the sea. He was terrified of being whipped, and I reckon if I had not taken the blame, he would have been whipped to the bone, the kid hardly has an inch of muscle on him. The boy is of no use to the Captain and is too young and scrawny to help in any way. At any rate, my guess is, the boy will be far more careful about his pipe in the future after seeing what the Captain did to my back." He shrugged.

"That was noble of you. You are probably right, there would have been nothing stopping Thomas from beating the lad half to death, though by the stain on your shirt, looks like you did not get off so easily either." Lucas pointed to Ethan's tattered shirt. "What brought you on board this particular vessel? You don't appear to be the average sailor bouncing from ship to ship." Lucas observed.

"I confess I am not. I am with the Royal Navy, yet another reason I believed the whip would have been far too severe of a punishment for a young lad. On the Navy ships, a young boy like that would have been bent over a barrel and been caned or maybe birched. He would have had a sore arse for a while but would have been none the worse for wear. Most of us can say we probably suffered through something similar as lads."

He chuckled. Growing serious again, he continued. "I

took leave from it for a time. Last year while I was away at sea my sister was assaulted on her way home from a dinner party at a friend of ours' estate. When I returned home, it was a couple months after the attack. She would always stay with a friend when I was away on duty. I was afraid she would get lonely or bored if she was in the big house alone. We have no relatives, our folks passed a few years ago." Ethan let his hands drop, walking over to the bars that divided the two cells. "They had sent a couple letters, explaining what happened, but I never received them."

"How is your sister fairing now? Was her attacker found?" Lucas stood, walking closer to Ethan.

He shook his head. "My sister did not make it. She was fifteen. The coachman was knocked off his seat. He hit is head hard on the ground, rendering him unconscious. When he woke, it was nearing early morning. My sister laid by the carriage; her clothes torn." He swallowed hard. "She succumbed to her injuries after the bastard left her laying there on the street." His jaw worked.

"Her attacker is the reason I am on this ship. The coachmen did not see much of the man. He saw him from behind, said he had blonde hair and resembled a pirate. I knew if I were to find the man, I would have to go where a pirate was most likely to be." He stretched his arms out. "A ship like this seemed like a good enough place to start. I hoped to be able to get to know the crew, question them slowly about a pirate they might know that would have done that. I was not getting very far. I had a suspicion that it might have been our dear friend, Thomas."

"The bracelet, the one with the rubies." He paused disgust in his voice, "I gave that to my sister, Helena, before I left. It was the last time I spoke with her." He looked towards the hatch again. "It was him, you heard what he said about that Baron's daughter and about the collection of jewels on his wrists." Ethan slammed his hand against the bars. He turned and slowly paced the tiny cell.

"Aye, I would not put it past the man." Lucas watched Ethan closely. "I suspect a battle is to come in a day or two. My men will be coming for me, when they do, I will make sure you are set free and if Thomas should live through the battle, you are welcome to join my crew. No man like him should be allowed to live, not for long at least."

Ethan nodded. "My thanks, I only hope that when he gets what he deserves, it will be by my hand." His voice was hard.

They both fell silent, listening to the sounds filtering down from above deck. Lucas leaned against the damp, back wall of his cell. He rubbed his knuckles together, worried about his crew and most of all Catherine. He knew what Thomas would do to her if they failed.

There was no way around a battle. He was not about to let Catherine's estate go or allow his crew to be sent to the gallows for failing to carry out the Governor's orders. He thought about the girl aboard his ship, how her lips had felt when they had kissed. Her hair was as golden as the sandy beaches and just as soft as the small waves that washed over them.

There were footsteps drawing closer and a hatch clanking that led to the brig. It slowly opened. A sailor came in, muttering profanities as he stepped down the steps, sloshing what looked like grey broth with bit of salted meat in it out of the wooden bowls. The man had a jagged scar on his face and looked to be a good thirty to forty years older than Lucas, his thin hair hanging loose about his shoulders. There was a square opening in the bars of the cells to allow food to be passed through the bars without having to unlock the cell and risk the prisoner escaping. Limping, the old sailor slid the bowls through the small openings at the bottom of the cells. He stood up, trying to wipe the spilled stew off his grungy, torn shirt.

"Best eat up lads, that will be all you are havin' and you won't want them rats gettin' to it first." He gestured to the bowls and hobbled towards the hatch.

Shooing a couple rats away with his boot, Lucas reached down, grabbing the bowl from the ground. He scrunched his face. He had eaten some pretty questionable meals over the years. Ship food could get rancid and hard in a short time, Cooks usually pickled or heavily salted the food to hide the souring taste. Running a wooden spoon through the stew, the small piece of meat felt as hard as the spoon. Taking a tentative bite, Lucas coughed and spat it right back out. He quickly put the bowl through the opening and watched as the rats scurried and squeaked towards it.

Ethan chuckled, "I suppose this is meant to be our punishment." He took a small bite. "To be honest though, the food was not much better above deck either." He said, choking down another bite. "So tell me, what is the deal with this deed and who is the Baron's daughter that the Captain mentioned?"

"Ha, well," Lucas let out a low laugh. "When I left for France under the Governor's orders, I took on a few new recruits, one of which was a particularly young sailor, I and the rest of the crew believed to be fourteen-year-old Allen." Lucas shook his head. "The young sailor did very well, a lot better than many do at that age. One night there was a nasty storm, the sailor was told to remain belowdecks and assist the others with leaks and holes."

"Next thing I knew, the sailor was scrambling towards a belaying pin that was loosening. In an attempt to save the ship the sailor almost went overboard. The next morning, I went to the surgeon to check on the patient, that was when I was informed that our young Allen was in fact, Miss Catherine Benedict. The daughter of a Baron. She had dressed as a lad so she would not be recognized, she had intended to board a passenger ship but through a bit of confusion and chaos at the docks, she landed aboard *The Trinity*. That's my ship, *The Trinity*. She continued her disguise for fear of what would happen to her if a ship full of men discovered her identity. After she got to know us a bit better though, I believe she was relieved when we found out who she really was. I am sure she was tired of putting on the façade for so long."

His tone turned sober. "Their estate and entire plantation is at risk of being handed over to a wealthy man in France. I am to take the deed to the man, they in turn will lose everything they have. Of course I did not know it was a deed at all, let alone the deed to Miss Benedict's plantation. I only recently learned that. I have been devising a plan to save the plantation as well as try and keep my Letter of Marque. I about had it all laid out when Thomas and his cronies took me." He scoffed. "I knew he was at the port, but I did not worry much about it. I knew Miss Benedict was safe on board my ship, last thing I had expected was the bastard to kidnap me."

Lucas laid his head back against the damp wood, letting his eyes close. It would not be long before Alaric and the rest of his crew came. He felt the ship slow and heard the heavy anchor lower into the sea. Now all they could do is wait.

Lucas woke the next morning to the clanking of the hatch being opened. He sat up straight and blinked back the sleep from his eyes. A young man quickly came into the brig.

"Ethan," The young sailor whispered. "I brought you a bit of dried meat. It's not much but it will have to do." He walked over to where Ethan stood at the bars.

"Thank you, Nick. I appreciate it." The boy reminded Lucas a lot of young Benjamin. Ethan handed one of the pieces over to Lucas.

"There is a bit of a ruckus on board. All the men are focused on the ship that was spotted on the horizon. The Captain is in a strange mood. I heard one of the men say it's his ship, come to make a trade." The young sailor pointed towards Lucas. "I best get back up there, likely someone will be coming down soon to fetch him."

"You be careful, Nick. Thanks again for the food." Ethan looked over to Lucas, grinning.

Despite his unease about Catherine possibly being involved in a ship battle and his men being at risk. Lucas felt confident his crew had things well in hand. They probably had Catherine tucked away safely out of sight of Thomas and his crew and away from any musket fire.

Lucas stood at the door to his cell, his arms draped through it, resting on the cross bars. They listened carefully and estimated *The Trinity* to be getting close enough to board. Lucas stood up straighter, the men above had all but gone silent. He glanced over at Ethan; his brows pulled together. Lucas felt the ship sway, indicating *The Trinity* had come up alongside Thomas's ship. He heard the scraping of wooden planks being pulled between the two ships.

"We will make the trade with you, but first, we need to see Captain Harding and make sure he has not been harmed." He heard Alaric's commanding voice travel over the ship and through the hatch.

"Very well, if you insist. Show me the deed." Thomas replied, fury in his voice at being challenged once again. There was a moment's pause. "Harris, go get Harding."

Lucas shifted his gaze to Ethan, "I will see that you are released. Once on board my ship, we can discuss what you would like to do about Thomas. I do not wish to risk my crew or Miss Benedict if this can be done without a fight right now."

Ethan looked to be in anguish. He did not want to wait any longer to approach Thomas about what he had done to his sister, but Ethan also knew he had little choice.

"Aye, alright." He said, taking a bite out of the hardened meat. "Good luck, Mate."

A big man ducked in the hatch, covered in tattoos and a gold earring hanging from his ear. He walked over to Lucas's cell, rubbing a hand over his bald head. "Looks like it be your lucky day, Harding." The man fiddled with the rusty lock, finally it clicked free. "Come along, let's not keep the Capt'n waiting and don't even think of trying anything funny, our cannons be loaded and we ain't afraid of sinkin' that ship o' yours down to the depths." He grabbed tight to Lucas's arm.

Lucas bit back a retort and clenched his fists. The sailor led him through the hatch and out into the bright sun. After his eyes slowly adjusted, Lucas scanned the deck of Thomas's ship, looking for any indication of Thomas not keeping his word. He turned his gaze over to The Trinity, he swallowed.

He could scarcely believe what he was seeing. There she was, still dressed as a lad, wearing one of his white shirts which rippled in the warm breeze. Small tendrils of her hair whipped around her face. She confidently stood next to Alaric, wearing Lucas's Captain's hat. Despite his fear at seeing her standing in the open, in front of Thomas's entire crew he chuckled. He caught her eye and grinned, giving her a wink.

Lucas watched Alaric give a brief nod to Catherine, who stared straight at Thomas as she slowly walked across the plank. Lucas tried taking a step forward but the large man holding him did not let him move. He did not like her stepping onto the other man's ship. He shot a look to Alaric, who simply raised an eyebrow and nodded just enough for Lucas to notice. He looked back to Catherine who was now standing in front of the other Captain.

"Release Captain Harding and I will hand over the deed." Her voice was steady. Thomas signaled to the man who still had his meaty hand around Lucas's arm. The sailor reluctantly released him, shoving him forward. Catherine cautiously handed the deed over to Thomas.

He snatched it out of her grasp, greedily grinning. He unrolled it and looked it over. "Very nice, you can have your precious Captain back." He spat at Lucas's feet.

"Catherine, no." He shook his head, he could not bear her giving up her estate for him. "Do not do this. You do not need to give him the deed."

"You are right, I do not need to." She said, sounding as confident as she looked. "Join your crew sailor," she ordered. Lucas grinned, he could hardly believe she had just given him a direct order in front of his entire crew.

"Best do as she says." Alaric responded, crossing his arms over his broad chest.

"Just one more thing. Allow me to take the prisoner down there, off your hands. He is just one more mouth to feed. After all, you will not want to have to explain to the Governor that you almost lost your ship to a fire. He will not likely grant you a Letter of Marque if you and your crew appear so careless." Lucas said casually.

"He is of no use to me, now that I have what I came for, you can do what you like." He waved a hand in the air, clearly ready to be on his way. "Go fetch him." He demanded of the brawny man.

Not a minute later, Ethan strode up on deck. He walked over to Thomas, "I'll be seeing you again." His tone sounding more than a little threatening. Not waiting for a response, he turned and walked aboard *The Trinity*, stopping only to shake hands with Alaric.

Lucas walked to Catherine, placing a hand on her back.

He steered her onto to his ship. As soon as they set foot on deck, the planks were removed, and the order was given to raise the sails and pull in the anchor.

20

Her heart lurched when Lucas emerged from below the decks of Thomas's ship. She imagined him being beaten and bloodied. Struggling to keep herself composed, she was determined to appear as confident as Lucas and Alaric did. She helped Alaric devise the plan and spoke to him and the other men about various battle tactics; she was not about to back away and hide when she had helped them this far.

She locked eyes with Lucas, his wink causing her already pounding heart to thud even faster. Catherine expected him to argue when she handed the deed over, hoping that he would not give anything away or that she would not say anything that would make Thomas suspicious.

The sails unfolded loudly in the wind, pulling *The Trinity* forward with a slight jolt. Catherine stepped closer to Lucas. "I think this belongs to you." She smiled and placed his Captain's hat on his head.

"It did look rather nice on you though." He grinned down at her and squeezed her. "Alaric," Lucas said, walking up to his friend and clapping him on the shoulder. "I thank you."

Alaric raised his hands, "Don't thank me alone, it was your lass there that came up with the plan." He said, pointing a finger at Catherine.

"Well, that is not entirely true," She shrugged. "I found the fake deed you were writing, I thought it was a great idea. I figured, if you believed Monsieur Dupont would be fooled," she lifted a hand in the air. "Then why not Thomas?"

Lucas barked out a laugh. "Unbelievable. I admit, that was the last thing I thought would be the plan to get me out." He looked about his crew and exhaled. "Ethan, why don't you go see Doc, he will get your back fixed up proper. Then go find yourself a hammock, I will have Cook bring you down a bowl of food. Believe me, it is far better than the grey rat food." He gestured for Ethan to head below decks.

"Much obliged, Captain." He nodded his thanks and headed for the hatch.

Catherine turned her face into Lucas at the sight of Ethan's blood-soaked shirt. "How is he not in pain?" She whispered.

"I reckon he is, and likely was in an even greater deal of pain during the flogging. It is a miracle he did not get a fever, many men do." He squeezed her tighter. "Let's set a course to France." He bellowed to the crew. They all cheered in response.

Catherine led Lucas into his cabin, "I put a fresh bowl of water on the cupboard over there so you can wash up. I will go and see if the meal is ready. I will not be long." She said, reaching up to give him a tentative kiss. His arms circled around her, drawing her to him. He deepened the kiss a moment, before releasing her.

"You are probably right; I likely smell like a mix of rat and moldy brig." He took a step back and turned to the water bowl.

He splashed some cool water on his face, exhaling. Running his hand through his hair, he dunked his head into the bowl and grabbed for the small bar of rough soap. Catherine walked through the hatch and towards the galley. The aroma of fresh food cooking wafted down through the hall. She took a step in. Cook was humming and all but dancing as he prepared the meal. She laughed, "What's got you in such a glorious mood?'

"Well now, what do you think, Mademoiselle? Your plan worked, our Captain is safely back with us and we are headed to France." He said with flourish of his hand. "Just wait until you see it, it will amaze you." He grinned, spooning a large portion of fresh meat, potatoes, carrots and onions onto a platter, he added a bowl of fruits, some of which Catherine had never seen before.

"I bet. After all, it will be the largest city I have ever seen. I have heard, the customs and dress are quite different from Barbados." She replied, taking the platter laden with food out of Cook's hands.

"Oui, that sure be true, Miss. I will be a happy man once we get there. It will be good to visit my home country again." He smiled, wistfully. "Now you best get that food down to the Capt'n and I will have Benjamin take this one to the new fella." He said, pointing to another tray.

Catherine nodded and headed back to the cabin. "Supper is ready." She said as she strode through the low hatch. Her foot paused in midair. He was standing by his desk, wearing a fresh, clean shirt that gaped open on his chest, pouring two glasses of whiskey. He turned and grinned at her.

"Mmmm that smells amazing." He said, gesturing for her to sit down at the table.

Catherine watched quietly as Lucas enjoyed the meal. She had been so worried about him. Had imagined every possible, horrible thing Thomas could have done to him. Relief enveloped her when she saw him. Now he was safely back on *The Trinity* and they were heading to France to sort things out.

Then they would be headed back to Barbados. It would be

another long trip but once they got home, then what? Would she ever see Lucas again? Would he simply bid her farewell and sail back out to sea? Would she be pushed back into the plantation and be tucked away or be forced to marry one of the rich men her father told her to marry? Would they be able to keep their plantation or would a man even still want her after finding out she had spent so many nights alone on a privateer ship?

"You look deep in thought and none too happy at that." Lucas said, breaking the silence.

"Oh, I am sorry," She tucked a bit of hair behind her ear and looked down at the cup in her hand.

"Is it that miserable to have me back?" Lucas teased.

"Of course not. I missed you more then you know. I was so worried about you." She blurted out. Tears spilled from her eyes as she buried her face in her hands.

"Come on, luv." He said gently as he coaxed her out of the chair and into his arms. She had not even heard him get up. "You are tired, it is understandable."

She smiled; he had never called her that before. "I am sorry, I will be alright. I am just a bit tired I suppose." She wiped her eyes. "I'll take the tray back to the galley; Cook is probably expecting it."

"No, leave it. It can wait." His voice was low and husky. Lucas kissed her then.

Catherine closed her eyes and sank into his arms. He smelled of the salty sea, soap and the ship. She breathed him in. Lucas lifted her chin, she felt herself sway. His arm wrapped around her waist a bit tighter as he lowered his lips to hers.

She jumped at the sudden knock on the hatch. Lucas groaned and gave her one more kiss before bidding Benjamin entrance.

"It had better be good, lad. What is it?" He said, curtly. Catherine, red faced, stood next to Lucas.

"It's Thomas, Capt'n. He's at full sail and headed straight for us. Alaric says you better come on deck." Benjamin explained.

"Damn!" Lucas clenched his jaw. "I'll be right up." He said, excusing Benjamin.

He turned to Catherine. "I am sorry, lass. I am sure it will be alright, why don't you get some rest. I will come back down in a bit and let you know if anything has changed. It will be awhile still before his ship is upon us, anyway." He ran a hand slowly through her hair and bent low to kiss her once more.

Catherine swallowed back the lump forming in her throat. She wanted to be nearby, but he had been right, she was exhausted and would not be any good to him on deck at the moment.

"Alright, but please be safe and come to get me at once when his ship nears." She put her hands on his chest. She bent forward, kissing him on his bare chest.

"Aye, luv. I will. Try and rest." He picked up the spy glass on his desk, strode to the hatch and flung it open.

21

Knowing Thomas was heading for them, Catherine felt drained, but restless. She walked over to the bed that sat in the corner of the cabin. Pulling down the cool sheets, she crawled in and let her head relax on the pillow. Inhaling deeply, she tried to rid her thoughts of Lucas being shot or killed by Thomas's blade. Running her hands through her hair, she strained her ears, waiting for a command that would indicate the other ship nearing. She knew it had only been a few minutes, but it had felt like an eternity, waiting below.

Catherine flung the covers off, she quickly realized that there was no way she would be getting any sleep. She paced the room, occasionally walking over to the small, rectangular window that sat at the back of the cabin, just behind the Captain's desk. It made her feel less alone, less trapped.

"Catherine." The hatch opened suddenly. "The ship is getting closer, he has speed on his side but nothing more." Lucas said, as he gently grabbed her arms. "I want you to stay with Doc, if someone comes down, looking for you to get leverage over me or to find the deed, they will first check here. They will not think to look with Doc. Benjamin will be with you as well, he may be young, but he is a fair fighter. Here, I want you to take this." He reached for his gun belt and pulled out one of his flintlocks. The weight of the gun caused her arm to drop. "If someone comes into the surgery, you stay behind Doc, if it comes to it, do not hesitate to use this."

"Yes, Captain." Her voice quivered. She could not believe this was happening.

"Here, look closely." Taking her hands, he raised the gun up. "You will pull this back, once it is fully engaged, it will be ready to fire. I already loaded it for you. It will be alright. You will be safe; this is all just an added precaution." His lips met hers.

Catherine reluctantly pulled her mouth from his. "Promise me you will be alright, that you will not be harmed. Promise me." She urged.

"I will do my best, lass, you have my word." He bent down, kissing her forehead. "I want you to have this as well. My father gave it to me when I was a small lad, tuck it away." He handed her a small dagger. She wrapped her hand around it tightly before shoving it into her pocket.

"Come on, let's get you to Doc." He said as he pulled her along through the hatch.

Once in the surgery she glanced around. Doc had several bottles of ointments, powders and oils set out. Bandages, clumps of lint and various surgical instruments lined the table. He was wiping a few down still as they entered.

Lucas simply nodded to Doc, who returned the gesture. Then Lucas squeezed her hand, giving her a wink before heading back on deck. Now, he wore a long sword at his side and two more pistols. She swallowed back her fear and tried focusing on a roll of bandages Doc handed her as Lucas walked out the door.

"It will be just fine, Miss Catherine. They are all very skilled fighters and have been through countless battles. Only worry the Captain has, is you." He said, as the door opened once more.

Benjamin came in. "I see we get the highest honor and the very most important duty this fight, Doc." He bowed dramatically and grinned. "At your service, My Lady. It is my pleasure to be able to protect such a lovely Lady this day."

"Oh, get on with you, lad." Doc chuckled. "Here, help Miss Catherine fix up these bandages."

Benjamin scoffed. Despite herself, Catherine felt a bit lighter and laughed. It was better keeping her hands and mind busy with preparing the surgery rather than pacing back and forth in the lonely cabin.

The three of them cleaned surgical instruments, some made Catherine's stomach turn at the thought of possibly having to use them. It also occurred to her while she was washing a Capital knife with boiling water that she might be in the same room with the Doc as he used the instrument. The bone saw, forceps and curved needle seemed to stare back at her, causing her to waver.

"You do not need to worry, Miss. No one aboard this ship will be needing those this day. I only had you clean them off to keep you and the lad busy." He said, pointing a stubby thumb at Benjamin.

Catherine felt her stomach turn at the thought of them having to be used on any of the crew members, whether she was present or not. The vinegar smell was strong in the cabin, Doc explained that many of the bandages were soaked in vinegar and used for cleaning wounds. Many of the surgical tools were also dipped in the vinegar and water mixture. It kept things cleaner and if dirty tools were used or wounds were not washed out properly, then fevers were more likely to develop. The tables were spread out and hammocks strung up. They waited for the battle to begin.

Doc seemed perfectly at ease. His strength gave her more

confidence. Not only was she terrified for the Captain's sake, but she knew she would have to assist in mending far worse wounds then what she had been doing. Doc had been teaching her over the past several weeks but nothing more serious than burns, slight illnesses, splinters, and a few cuts that needed stitching. She had never dealt with musket balls digging deep into flesh and bone or wounds that bled so much the patient turned ashen and did not wake again. Doc warned her that such a long voyage was unlikely to go without some sort of fight. He had done his best to prepare her in case they were met with such an event.

There was a thunderous blast, followed by a splash and shouts from above deck. She could barely make out Lucas's voice as he shouted, "Turn her around, mates." Catherine put her hand to her throat. It suddenly got hard to swallow and breath.

"Take a sip of this, Miss Catherine. It will calm your nerves." Doc's hand was on her shoulder and the other was holding a small glass of whiskey. The smell was potent but she did as Doc bid and drank the amber liquid. A warming sensation overtook her as it trailed down her throat and settled in her stomach.

She took a steadying breath in. "Thank you Doc, it does help. What do we do now?" She asked, uncertain of how to keep her mind off of the shouts and cannon blasts. The ship rocked as one of the heavy, iron balls shot from the cannon of the other ship, splintering into the hull of *The Trinity*.

Catherine gripped Doc's arm. He simply patted her hand and informed her that was certainly not going to be the only cannon ball to put it's mark upon their ship. He looked a bit grim, but did not seem overly bothered. Benjamin had gone a bit paler, but his usual smile spread across his face as he met her gaze.

"We calmly await our first patient and hope for the best," he adjusted a bottle of some sort of powder that had slid to the edge of the table during the last cannon blast. "And that this battle will not last long."

The blasts from the cannons were far too loud and the pounding feet overhead drowned out what was being yelled above deck. The ship rocked again, but this time the blasts came from The Trinity's cannons.

"It won't be long now; men will be filing down to be fixed up and Thomas's men will meet ours with swords and muskets." He nodded to the hatch that led to the upper deck.

The words hardly left Doc's lips when Catherine heard more shouts as the cannon blasts ended. By the sounds of the scraping wood, she knew they were being boarded. Muskets fired and blades clanked together. Catherine squeezed her eyes together, dreading seeing any of the men from *The Trinity*, that she had begun to care for and consider friends, being brought down dying or gravely injured.

Catherine felt an arm come around her shoulder, "It will be alright. I mean, well…Catherine, it won't be easy." Benjamin's voice broke. "I don't want to see them hurt either, they are all I have and they are my family. They know what they are doing. We need to be here for them, down here, and help them when they come pouring in. Doc has taught you far more than anyone else on this ship knows and he is going to need you. Our crew is going to need you, Catherine." He squeezed her closer.

Pulling in all his strength, she knew he was right and felt herself growing more confident. She had to be ready for the injured men and needed to focus. She turned to Doc and nodded, "Thank you, both of you." She smiled up at Benjamin, "Let's get ready for our patients."

"Well done." Doc praised. "Looks like we will not have to

wait long for our first patient." Doc said, gesturing towards the hatch.

Ol' Shorty came down, practically dragging a sailor. The man's face was covered with blood and his head hung low, swaying from side to side. "A sword got him Doc. Down the side o' the head and caught his shoulder." He quickly explained as he shot Catherine a sympathetic glance before racing back on deck.

"Catherine, quickly. Grab the needle, thread, plenty of bandages and lint." He commanded as he poured water over the wounds, careful not to get any in the sailor's eyes. As the blood washed away, she recognized him as Jim.

Her throat tightened. Jim was one of the sailors that encouraged her by telling her tales of the sea and of his adventures. She handed Doc the bottle of vinegar water to cleanse the wound. Jim groaned as the liquid ran along his head and shoulder. Doc prepared the needle and thread then nodded to Benjamin who obediently held Jim's shoulders down in case the man gained consciousness in the middle of being stitched up.

The hatch flew open again, three more sailors piled in.

"Catherine, you take over here. Finish sewing him up and bandage his shoulder and head when finished. After that, you and Benjamin attend to the next patient." Doc spoke quickly, as she hesitantly took the needle from him.

Catherine tried working with as much efficiency as Doc had. She glanced up at Benjamin briefly. "It's nothing new, I've seen you stitch the men up a couple times."

"I suppose." Focusing her attention on the sailor laying limp in front of her was different. Doc had been standing right next to her and guiding her the entire time. Those wounds were minor and not life threatening. Jim could have easily died from this injury if it had cut a bit deeper. Even with his cut being cleansed and stitched, infection was still a very real danger.

    She finished up and tied off the last stitch. Benjamin let go of Jim's shoulders and went to assess the next sailor that was sitting on a table nearby. This sailor was holding his side, blood seeping between his fingers. Catherine quickly wrapped the bandages over Jim's head and shoulder. She picked up the needle, putting it aside to be cleaned and used again later.

    "Catherine, a musket ball grazed his side fairly deep." Benjamin explained.

    Catherine removed the man's hand from his wound, causing more blood to flow out.

    "Right, let's get that shirt off of you and clean up the wound." Not bothering to wait for the man's response, she grabbed a small pair of suture scissors and cut the shirt away from his body. Catherine did not want him lifting his arm too high for fear it would tear the wound even more, not to mention the pain it would cause him.

    "There," she said soothingly, "it is almost cleaned." Pouring a bit of vinegar water over the wound, she grabbed for the needle. As she bent over, the sailor rested his forearm on her shoulder so she could see the wound. Benjamin made a move to hold onto the man but the sailor simply shook his head, dismissing Benjamin. The man flinched slightly when the needle punctured his sensitive and raw flesh, but relaxed once she continued. "I am sorry if it is causing you more pain." She said sympathetically.

    "Nah Miss, I have had worse injuries and you are far gentler than that old Doc over there." He commented loud enough for Doc to hear. Doc merely scoffed and continued working on a more serious musket injury.

    Catherine smiled as she wrapped up the sailor's side.

"You are all set."

"Thank you, Miss." He said, stepping onto the floor and grabbing his weapons.

"Where are you going?" She demanded.

"Back up top, they need as many men as they can get." He said, nodding to the next group of injured sailors that piled in.

Catherine was speechless. "He will open his wound again, surely he cannot go back up."

"He will be alright, this is what happens every battle, some that cannot fight but are not gravely injured will help us down here as well." Benjamin assured her.

Men were bleeding and groaning about the now crowded room, some were already unconscious. She tried picking out the men that needed more urgent care.

The afternoon and night blurred together. She quickly lost count of how many men she sewed and bandaged up. A few lucky ones had simply been knocked unconscious and had been brought down to keep them safe until they woke. Men came and went, Catherine tried to keep her mind off Lucas and desperately tried to do her best for the sailors that needed her help. With every sailor she fixed up; her confidence rose.

An extremely pale man was laying on one of the tables, blood trickling out from what looked like a musket shot in his stomach. She checked his breathing and pulse, like Doc had taught her. She gasped; he felt cold and there was no pulse. She looked up; Doc was now standing next to her.

"I am sorry, Miss Catherine." He rested a hand on her shoulder. "You go see to our other patients."

Feeling herself sway, she glanced around the room once more. Most of the men had been fixed up and were either laying down resting, unconscious or they had been bandaged and had simply headed back through the hatch.

Catherine walked over to a man that was laying on one of

the many tables, clutching his leg. "Here let me have a look," She whispered. The sailor nodded in response. "Red, isn't it?"

"What's that?" He replied gruffly.

"Your name, it is, Red, isn't it?" Catherine asked a bit louder.

"Aye, that it is." He groaned as she cut away more fabric to access his wound.

"Doc, will you come over here?" She called out, glancing up at Red who was laying back with his eyes closed. He probably knew the musket ball had not gone clean through and therefore needed to be removed. Doc explained how a ball was to be taken out but she had never done it and was not entirely sure she wanted to do it alone.

"The musket ball did not go through his leg, it will have to be removed, I think."

"Aye, you are right." He said, quickly examining the injury. "Best get to it, I will assist you but I want you to do it, you need to know how." Doc explained. Catherine glanced nervously from Doc to Red.

"Do not worry yourself, lass. Red is a tough old bugger and will hardly feel a thing." Doc reassured her, handing her the bowl with instruments and bandages.

"Right then," Catherine exhaled and began to cleanse the wound. She hesitated before grabbing the scoop and hook that was used to grip the ball and bring it out. With a steady breath, Catherine slowly and as gently as she could felt around the small, and perfectly round wound for the musket ball. Red laid perfectly still, sweat beading down from his forehead, just below his hair. If she did not see the steady rise an fall of his chest she would have thought him dead. Catherine moved the hook and scoop in a bit further, finally feeling the hard ball at the tip of the tools.

"I found it." She stated, not sure if she was telling herself, it was nearly over or if she was letting Doc and her patient know. Carefully, she pinched the musket ball between the hook and scoop and drew it out from the wound. She dropped the ball in the bowl with a clink. Doc quickly covered the wound with a bit of lint to stop the blood that was flowing from it again. Both Catherine and Red let out a sigh.

"Well done, very well done. I could not have done it better myself." Doc said, "Now, finish closing up the wound and…" Doc fell to the ground as an ear ringing shot blasted through the surgery. Catherine dropped to the ground next to Doc who laid there bleeding from the arm. Catherine bit back fear as her vision blurred with tears.

"Doc, oh please, Doc." She choked out. She ran her hands along his face and pressed her hands against the bleeding wound.

Another shot rang out and she heard a body fall to the ground. "Stay down, Miss Catherine." Doc groaned, lifting his other arm up and grabbing hers.

Sobbing with relief, she knew that Doc was alright. Daring to glance under the table she gasped as Benjamin narrowly dodged a blade that was swung at his chest. He stepped back for a moment before lunging forward, his own sword driving through a man's stomach. Benjamin did not pause for even a second, he swung around, his sword meeting the other sailor's blade.

Catherine was terrified. She looked around for a weapon, surely one of the injured men brought a musket down. Lucas had given her one but she had set it down at the table she had started at, across the room. All she had was the small knife and that was going to do no good.

There was a grunt, followed by the sound of another body hitting the ground. She looked back; afraid she would see Benjamin lying lifeless on the ground. She raised a hand to her mouth. Benjamin had killed the last man but was heading for the hatch, his sword drawn.

Lucas and Alaric needed Benjamin below to look after her and Doc, in case something happened to them and Thomas's men got below. If his men had come for her, that meant something had to have happened to Lucas and Alaric. Catherine's heart leapt to her throat. She grabbed a handful of lint and pressed it firmly to Doc's wound. She checked his breathing, it was slow but steady, he had become unconscious. "I will be back, please be alright." She whispered to his still form.

Catherine stood up and rushed for the hatch, she needed to see if Lucas was injured or worse. Yanking the hatch open, she sprang onto the deck. It was a blur of men swinging swords and muskets going off. Thomas stood a few feet from the hatch, his musket raised. She turned to see who he was pointing it at.

Catherine screamed as the shot fired. Benjamin's eyes widened, he put his hand over his chest where the ball had entered. He staggered backwards, his eyes meeting hers before he fell over the railing and into the waters below. Catherine had tried running to him, but an iron grip wrapped around her arms and body. She heard a chuckle in her ear that made her skin crawl and felt the cold metal of a musket barrel against her cheek.

22

Lucas grinned as the shots from Thomas's ship fell short and splashed into the sea. He knew that Thomas was in such a rage that he would not have full control of his ship or his crew. Lucas signaled and gave the order for the crew to steer the ship around.

"Fire!" He bellowed, glancing at Alaric. Thomas would not allow his ship to be destroyed, he would attempt to board *The Trinity* before that happened. Lucas did not want to see his ship damaged either and did not want to risk a stray cannon ball blasting through the surgery. He would let Thomas board *The Trinity*. Lucas and his crew would be ready for them.

The planks slammed against the railing, allowing the men to swarm over the deck. Swords clanked against each other and muskets fired. Lucas kept an eye out for his men, trying to make sure that the injured were made to go below. Many of his crew had been through countless battles with him. They all knew each other well, their strengths and weak points. Alaric stuck close to him like they had since they were young lads, they watched each other's backs, and always kept each other in sight.

He scanned the deck for Thomas. He had spotted him at the railing as they neared but he had disappeared as soon as the ships got close enough to board. He figured the coward all but ran off to hide until the battle ended.

Lucas swung around, blocking a blow from a large sailor, his body covered in markings. He wore an old torn up vest, his lips curled up in a vicious sneer, showing several gold teeth and several missing ones. The sailor's blade came down heavy against Lucas's, causing his hands to ache. As the blade rose once more, he prepared himself for the blow. Only this time he slid to the side, drawing his blade against the man's exposed stomach. The sailor dropped to the planking of the ship, his blade slipping from his limp fingers. Lucas exhaled, he drew his musket and fired at a scraggly man that stood above Eddie. The man fell forward, nearly landing on Eddie. He shoved the man aside and stood up, nodding his thanks to Lucas.

Lucas tucked his musket back away, lunging at another sailor. The blade sliced easily through the man. There was a hiss behind him, swinging around he saw four men coming at Alaric. His arm was bleeding and tucked against his side. "I'll take the smaller one." Lucas grinned.

"No mate, you got the smaller one last time, it's your turn to take on the behemoth this time." He pointed his sword at a very large man in the middle of the four men. "Don't fret, the large ones are always slower." The large man snarled at them, charging forward with as much force as he could. Lucas and Alaric leapt apart, causing the big man to fall between them and onto Lucas's waiting blade. Alaric lifted an eyebrow to Lucas, "Perhaps a bit too easy. Maybe the others will give us more of a challenge."

Lucas turned to the three remaining sailors, opening his arms wide, "Let us see what you've got, lads." A grin spread across his face as the three sailors eyed them, an equal amount of caution and fury flashing in their eyes. Lucas adjusted his grip on his sword and readied himself for the attack.

The three men sprang forward in one fluid motion, swinging their blades. Lucas knocked the blade from the smaller, rat-faced man who quickly drew a musket. He fired it. Despite being so close, missed his mark. Lucas brought his sword down against the sailor's chest. He turned to the side to avoid being stabbed by the other man's blade but was not quite fast enough. The blade sliced through the tender flesh of his side. His shirt draped open, the warm, sticky blood trailed down his side, soaking the edge of his breeches. He sucked in a breath at the sting. He rushed his blade forward at the same time Alaric did, the sailor's eyes grew wide. He dropped to the ground when they withdrew their blades.

"You had better get that arm looked at." Lucas nodded to his friend's bloody arm.

"Your side is far worse; I will not go below until you do." Alaric challenged.

"Very well, looks like we both will be bleeding the rest of the fight." Lucas slapped Alaric on the shoulder, causing his friend to wince.

A shot fired behind them, followed by an ear piecing scream. The two men whirled around; Lucas's breath caught. He took a step forward.

"Let her go, Thomas!" He bellowed. The battle around them coming to a complete halt.

Thomas laughed. He kept an eye on Lucas as he bent his head down, burying his face in Catherine's hair that hung down past her shoulders. Lucas growled and took another step forward, careful not to move too fast. He was not sure how far Thomas would go. He did not put it past the man to use the pistol that sat up against Catherine's cheek.

"Not another step." Thomas pushed the musket harder against Catherine's face, causing her to squirm. "She's not bad at all, Harding. I see why you want to keep her to yourself."

"You lost Thomas. Release her. You are outmanned and we both know your crew holds no loyalties towards you." As he said this, Ethan stepped forward from the crowd of men, followed by the boy Lucas remembered from the brig.

Thomas's eyes shifted between the men. "You and your whore will pay. The deed was a fake. The bitch signed her name and I saw no seal from the Governor on it." He spat. "You both will get what you deserve. See, the way I look at it is, I kill one of you, the other will suffer as well." He pressed Catherine's body closer to him. "Seeing as how I still want a chance to get to know your woman a bit more, I guess it will be you that will die today." He ran his hand over Catherine's body. She flinched and tried pulling away from him. Thomas grabbed a handful of her hair, yanking her head back. He raised his pistol from her cheek and pointed it at Lucas.

The men around Lucas raised theirs in unison, the sound of multiple clicks from muskets being cocked echoed, eerily across the deck. "Kill me and you won't make it off this ship alive. You only have one shot in that musket, that is, if you haven't already spent it." Lucas said, his grip firm on the hilt of his sword, the other hand fisted tightly. He took another step closer, the wood creaking beneath his feet.

Careful to keep Catherine in front of him, Thomas looked about the ship. He stepped back, his body hitting against the railing. Shoving Catherine forward, he flipped himself backwards off *The Trinity*. Lucas bolted forward, gathering Catherine in his arms before she could hit the hard planks of the deck. Alaric and Ethan rushed to the railing.

Ethan fired off a shot. "Damn you!" He yelled after Thomas who was holding onto a skiff that was waiting for him. Ethan threw his musket at the man, causing the water to splash up next to his head. Thomas's crew rushed from the ship, readying to pull away.

"Are you alright?" Lucas cupped Catherine's face in his hands, his fingers brushed the tears off her cheeks.

She nodded but quickly shook her head. "I...I am not hurt." She choked back a sob. "Benjamin, he..." She buried her face in his chest.

"Catherine, what about Benjamin?" Alaric's voice broke. "Catherine, where is he?" He asked desperately.

Lucas rose her to her feet. "Catherine, what happened?" He asked gently.

"Thomas, he shot him. I tried running to him, but Thomas had already grabbed me." She put her face in her hands, Lucas's arms still around her. "Benjamin fell over the railing." She whispered.

Lucas looked over at Alaric, his face pale. Alaric stumbled backwards as if someone had punched him. He turned to the railing, frantically searching the water for the boy he had taken in and grew to care for just like a son. "Alaric..." Lucas whispered, placing a hand on his shoulder.

"Don't," Alaric said, shoving Lucas's hand off him, his voice hard. "Take her below, I don't want to see either of you."

Lucas glanced at Catherine frozen to the spot. He looked back to his friend. "Alright," He did not know what else to say. He knew his friend blamed them. If he had never marooned Thomas, he would have never sought revenge and if Catherine had given him the real deed, he would never have attacked, and Benjamin would still be alive and well.

"Come on, let's get you cleaned up and check on the rest of the men." Lucas put his arm around Catherine, leading her to the hatch. He glanced over his shoulder, "I cared for the lad too." He said, just loud enough for Alaric to hear. They ducked through the hatch and headed towards the surgery.

23

Catherine's mouth went dry. She could hardly get the words out to tell Alaric what had happened. Her heart ached. Benjamin had told her how Alaric had saved him and had taken him in. Alaric must be feeling unimaginable pain right now. She blamed herself for not being able to save him, for not being able to stop Thomas. As they made their way down to the surgery, she clutched Lucas's shirt. She needed to check on Doc and could not bear to watch Alaric stare into the water, hoping to spot Benjamin.

They entered the surgery, Lucas's arm was still around Catherine, keeping her close to him. Doc was awake again and sitting on the table. He held a fresh batch of lint up to his arm that looked to still be bleeding. Doc was pale, sweat had soaked his hair and shirt. He looked like he was in more than a bit of pain.

"Oh, Doc. I am so sorry. Let me see it." Catherine said, gently removing his hand and the lint from the wound. Blood trickled from the hole and washed down his arm as Catherine poured the water and vinegar over it.

"What happened?" Lucas asked, his voice sounded strained.

"Some of Thomas's men came in, one of them fired, hitting me in the arm. Benjamin shot one of them and then fought the other two." He smiled weakly. "The young lad sure can fight, Alaric taught him well."

Catherine swallowed the lump forming in her throat. She sniffled and wiped away the fresh tears that began to flow again. Attempting to focus on fixing up Doc's injuring but her vision blurred from the tears. She felt Lucas put his arm around her shoulders again.

"What's wrong?" Doc asked, concern spreading across his face.

"It's Benjamin, he…" Lucas sighed, looking away. "He didn't make it, Doc."

Doc shot up from the table, "What do you mean? Where is the lad? I might be able to help. Take me to him." Doc asked frantically, slightly swaying at the pain and loss of blood.

"I'm sorry, Doc. There isn't anything anyone can do. He fell over the railing." Lucas's voice was barely a whisper.

Doc slowly sat back down, staring at the floor, shaking his head. "Alaric?"

Lucas nodded. "He knows, he has a cut on his arm he needs stitched, but I don't think he feels that right about now."

Doc nodded, "I imagine not. Catherine, you will need to remove the ball from my arm, afterwards, please check over the men again. I will see to Alaric."

"No, I can sew myself up." Alaric's loud, angry voice filled the cabin. Catherine did not know how long he had been standing there. "Give me a needle and thread." He said, rummaging through the medical supplies, a bottle of whiskey in his hand.

Catherine looked at Lucas, he nodded. She walked over to a bowl with bandages and a needle and thread in it. She handed it to Alaric who refused to look at her. He turned and walked out the hatch without another word.

"He will be alright. He just needs a bit of time. Let's get the musket shot out of Doc." Lucas gestured to Doc, who obediently laid down on the table.

Catherine wiped away the blood gently. Grabbing the hook and scoop from the bowl, she eased them into the wound in his harm. Doc flinched. Catherine bit her lip, trying to find the ball as quickly as possible and get it out.

"You are doing fine." Doc breathed out, his eyes closed tight against the pain.

Catherine felt for the ball and found it. Clapping it between the tools and pulling it out. She dropped it in the bowl and applied more lint to the wound. It had begun seeping blood again, just as Red's had. After stitching and wrapping it up she slowly assisted Doc in sitting upright.

"Mighty good job, Miss Catherine. You are a fast learner, good thing too. You will have to be the main surgeon on *The Trinity* until I am able to use my arm again." He smiled at her. "Now see to your other patients and then go and get some food and rest." He ordered her, placing his palm on her cheek.

"Thank you, Doc." She blinked back the tears and walked over to Red, checking his leg before moving onto the next sailor. Lucas walked around the room with her, talking to his men and making sure they were comfortable enough.

"I will be right back; I am going to see if Cook needs anything and see about getting the men some broth." He gave Catherine a kiss on the forehead and walked out. Catherine busied herself tending to the men, occasionally checking with Doc about different injuries that she was not sure on how to treat.

One of which was a broken arm. The cannon ball had shattered into the railing, causing a large piece of the wood to fly off and hit one of the sailors. Catherine knew what needed to be done. Doc had showed her several pictures and had gone over the procedure with her. She carefully felt the young man's arm. He was one of the new recruits on the ship.

"Alright, Joseph. I am going to feel around a bit. I need to feel exactly where the bone is broke. Then I will ask one of the other men to help me as I realign the bone. Here take a long drink of this." She handed him a bottle of rum that was being passed around. Joseph did as he was told and took several gulps from the bottle.

Slowly, she ran her fingers down his arm, starting at the elbow. She was almost to the wrist when she felt a bit of give in the arm. It felt different from that same spot on his other arm. Joseph, who was only a few years older than her, winced. He was also from Ireland, not far from where Lucas and Alaric had grown up. Unlike them, Joseph's hair was not dark, it was an incredible shade of orange and red. Catherine had never seen hair so bright in her life and had been shocked the first time she saw him on the ship.

Catherine went over to Doc and clarified with him what needed to be done. Doc got up and walked over to Joseph. "Henry, go on and hold him steady, if you can." Doc instructed. Henry had been one of the more fortunate sailors that had been knocked unconscious during the battle and other than a nasty bump on his head. He was just about ready to get up and go about fixing the ship.

"Aye, Doc." He strode over to Joseph, wrapping his arms around the younger man. He nodded when he was ready.

"Mind you, you need to keep him as steady as possible. Miss Catherine is going to steadily pull the arm until the pieces are back in place." Through his spectacles, he peered down at the two men in front of them. "Miss Catherine, grab hold of his arm and slowly pull, you will likely need to pull rather hard in order to reposition the bones."

Sweat forming on her forehead and lips, Catherine did as she was told. The sailor let out a low moan. The moment the bones lined up, she stood up straight and firmly wrapped the bandage around the arm and the wood that Doc said would assist in keeping the arm straight while the bone mended.

"There you go. you will be as good as new before you know it." Catherine smiled at Joseph who was slowly regaining color. He took another drink of rum and thanked Catherine.

"Well, I think that does it. I will go and see how the Captain is doing and where that broth is." She told Doc, untying the big apron and laying it in a bucket to be washed later.

Catherine entered the galley and looked about the room. "Cook, where is the Captain? He mentioned the crew might like some broth. Would you like me to make it?" Exhaustion was creeping over Catherine but she was not ready to sit and think about all that had happened. She wanted to keep her hands and her mind busy.

"No, Miss Catherine. I have the broth all done and steaming over in the pot." He pointed to a large pot on the other side of the room. "The Captain came in, asked for the broth, but I have no seen him since." He turned from what he was doing and looked at her. "Are you doing alright, Mademoiselle? Today must have been quite a shock." His voice was gentle. He went and ladled a large helping from the pot into a bowl. He handed it to her and gestured for her to sit.

She let out a breath and reluctantly sat. "Yes, it was. Though, I am not sure it has all quite sunk in yet."

"That is to be expected. From what I hear, you did a mighty fine job and many of the crew owe you their lives." He turned his back to her again and continued doing his usual Cook duties.

Silently, she quietly sipped the broth. The warm liquid

filling her empty stomach, warming her entire body and relaxing the muscles that ached from bending over patient after patient. Draining the last of the broth in her bowl, she rested her head against the wall behind her, still holding onto the wooden bowl. Her mind slowly began replaying the events of the last few days. Her arms and legs now felt as heavy as the cannon balls that had ripped unforgivingly through the ship. Her face felt swollen from crying and she knew she must look an absolute mess.

At some point she had found a string that she had used to tie her hair back with so it would not continue to spill in her face while she fixed up the patients, but it had come loose when Thomas had grabbed her. She shuttered at the thought of the man. Her heart ached at the memory of Benjamin looking at her in shock and confusion before he fell over the railing.

"Catherine. Catherine, it's alright. It's over." She woke slightly, feeling a strong body next to her. She rolled over and laid her head on Lucas's chest, he pulled her closer. "Try to get some more sleep. The Trinity is repaired enough for us to continue to France. It will be a while still before we arrive." His voice was low and gentle. Catherine felt her eyes closing again as her breathing relaxed once more.

Catherine rolled over, her arm feeling the bed next to her for the Captain. Opening her eyes, the spot next to her was empty. The Captain was gone. The light streamed in through the small window behind the Captain's desk, she was not sure how long she had slept. She slid the covers of the bed back and stood. The last thing she had remembered was sipping the broth in the galley, then waking and feeling Lucas next to her in the bed. Had she imagined it?

She walked over to the bowl, pouring some water into it from the pitcher. The water was cool and refreshing against her skin. She was finishing up when the hatch opened. Lucas came in carrying a tray of food, her stomach gave an unbecoming growl. She put her hand over her belly to quiet it.

Lucas chuckled and beckoned her. "Did you sleep well?" He asked, his eyes twinkling as the flush spread across her face at the memory of laying in bed with him.

"Yes, thank you." She looked down at the food, picking up a bit of cheese and popping it in her mouth. "How long was I asleep for?"

"Almost two days." He chuckled. "Don't worry, you needed the rest and you certainly deserved it. The crew says you are just as good as Doc, only far easier on the eyes." He winked at her, causing the color to rise in her cheeks again.

Catherine ate. "Are we near France, now?" She asked, trying to steer the conversation in a different direction.

Lucas' grin broadened. "Aye, the wind is with us and we are making good time. It won't be too long now."

"That's good." She looked up at him, her fingers picking at a biscuit. "What will happen with Monsieur Dupont? We can't very well attempt the same trick we tried with Thomas."

"I agree," he nodded, taking a bite of fruit. He sat forward, resting his arms on the desk. "We will figure something out." Catherine could not hide the smile forming on her lips. "What is it?" He asked.

"You said, *we*, will figure it out." Catherine felt her heart swell.

"Well, you have already proven you can come up with a fair plan. Besides, I could use your help and I quite enjoy your company." He stood and walked around the table. He reached for her hand and she stood, looking up at him. He bent his head down, pausing before touching his lips to hers.

"You had best finish your meal," he nodded to the tray on the table. His hands still on her back. "The men will need help changing their bandages and Doc can't do much of any of it yet." He ran a finger along her cheek, tucking a strand of hair behind her ear. "I need to go on deck and make sure we are staying on course. I will come to the surgery after a while and see how you are fairing."

"Alright," She was actually looking forward to working in the surgery again and helping Doc. She was also excited about finally reaching France and hoped they would be able to convince Monsieur Dupont to not take the plantation. As Lucas headed for the Quarter deck, she took a few more quick bites before picking the tray up and taking it to the galley.

"Cook, I wanted to thank you for the broth the other day and apologize for falling asleep in the galley." She still could not believe she had allowed herself to drift off like that.

"No need to apologize, Miss Catherine. I hope you were able to get a bit of rest. You will need all your energy to be able to tend to the crew and will want to be well rested for when we reach France." He took the tray from her and sat it on the table.

"Thank you," She smiled at him and headed for the surgery.

It did not take her long to change the bandages and check the injuries. All looked good and only one or two of the men had slight fevers, nothing too concerning. When she had finished, she realized she had not seen Alaric. She had forgotten to ask Lucas how he was doing. "Doc, have you seen Alaric today? I meant to talk to Lucas about him and see how he was holding up and if his arm is alright but I forgot to ask."

"No, I have not seen him. I am worried about him too. The lad meant a great deal to him, to all of us." Doc's voice cracked. "Alaric was the only father the lad truly knew."

"I know, Benjamin had told me his story." She replied softly. "I will go see if I can find him and see if he needs anything. Alaric helped me when the Captain was taken. He included me in the plans and did what he could to make me feel better about the situation. I owe it to him to help him now." Catherine said, grabbing fresh bandages and vinegar water to rinse Alaric's cut.

Catherine walked through the companionways, looking for any sign of Alaric. She had gone above deck to see if he was up there, but no one had seemed to have seen him since the other day. Catherine continued weaving through the different cabins and storage areas.

There was a shuffle in the corner of one of the cabins that held netting and other items. Catherine had passed it but had not seen anyone in it. She went back to the small cabin and peered in. It was dark and she could barely make out the figure that lay on a bunched-up pile of nets. Catherine slowly walked in, "Alaric, is that you?" She asked quietly. "I brought some things to clean your arm up with."

"I don't need it." He replied gruffly. "I can tend to my own injuries."

"I am sure you can but sometimes it is nice to let someone help you." She coaxed, walking in the cabin. He snorted with impatience. As she neared, he looked flushed and out of sorts. She was not sure how much of it had to do with the drink or his injury. There were several empty bottles laying around him. She knelt beside him and placed a hand to his forehead.

He jerked away, "Leave me be."

"I will do no such thing. You are burning up with fever. I have to get you to the surgery." She said sternly.

"I rather stay here, if you don't mind." He snarled.

"Actually, I do mind. I owe it to you to help you and you are making it rather difficult." She sat back on her heels and let out a slow breath. "Benjamin was my friend, and he saved my life. I know you loved him a great deal. He loved you too.

He looked up to you. I imagine you knew him far better than me, but one thing I do know is that he would not want you laying down here and dying of a fever from a measly little cut on your arm."

Her voice rose as she spoke, trying to hide the emotion in her voice. "You helped me find my courage once, let me help you now." She put her hand on his shoulder but he refused to look at her. Gently, she tugged on his elbow and he stood with her. They walked in silence back towards the surgery.

Once through the hatch she led him to a hammock, which he mutely sat in. His cut was not wrapped and the stitching was done surprising well for him having done it himself. Catherine carefully washed up his arm and wrapped it up. She grabbed a jar with several different herbs that when made into a tea could help fight off the fever. Doc had explained the different herbs, but she could not remember what two of them were called.

"I am going to have you drink this, it will help with the fever and the pain. It has yarrow and willow bark in it." She explained, though she was not sure if he was listening. She reached for the metal pot that had heated water in it and poured it into a wooden cup. When she handed it to Alaric, he obediently took a long drink of it.

"Thank you, Catherine."

Catherine was relieved. Lucas would be glad to hear his friend was doing better and was resting. "I will be back. I am going to check on the others." She went to see to her other patients.

"Looks like the other two men have been able to fight off the fevers. We will have to watch Alaric closely for the next few days but I think he will pull through." Catherine whispered to Doc.

"Yes, I believe he just might. I am not sure what you said

to him to get him to listen but well done. The Captain will be very relieved to see him doing well."

"I will go tell him now." She said, turning to leave. She reached for the hatch as Lucas opened it.

"Where are you off to?" He asked.

"To find you actually." Catherine replied, her hands on her hips.

He chuckled. "Is that so? Why's that?"

"I thought you would like to know that Alaric is doing better. I convinced him to let me help him. He's over there, sleeping in the hammock." Catherine whispered, not wanting to wake Alaric or the other resting men.

Lucas looked from her to the hammock and then to Doc who nodded to him. "Thank you, Catherine. For everything you have done, truly." He reached for her hand and squeezed it.

24

A heaviness lifted from Lucas's chest when Doc and Catherine told him that Alaric was on the mend. Alaric had never been so broken before and he had no idea how to help him. Lucas had gone down and tried to find him, but did not have as much luck as Catherine did.

It did make him feel better that Alaric had accepted help and not hiding away in the ship somewhere, drinking himself to death. Lucas had a tough time himself, trying to find a way to go back and change what happened. He had been there when Alaric took Benjamin in and had watch as they grew closer. He enjoyed having Benjamin on his ship, watching him grow, learn and become a very skillful sailor. Benjamin had loved sailing and felt completely at ease on the ship. Lucas would never forget the first time Alaric had allowed him to sail with them. The boy's excitement was evident.

"Why don't you come above deck with me. Fresh air will do you good and you will be able to see France." Lucas coaxed Catherine. A break would do wonders for her. He also was not sure what he would say to Alaric if he woke and was not sure he was prepared to face what had happened yet.

"Sounds wonderful," She replied hesitantly, looking back around the room at the resting patients. Many of the sailors had recovered and were already back at work. Even Lucas's cut from the sword did not cause him much pain anymore.

"They will be alright for a couple hours. Doc will call for you if he needs assistance." Lucas glanced at Doc.

"Of course I will, Miss Catherine. The men are all resting anyways so there is not much we can do at the moment." Doc reassured her, patting her hand gently.

"Very well, if you two insist." She smiled, slipping her hand around Lucas's arm.

They walked out onto the quarter deck. Catherine gasped at all the ships around them. A large British Man O' War was cutting through the water, heading out of the ports and into the deeper ocean . Smaller Schooners rushed about, delivering goods, fishing off the shores, and assisting in monitoring the waters near the ports.

"Incredible." She whispered, hair blowing in the breeze and mouth slightly hanging open.

"I agree." Lucas replied putting his hand on her back, "When we reach France, we will head to a place I know of where we can stay. There we will be able to clean up and change into something more appropriate." His eyes roamed her body. "From there, we will need to take you to the dress makers and get you a few more things. We will most likely be in France for a couple of days and will need to attend a dinner or two in order to meet with Monsieur Dupont," he added.

Catherine nodded, staring at all the ships coming and going.

"It will be a few hours before we make it into the port and ready to depart from the ship. Until then, you are welcome to stay above deck and take in the sights. Or if you prefer, you can do one last round and check on the injured." It felt odd leaving his ship and the injured crew. He was usually the one that stayed aboard, only stepping onto land for a few hours at a time and seeing to any business he might have at the various ports.

This time, not only would he need to make his appearance known and show his face in society, but he needed time to be able to approach Dupont. Lucas imagined Monsieur Dupont was likely a busy and very well-known man of the French nobility. Simply calling upon the man would not be enough to change Dupont's mind about the plantation. They would need to catch him in an agreeable moment.

He also wanted to make this short time in France special for Catherine. She had told him the reason she had tried boarding a passenger ship was that she had longed for adventure. That she had felt trapped in the estate, always waiting for her father to come back from his voyages but never allowing her to go along with him. Her loneliness prompted her to get out and see more of the world, even if it was just once. He understood her restlessness and admired her for doing what she had longed to do.

"I will find you when the times comes. I would like a chance to speak with Alaric before we reach port." He excused himself and left Catherine looking out at the sights.

Lucas made his way to the surgery and walked over to where Alaric was sitting up in a hammock. "You don't look like much." Lucas said lightly. They had been through a lot together but nothing quite like this.

Alaric turned to him, cocking an eyebrow, and looking him up and down. "I reckon I look a right sight better then you, and I'm the one with the fever. What's your excuse?"

Lucas chuckled and leaned up against the table near the hammock. He crossed his arms over his chest and looked down at the floor. "We are only a few hours from making port in France." Lucas felt his chest tighten; he knew how excited Benjamin had been to go to France.

"Aye, I figured as much." Alaric replied curtly. He stood up, running his hands through his hair. Grabbing a bottle of some kind of herb from the table, he threw it against the wall, causing the bottle to shatter and the contents to fly about the cabin.

Lucas ran his hand over his face, "Mate, I…" he dropped his hands to his sides. Trying to find the words to apologize for costing Benjamin his life and wishing there was some way he could bring the lad back.

"I know." Alaric turned and faced Lucas. "I am sorry, I was wrong to blame you and Catherine. I know you cared for Benjamin a great deal and I know Miss Catherine became good friends with him." He shook his head and looked towards the hatch. "He did good, he was brave that night. He saved Catherine's life and the life of the injured men." Alaric shuffled his feet. "He was too young. I should have waited until he was older to let him sail with us."

"No, you did the right thing. He was more than ready and he learned fast, despite his age, the crew respected him. He could not wait to be on *The Trinity* with you. Besides, we were about his age when we were thrown onto a ship. It is no one's fault, no one except Thomas Banning's." Lucas said, squeezing his friend's shoulder. "You are welcome to come with Catherine and I. We need to find Francois Dupont once we get to France. I am getting a couple rooms at the Inn until we hear from our old friend, the Marquis. My only hope is that he is here in France and not at his Château or in some other place on business."

Alaric and him had enjoyed several months with the Duke of Choiseul a few years back. They had come across him when he was traveling on business. He was a very influential man with friends all over and was a highly respected figure amongst the French court.

The Duke's ship had been attacked by two enemy vessels that hoped to gain information about the French King. Lucky for the Marquis and the King, the letters were never discovered but the Duke of Choiseul did lose a great deal and needed assistance. *The Trinity* came upon his ship as the remainder of the crew were trying to make much needed repairs. Lucas offered their help and the Marquis rewarded them by hosting him and Alaric in France for a time. During their stay at the Duke's residence, they met members of the French nobility and had attended countless parties and balls. It had been awhile since then. Lucas was not sure how many of the Lords and Ladies they had met were still prominent figures in French society.

Alaric chuckled. "It would be good to see the Duke again and his beautiful wife. We really enjoyed ourselves when we stayed with him last." Alaric said, kicking at a piece of broken glass from the bottle he had thrown. "I'll come with you to the Inn just in case you run into any trouble. As I recall, the streets of France are crawling with expert thieves and scoundrels." Alaric said. "I'll get my things together and prepare to dock." Lucas was thankful Alaric wanted to get off the ship and see France again. Perhaps it would take his mind off of what had happened, at least for a bit.

"I'm glad to hear it. Catherine and Doc said your fever is nearly gone and you would be ok to move about more. I was hoping you would accompany us." Lucas smiled and nodded to his friend. "I will see you on deck."

Lucas went to his cabin to collect some of the items. As Alaric had said, the city had many unsavory people lurking about. He strapped his flintlock to his belt and his small blade as well. Lucas reached into the chest and pulled out a fresh shirt. He had a countless number of shirts in his chest and with each voyage he still seemed to need new ones.

Sailors did not have much time to wash their clothes and they tended to get tattered and worn, fairly quickly. Therefore, most of the men carried several shirts on board. Lucas went over to the wall, pulling a plank out, it opened into a small closet like space where a coat and other clothes were stored. Clothes that were reserved for being seen with the Lords. He was not too fond of the garb and found it to be stiff and uncomfortable but there was not much he could do about that.

Walking over to the desk he grabbed the deed and tucked it safely in the inner pocket of the coat he wore. There was a knock on the hatch, "Come in." He said, shuffling through the papers on his desk. "Ah Ethan, what can I do for you?" He asked, as the man ducked in through the hatch.

"When we were fighting Thomas, I snuck aboard his ship to try and find him. I did not see him in the battle until the end, I had assumed he had gone to his cabin to hide." He explained, walking over to the desk.

"I assumed the same. I saw him on deck as they approached but also did not see him until he had Catherine." Lucas said, his anger rising.

"I went into his cabin to confront him about my sister. He was not in there, but I noticed his logbook on his desk and grabbed it." He placed the book on the desk and opened it. Lucas glanced down at it. "I thought that if I could prove he was in Barbados during the time of her attack, I could prove it was him and if I was unable to catch him myself or find him again, perhaps the Royal Navy could help me in his capture." He pointed to a date that was written in the logbook. "This is the date it happened." He said, watching Lucas scan the documents.

Lucas looked up at him in confusion, his brow furrowing. "I do not understand. You said it was a blonde man that resembled a pirate, or at least that is what the witness had stated.

You also say he has your sister's bracelet that you gifted her and I certainly would not put it past the man to do what was done to your sister," He paused, searching Ethan's face. "But in here, it says he was just off the coast of Africa when she was attacked. If this ledger is accurate, then he could not have been the man that harmed your sister." Lucas looked back down at the ledger in front of him.

"I know, that is why I brought this to you. I do not understand any of it. I was sure it was him when I saw the bracelet. I am not mistaken that that was hers. My only thought is that he must have stolen it or traded for it from someone else. Either that or it fell off her and Thomas found it and kept it."

Ethan shook his head, running a hand through his dark hair and turning his back to Lucas, walking around the cabin. "I thought I had finally found the man and even though he got away, it would be easier finding him this time since I had a name instead of just a vague description. Now I am doubting his involvement in it and I'm going to have to start over." He slammed the logbook closed.

"You had every reason to believe it was Thomas. It was a logical guess. I do not think the ledger is lying. I heard awhile back that a few ships had been hired by some of the rich plantation owners to travel to Africa and bring goods and slaves back. I am sorry you have to start your search over again. I have no doubt you will find the man, though. I wish you the best of luck and if there is anything I can do to help you, let me know," Lucas said.

"Thank you, if I can stay on with you until I find out more information, I'd greatly appreciate it." He reached out, shaking Lucas's hand.

"Of course, you can stay on as long as you need to. You are a fair fighter and an experienced sailor, I certainly have no objection to having you on my ship and a part of my crew,"

Lucas replied.

A few minutes later, Catherine came in through the hatch and into his cabin. "And what can I do for you Miss Benedict?" He asked, his eyes trailing over her.

She put her hands on her hips, "I am here to gather my things, Captain. Ol' Shorty said we are preparing to make port and that I should get ready to go ashore."

Lucas's chest rumbled, "Right then, you best do as you are told." He winked, enjoying the blush that spread across her cheeks. Lucas waited for her to gather the items she would need for the next few days in France. He led her on deck as the crew dropped the plank down to walk across and onto the docks.

"Well, Miss Catherine, welcome to France." He grinned down at her. The twinkle in her eyes made him tighten his jaw, trying to hold back from kissing her in front of an entire port full of merchants and sailors. He cleared his throat, "Let us head to the inn to get our rooms and clean up. We can eat there and I have a letter I need to post."

His hand rested on her back, keeping her close to him. People were rushing around, loading and unloading crates, barrels and cages, filled with goods, foods and animals from ports around the world. He watched Catherine as her eyes darted about, trying to take every sight in.

They made their way through the crowds of the docks and onto a street. They passed by stores, businesses, and taverns, winding through the streets. They eventually reached an inn that stood snug between a hat maker and a shop that sold various herbs, oils and remedies for all sorts of ailments. The wooden sign with a small orange and brown colored bird carved into hung just above the door. The edge of the sign was painted an off red color and the bright, white lettering read Le Merle.

"The Robin?" Catherine looked up at Lucas quizzically.

"Aye," he nodded, grinning. "The woman who owns the Inn is Madame Merle but we have always called her Robin and she loves those little birds, so she named her Inn the same." "We stayed here a few years ago when we were in France last. It is a nice place and very friendly." He looked back at Alaric who was grinning and shaking his head.

"Oh, she is friendly to be sure, just a wee bit," he cocked his head to the side, trying to find the right word to describe the owner. "Excited, I suppose you can say." He said, gesturing for Lucas to open the Inn's door.

They were hardly in the door when a rather plump and rosy cheeked woman came bounding towards them, squealing. "Well, if it isn't Captain Lucas Harding and his first mate, Alaric." She bellowed in a thick French accent, winking at Alaric flirtatiously, who looked slightly uncomfortable. The woman wrapped her arms around Lucas and embraced him in a bone crushing hug. Then she turned her attention back to Alaric, placing her large, round hands around his arms. "And as handsome as ever." She said, placing a kiss on his cheek.

"You haven't changed a bit, Madame Robin." Alaric laughed, "I am glad to see you are doing well."

"You two are a long way from the West Indies, what brings you all the way to France?" She asked curiously, her tight, brown curls bouncing.

"Ah, you have the Governor of the West Indies himself to thank for the opportunity to see us again." Lucas said, giving a dramatic bow.

"And thank him I will, it has been far too long since you two graced *Le Merle* with your presence." She beamed and ushered them to a table. "Oh? Qui est-ce?" Madame Merle turned from Catherine to Lucas, her hand resting gently on Catherine's shoulder. Catherine still wore sailor's clothes and though her hair was tied up with a thin rope, it still draped down in long waves against her back. She no longer bothered tucking it up in her hat to hide it.

"This is Miss Catherine," Lucas replied, putting his arm around Catherine's waist. "It is a long story, but she is with me and is now a valued part of my crew," Lucas explained.

"I see," Madame Robin giggled. "It was about time one of you found a feisty little slip of thing to keep you in line." She took Catherine's hand in hers and patted it. "Welcome to *Le Merle* Miss Catherine. If you should need anything at all you just let me know, Sweetie."

"Thank you, it is a pleasure to meet you. You have a wonderful place here." Catherine replied politely. Lucas was amused, Catherine did not seem the least bit surprised or awkward towards the exuberant woman. The last time they had stayed at *Le Merle* a few people were quite taken aback by Madame Robin's enlivened personality, but Catherine appeared completely at ease.

"Allow me to go dish up some food and drink. I hope you will be staying here tonight?" She asked, her hands folded in front of her, resting on her large cream dress, dotted with orange and yellow blossoms.

"Yes, we would greatly appreciate some food and lodging, though we are not sure how long we will be staying. We have some business to attend to and we hope to be hearing from the Duke of Choiseul very soon. In fact, I have a letter I need to get to him. Do you have a man that can take it to him?"

"Oui, of course. I hope you will be keeping out of trouble this time." She said, taking the letter from Lucas. "You should have seen them Miss Catherine, they certainly did have their fun. Stealing the hearts of all the ladies, dueling in the nearby woods, and causing quite the fuss." Madame Robin let out another giggle and nudged Catherine.

Lucas cleared his throat and looked at Alaric who was enjoying himself quite a bit at his friend's expense. Catherine's eyebrow cocked and a grin slowly spreading across her face. "Yes, that was some time ago."

Madame Robin threw her head back and let out a loud laugh, causing other patrons to look at them curiously. She turned and walked to the long counter. Going through a doorway that sat behind it, she emerged a few minutes later carrying a tray with three bowls of hot stew. She set the bowls down on the table and then sat the glasses of wine and an extra bottle down next to them. "Only the best for my favorite customers." She turned to Catherine, "I hope you enjoy the stew. The wine is the best around. When you are finished, I will have a hot bath set up in your room." She smiled at Catherine and patted her shoulder.

"Oh, thank you. The stew looks delightful." Catherine replied.

"Oui, prendre plaisir." She said and bustled off to help a group dining at another table.

The food was indeed delightful, and the wine was suburb. Lucas had not cared for wine until he had to drink so much of it when they had stayed with the Duke of Choiseul. By the end of their stay, him and Alaric had grown accustomed to the taste.

Catherine sunk deeply into the warm water, causing some of it to spill over the side of the large tub. Closing her eyes, it felt as if her whole body was simply floating weightless in the tub. The last time she had a warm bath was when the Captain had taken her to the pond and waterfall. The water had been warmer than she had expected.

Heat rose in her face when she thought of how he had sat on the hot rock and guarded her, making sure no one came down the path. He had not looked, not until the end, when she was drying out her hair. The look on his face burned into her mind, she could not explain what she saw in his eyes at that moment, she only knew she had felt the same.

Catherine grabbed for the bar of rough soap and scrubbed until she felt all the salt and sand was completely washed from her skin and her hair. Running her hands through the water, she leaned her head back and relaxed. It was beginning to grow cooler; it was time to get out, she sighed and slowly stood, letting the water roll off her.

Stepping out of the tub, she reached for a thin cloth that lay neatly folded on a stool. Catherine patted herself dry and undid the bag she made out of old sails which held the dress, brooch, and undergarments that Lucas had purchased her. She pulled out the soft, white shift. As much as she had enjoyed the freedom of the scratchy breeches and the loose white shirt, she found herself excited to be able to wear a soft and delicate shift again.

Grabbing the brush off the table with a mirror on it, she tried to loosen the horrid knots that had developed from the ever going breeze on the ship. Robin had to have put them there for her and she made a note in her head to thank the kind woman.

Catherine sat the brush down, it had taken far longer than it had in the past to brush out her hair. There were more tangles and knots then she had realized. There was a knock on the door. She quickly ran over to the bed and grabbed the small quilt off of it and draped it across her shoulders like a shawl.

"It's me, Catherine." Lucas said quietly from the other side.

She opened the door, bidding him entrance before someone could see her in her shift. She had grown used to the thick breeches and now felt far more vulnerable in the thin material.

"I am sorry to disturb you," He said, running a hand over his face. "I just wanted to check on you and make sure you were alright. I know you should be quite safe in here, but I was uneasy about the men that are coming in, now that it is growing late." He stepped closer, putting a hand under her arm. "Are you doing alright?"

Catherine swallowed, "Yes, thank you. I will be just fine." She was sure he could hear her pounding heart. She looked down at her hands, they were pulling at the fabric of the quilt. She looked back up at him, her eyes pausing briefly on his lips.

"I will be next door if you need anything." He said, lifting his hand and gently touching her face. "I'll see you in the morning."

Mutely, she simply nodded, unable to take her eyes from him as he exited her room. Trying to calm her nerves, she let out a slow breath and put her hand to her stomach. The open window beckoned her, so she sat, looking out on the street and surroundings. Occasionally someone would pass by or stumble out of the inn roaring with laugher and hobble down the street trying to keep their footing.

It reminded her of the night the crew had enjoyed themselves when her father and Captain Lester dined on *The Trinity*. As she watched people pass by, enjoying the cool night air, she could hardly believe all that had happened thus far and that she was standing at the window of an inn in France.

Sunlight streamed lazily through the window waking her up. She threw the covers back and got out of bed just as there was a small tap on the door, "Miss Catherine, are you up?" Madame Merle's cheerful voice filtered through the wooden door.

"Oh, yes, please come in." Catherine said, glad to see the lively woman again.

"I thought you might need a bit of help with your dress and hair. Would you mind if I assisted you?" She asked guiding Catherine to the stool in front of the small table that held the brush, mirror and a few pins.

"Not at all. I would be glad of the help," Catherine beamed.

Catherine and Madame Robin chatted as she skillfully did Catherine's long hair, pinning it up in the proper French fashion. Catherine slid into the dress and was surprised at just how well it fit her. She ran her hands over the delicate material.

"Belle!" Madame Robin exclaimed, "You will have all the heads turning. Captain Harding might just find himself in another duel or two." The woman laughed, "If you are all set, my dear, let us go downstairs and I will get you a bite to eat."

"Just one last thing," Catherine quickly pinned the brooch to her dress. "There," beaming, Catherine followed Madame Robin down the stairs. Lucas and Alaric stood when they saw her. Alaric grinned and slapped Lucas on back, before sitting back down to watch the scene unfold in front of him. Catherine was suddenly feeling far more self-conscious then she ever had before. She touched her hair then dropped her hand back down. Alaric coughed loudly, bringing Lucas back to his senses.

"Catherine, I, uh, you," he stepped over to her. "You look breathtaking," he whispered, his voice low and deep. "I am glad to see that it fits you," His eyes caught site of the pendant, a pleased look on his face, "You wore the brooch." He said, his voice holding something Catherine could not quite explain.

"Of course I did," She said, running her fingers gently over it.

"Come now, your food will not last long if you just stand there gaping at her." Madame Robin exclaimed as she strode through the back door with another plate of food. Lucas smiled politely and gestured for Catherine to take the seat next to him. "Ah, I almost forgot. This came for you this morning, Captain." Madame Robin said, digging into the folds of her gown and pulling out a small white paper with a red seal on it.

"Thank you," he took it from her and glanced at Alaric. "It's from the Duke," he bent the letter ever so slightly, causing the seal to break in half and allowing the letter to be opened. Lucas scanned the paper and grinned. "Fantastic, he is at his estate and asks that we join him and his wife at their place, the *Hôtel Delaunay,* for the remainder of our time in France."

"I will ask to have our things taken over there," Alaric said, wiping his face with a soft, orange napkin. He placed it back on the table and stood. "I have some things I would like to do, afterwards I will meet you at the Duke's," he told Lucas. Turning to Catherine, he grinned, "you look absolutely stunning." Catherine's face flamed at the compliment. They watched him walk over to Madame Robin, no doubt saying his good-byes and asking her to have their things sent over to the Duke's estate.

"We best get going as well, we have a few things to do ourselves today." Lucas stood, pulling her chair out for her. He led her over to Madame Merle. Though they had only just met, Catherine liked the friendly woman a great deal. She hugged Catherine and sniffled.

"I would greatly enjoy hearing from you. Please write me." Madame Robin dabbed her eyes and sniffed again. "You make sure that rogue of a Captain takes good care of you." She said, shifting her gaze to Lucas and patting his cheek.

"Thank you for all you have done. I would be honored to send you a letter as soon as I reach Barbados again." Catherine smiled, squeezing Madame Robin's hand.

"It was very good to see you again. Thank you, you take care," Lucas gave the woman a quick hug.

Catherine and Lucas wound their way between buildings and through the city. Catherine could not get over the huge structures and numerous, colorful shops. People weaved in and out of the shops, women dressed in silks and satin gowns with various styles of hats, chatting as they strolled down the stone streets. Others tended to stalls that sold baskets, food, and less expensive cloth.

"Madame Merle speaks very good English. Has she lived in France all her life?" She asked, looking up at Lucas. Her hand resting snuggly in his arm.

"Very observant of you, Miss Catherine," Lucas held in a laugh. "Her father was French but her mother was from Scotland. As far as I know, she did grow up in France, but she was close with her mother. They ran the inn for many years together."

"I see," Catherine replied. "I enjoyed her company. I believe she is one of the friendliest people I have ever met."

Lucas laughed, "That she is. I think you will enjoy our friend, the Duke of Choiseul. I am sure you will get along with his wife as well. She is a kind woman. They will most likely be having a dinner party tonight and after talking to the Duke we will see where to find Monsieur Dupont." He explained, steering her into a dress shop with a lavish gown of reds and golds in the window.

Catherine looked about the shop, she had never been in a place like it before. There were a few dress makers in the West Indies, but nothing quite so stunning. Fabrics of all kinds and colors were stacked on the back wall. An open book stood on a tall table, showing various designs and cuts.

"Comment puis-je t'aider, Madame?" A lady came forward from behind the long counter. She had been hidden behind a stack of velvet material.

Before Catherine could speak a word, Lucas spoke up, "Good morning, this is Lady Treadfast," the corner of his mouth twitched. "She is here to purchase a couple new gowns." Catherine began to speak up to protest but Lucas continued, "Please have the gowns ready as soon as you can and have them and the bill sent to *Hôtel Delaunay,* we will be staying there." Lucas looked down at Catherine and winked, "I will explain later. In the meantime, choose anything you like," he whispered. "I will be just outside. Take your time."

"I am Madame Bette, please come in and tell me what style of gown you like. Then we will have a look at the fabrics." The woman wore a pale green gown with a bright yellow ribbon laced around her slender neck. She curtsied to Catherine and quickly led her to the open book. Catherine felt bad about Lucas buying her new gowns but also knew that if they were to be in company of the Duke and his wife as well as Monsieur Dupont then she needed a new gown or two.

The next couple hours Catherine and Madame Bette went over several styles, designs and colors of the latest fashion. They eventually decided on two new dresses. "I will have them to you by tomorrow morning, Lady Treadfast." She curtsied again and rushed into the back room with a bundle of fabrics in her arms.

"I do not know how to thank you. You have been so kind to me, and I have given you nothing in return." She had walked out the store to find Lucas standing against the wall of the store. He had his knife out and was chipping away at a stick. "I came on board your ship and lied to you from the start, pretending to be a young boy, instead of a Baron's daughter." Catherine spoke faster, letting the words spill from her lips. She stared down at her feet.

"Catherine," he began, putting his knife away and tossing the stick to the ground. He stood on a small space of grass. Catherine noticed that many of the stores on the street had patches of grass or trees around them. "I will be the first to admit, you have been far different than any sailor I have ever had sign onto my ship. You disobeyed my orders during the storm and not only could it have cost you your very life but the life of others that might have tried to save you." He drew her closer to him.

"You have also saved the lives of my crew, including my best friend, not to mention my own. You came up with the plan and rescued me from Thomas's brig and gave my crew the time we needed to defeat him. Catherine, you are worth far more than a couple new gowns." He wiped the tear away that began to roll down her face. "We need to head over to the Duke's. I will hire us a carriage." He said, guiding her into a street and over to an awaiting carriage.

The man jumped down from his place behind the carriage and quickly opened the door for them. "To the *Hôtel Delaunay*, please." Lucas told the driver as they were seated.

"I almost forgot. Why did you say my name was Treadfast?" She asked.

"Ah. It is to protect your reputation as best I can." He grinned, "I do not want word getting out that you are the daughter of the Baron who owns the land Monsieur Dupont is trying to take. If he were to find out that you are not only here with me but will also be attending the parties where I will speak with him about your father's plantation, it will appear that your father hired me to convince the Marquis not to purchase the plantation. It could also cause quite a stir for your father. So, while we are among the Lords and Ladies of France, you will be Lady Treadfast from England." He smiled and rested his head against the red velvet seat.

"Alright, I can do that. After all I was a Treadfast for several weeks before. It could be exciting being Lady Treadfast this time." Lucas chuckled. Catherine's eyes filled with excitement. "Why did you tell Madame Merle who I was but not Madame Bette, neither of them are French royalty?"

"Because I know your name is quite safe with Madame Robin. She will not say a word. The French Lords and Ladies have not been known to frequent inns and will not suspect we stayed there. Madame Bette, on the other hand is a well-known and much liked dress maker of the Ladies here. The chance she might say something to one of them, if asked, is far greater." Lucas said.

"I see. You have thought of everything," Catherine marveled. The carriage slowly came to a stop in a large courtyard. Catherine looked out the small window and up at a large and grand estate. The door opened and a footman grabbed a small block from below the seat, placing it on the ground before holding out a hand to assist Catherine down from the carriage.

"Captain Harding, it is good to see you again. When I received your letter that you were in France I was overjoyed." A slender man with a round face and a friendly smile came out of the door of the estate. He wore the typical wig that most of the Lords wore. Her father wore one on occasion but had said that they were never that comfortable and preferred not to wear one if he did not have to.

"Monsieur Choiseul," Lucas said, stepping out of the carriage, his arms open wide. "It is great to be here again." He looked at the woman that stood behind the Duke. "Madame Choiseul," he bowed and kissed her hand gently. "Thank you for hosting us for the time we will be in France. I would like you to meet a friend of mine, Lady Treatfast." Lucas said, turning slightly away from Madame Choiseul and holding a handout to Catherine.

She smiled politely and stepped up to Lucas. She curtsied, "It is a pleasure to meet you, Madame Choiseul."

Madame Choiseul took her hands. "The pleasure is mine. And please, call me Louise." She laced her arm around Catherine's and led her into the large house. Catherine looked over her shoulder to see if Lucas was following. He nodded to her, following with Monsieur Choiseul close behind them.

"I will show you what room you can stay in while you are here, then you can relax for a while before everyone joins us. We are having a dinner party tonight, so you arrived just in time." She said, patting Catherine's hand and leading her up the staircase and to a large room, about the size of her own back in Barbados. She spotted a shelf lined with books. "I hope it is to your liking, Lady Treadfast." Louise said, watching Catherine closely.

"It is absolutely wonderful." She walked over to the books, running her fingers along them.

"Captain Harding told my husband that you enjoy reading, so I had a few extra books put in the room." She said, walking over to Catherine and looking at the books on the shelf.

Catherine turned to Louise, curious. "Captain Harding told the Duke that I enjoy reading?"

Louise laughed. "He did, in the letter he wrote to my husband, telling him he was in France and that Mr. Stein and a lady would be accompanying him."

Catherine wondered just how much Lucas had told his friends and how much she should reveal. "Mr. Stein?" She asked.

"Yes, Captain Harding's first mate, Alaric Stein."

Catherine blinked, it occurred to her she had only known the man by his first name. "Oh, of course. I am sorry." She let out a little laugh. "It was very kind of you to have the books brought in and please, call me Catherine." She squeezed Louise's hand.

"Very well, I will let you get some rest. You much be exhausted from such a long and eventful voyage." She turned to leave, looking over her shoulder, a single long curl swayed on her shoulder. "I will have Madeleine, one of the maids, attend to you. She will see to it that you are ready for the party." She curtsied as she closed the door behind her.

Catherine had grown so accustomed to the confining spaces of the ship that she hardly knew what to make of the spacious room. The green walls resembled the leaves on the rose bushes her mother had loved so much. A yellow arm bench sat under a window against the back wall. Overwhelmed by Lucas's thoughtfulness, she grabbed a dark red book from the shelf, clutching it to her chest and went to sit down on the bench.

She missed her father, Emma and their plantation and could not wait to see them again. As much as she wanted to be back at the plantation, she knew that that would mean the end of her voyage. Lucas would leave once again on *The Trinity* and she would be left to marry Lord Anderson. Once they arrived in the West Indies, she would have to say goodbye to Lucas and the thought of that tore at her.

She wiped away a tear. She had made a promise to her father. She had told him in the letter she had left him, that once she returned she would marry Lord Anderson. It would not be right to break her promise to her father, especially with all that she had put him through these last few months. She guessed that by now he had received a letter from their butler and was likely searching for her.

There was a knock at the door, "Come in," Catherine said, placing the book on the bench and standing up.

A small young woman came in, probably about the same age as Catherine though a few inches shorter. Her hair was pinned up underneath a white cap and she carried several white boxes. She curtsied, "I am Madeleine, I am here to get you ready for the dinner party. Your new gowns just arrived, I thought perhaps you might like to wear one of them tonight." She said, her voice soft and thick with a French accent.

"Oh, wonderful," Catherine exclaimed, going over to the girl, and opening the box on top. "It is lovely. Come, let us lay them out and you can help me decide which one will be best for this evening."

Catherine examined the two gowns Madeleine obediently laid out. One, a midnight blue and made from the smoothest satin. A large bow of the same color sat just at the edge of the dress where it ran along the chest. The other was of a similar material but a yellow this time. The yellow satin parted as it ran down the dress, exposing a cream skirt decorated with small flowers that had been tediously sewn into the fabric. She could not help but wonder what the Captain would think of the new gowns.

Catherine walked into the room, people were gathered in small groups, engrossed in conversations and sipping on the wine that was being passed around in clear glasses. She searched the room, hoping to find a familiar face. Unsure of herself, she ran her hands along the new, blue dress.

"You look gorgeous," Lucas whispered in her ear, placing his hand on her lower back. Catherine's stomach flipped. He came around her and bowed. "Lady Catherine, you are one of a kind." He said, pulling her hand up to his lips.

She giggled and curtsied. "Thank you for the compliment, Captain Harding. I must say, you do not look so bad yourself." She commented, boldly letting her eyes run up and down his body. She had never seen him with a vest on, let alone a coat. She was only used to seeing him in the thin white shirts.

Lucas chuckled, "How do you like your room?"

"It is wonderful. In fact, I wanted to thank you, I am enjoying the shelf of books. Louise told me; you had suggested it." She whispered.

"I am glad. I wanted you to feel comfortable here. I know we will only be staying a couple nights but I thought it might give you an escape from all the excitement." He explained.

"So the rumors are true. Captain Harding is back in France, and not alone." A woman walked up beside Lucas, looking Catherine up and down, her lips pursed. She was about the same height as Catherine, though perhaps a few years older. Her features delicate, her hair pinned up in the typical fashion with one long curl hanging over her shoulder, her dress dipping just a bit too low.

The look of surprise on Lucas's face told Catherine he had not expected to see the woman standing next to him.

26

"Lady Camille," he replied, cringing. He had all but forgotten about the woman from years ago. "Let me introduce to you, Lady Treadfast." He said, giving a quick bow and gesturing to Catherine. He looked from Catherine to Camille and back to Catherine.

There was a time he had found Camille to be a rather attractive woman, and he supposed, in her own way she still was, but his thoughts were on Catherine. She was completely different then Camille or any of the other Ladies he had ever met. He watched the woman who had effectively become a valued part of his crew and was quickly becoming just as valuable in his life. The new gown she wore fit her body perfectly, outlining almost every curve. He admired the confidence that emanated from her. Even though she had been through numerous, trying events over the past months and now in a large, new city, meeting countless Lords and Ladies, she still did not waver.

"A pleasure," Catherine nodded to her and curtseyed.

Lady Camille thinned her lips into a forced smile. "The pleasure is mine, I am sure." She turned to Lucas, "Captain, you have not changed a bit, I see." The look in her eyes made Lucas squirm. "When I heard you were here, I had to come. It has been far too long since you were here last." Lady Camille reached out, gently adjusting the seam on Lucas's shirt that had been creased to perfection.

Lucas cleared his throat, "I see you have not changed a bit either." The smile on his face, not quite meeting his eyes. Catherine's chin sticking out a bit further then it had been a moment ago. He almost laughed but quickly composed himself.

A bell rang echoing elegantly through the room. "It must be time to go in." Lucas said, relieved of the awkward situation. Since they had arrived at the Duke's house, he felt like he had hardly had a moment alone with Catherine. He was also glad to be steering himself and her away from Lady Camille.

They walked into a room with a long table, it's dark wood almost shining. Everyone found the seat that had been chosen for them by their hosts. Lucas realized Catherine was no longer standing next to him, in fact she was several seats down on the opposite side of the table.

"This is fortunate." Lady Camille sidled up beside him and sat down next to him.

Lucas groaned and looked back over to Catherine who was now seated between two Lords Lucas did not recognize. He searched the table for Alaric. He had arrived at the Duke's house shortly after they had. While Madame Choiseul was getting Catherine set up in her room, Alaric, Lucas, and the Duke spoke in his study. They quickly filled him in with all that had happened over the last several weeks.

"I have heard tell that Monsieur Dupont was possibly acquiring a sizable plantation in the West Indies for a very reasonable price. Though he has not said much about it nor does he seem particularly enthusiastic about it. From what I understand, the Governor there sent Dupont a letter. Apparently, they had met a couple years back while the Governor was here in France. I do not recall that I ever met him though it is possible that I have. Dupont had said that the Governor offered him this plantation at a reasonable price that he felt foolish to turn such an offer down."

The Marquis walked over to his desk, placing his hands on it. "Monsieur Dupont is always sniffing out new ventures that might help him acquire even more wealth. I do not believe he even knows much about owning a plantation. I suspect that with enough money, and he certainly has enough, he could hire a good enough foreman to look after the place."

"That is just it, the plantation has not produced enough crop the last few years to be lucrative. It will likely be another couple years and a lot of work to get it back to its former glory. It is one of the largest plantations in the Caribbean. If the Governor is telling Dupont he is giving him a very good price on it then I am willing to wager he has not told the Marquis about the plantations hardships." Lucas said, running a hand through his hair. "The Governor is much like Dupont, he is wanting more money, but also wanting powerful friends who can help him keep his seat as Governor of the West Indies. If Dupont believes the Governor is practically giving him one of the largest plantations, then he will have yet another influential friend. He already has several British Lords on his side, now it seems he is wanting to expand his reaches to France," Lucas concluded.

The Marquis waved his finger in the air, "Yes, yes. I believe you must be right. That is all very logical." He replied, looking over to Alaric.

"Our friend the Governor would be gaining a powerful and rich friend while the Baron loses everything he has, save for one or two of his merchant ships." Alaric said, looking at Lucas. "We were fortunate enough to meet the Baron several weeks ago. He is a good man and doing all he can to save his plantation. He said he is searching for someone he can trust that would be interested in being a partner for his plantation." Alaric was still watching Lucas as he spoke, slowly shifting his gaze to the Duke.

"I would love to help the man if I could. Unfortunately I am not in a position to be taking on that task at present. As a diplomat I spend most my time away, discussing France's military advantages, plans, and procedures." He said sympathetically, pouring himself a glass of wine and offering them each one.

"No, that is understandable, we do not wish to inconvenience you." Alaric responded, smiling at the Duke. "Let's drink to old friends." He said, raising his glass.

Lucas sat stiffly at the table, picking at his food. The meal was delicious, the company on the other hand was not so much. Alaric was enjoying himself though. France was proving to be a good way to distract Alaric from what happened to Benjamin. Once they set foot on the ship again and headed back to Barbados, Alaric would have a much harder time coping with the loss.

Alaric sat between two lovely young women, both completely enamored with him and his brave tales of the sea. Lucas chuckled and shook his head, Alaric certainly did not seem to mind the company at all. Across the table, Catherine sat, politely smiling, and making conversation with one of the Lords. Something the man said, made her laugh.

Lucas suddenly had a bitter taste in his mouth, remembering the Lord Anderson that Catherine said she was engaged to. Neither of them had spoken about the man since that night. However, that did not mean Lucas did not think of him every time he kissed, or wanted to kiss Catherine. He did not care for the idea of Lord Anderson marrying Catherine, but Lucas did not know what he could do about it, if there was anything at all he could do.

"Captain, you certainly do seem distracted this evening." Lady Camille whispered in his ear.

Lucas sighed, "I apologize, Lady Camille. It has been a long voyage and my thoughts were elsewhere." He replied, taking another bite of his meal.

"Yes, I can see that. Perhaps your mind is filled with thoughts of a particular English maiden." Lady Camille said, nodding towards Catherine. "I believe the last time you were here; I was the one that occupied your thoughts." She said, placing a hand on his arm.

"The last time I was here was some time ago." He said, gently removing her hand. From the corner of his eyes, he saw her purse her lips. He could not help but wonder what exactly he had seen in her before.

"Lady Treadfast," Camille said, loud enough to draw the attention of the rest of the room. Lucas grimaced and watched as Catherine's face flushed pink. "What a peculiar name. I do not believe I have heard of such a name before. Pray tell, how did you and Captain Harding meet?" She asked, a look in her eyes that made it seem as though smiling was quite painful. Lucas felt his heart racing, for everything he had thought of, he had not considered coming up with the story of how they met. His mind raced trying to think of some idea that sounded reasonable and would not jeopardize her reputation.

"Captain Harding and my father met while the Captain was still in the Royal Navy. I only met him briefly then." Catherine said confidently, taking a small sip of her wine.

"Oh, and how is it that you come to be in France with him, now?" Camille asked, tilting her head to the side.

"I was to meet a friend here. Unfortunately her and her husband were called away on an urgent family matter just before we arrived. My Father had asked Captain Harding to take my maid and I here since he had heard that the Captain was coming to France anyway. He had thought it would be safer if we travelled with the Captain since so many merchant and passenger ships have been set upon by pirates of late." Catherine explained. She shrugged as if it had been common knowledge of how they met and why they were here together.

"That about sums it up." Alaric spoke up, "We will be staying here for a night or two while Captain Harding and I finish up some business, then we will be returning Lady Treadfast back to her family and making our way to the West Indies." Lucas raised his glass to Alaric in a silent thanks.

"What business is it that brings you all the way back to France?" Lord Cardwell asked.

"Business for the Governor of Barbados." Lucas said, without elaborating.

They had all left the dining area and were now gathered in yet another room of the estate.

"Tell me, Captain. What is it like being a privateer? Is it quite dangerous? Do you have to often fight those vicious and unforgiving pirates Lady Treadfast spoke of earlier?" Madame Aline asked with a slight giggle and brazenly letting her eyes slowly roam over his form.

"I must say, it is not all as grand as that, Madame Aline. Being on a ship can be trying and one has very little conveniences on board."

"But you enjoy it all the same, no?" She asked, her thick accent flittering in his ear. Her potent perfume was enough to make his eyes blur.

"Yes, I enjoy it a great deal. Monsieur Stein and I have been sailing for many years. We have indeed fought countless battles, though not all of them being pirates." He replied, hoping that bringing Alaric into the conversation would give him an excuse to find Catherine and seek some fresh air.

"I am sure you must have many battle wounds to show from these challenges?" She said this as she touched his arm, squeezing it ever so slightly.

"Aye, we do." He said, looking over at Alaric who was trying hard not laugh.

"Our Captain here has a pretty fresh one too. A sword sliced across his ribs; he is lucky to be alive." Alaric's choked on his wine at Lucas's scowl.

"Aye, I do, but as I recall you too were injured in that battle. On the arm, was it not? You are lucky you did not lose it." Lucas grinning at his own rebuke as Madame Aline instantly switched her sympathy and flirtations over to Alaric.

"And both our wounds were mended and tended to by the lovely Lady Treadfast." Alaric responded, the corner of his lip turning up into a challenging smile as he eyed at his friend.

"Lady Treadfast, she mended your wounds?" She asked curiously, looking from Lucas to Alaric.

"That is correct, Madame. During our voyage we met with a few injuries. It is not uncommon, so we were well prepared and have a very skilled surgeon on board The Trinity. Lady Treadfast was a quick study and became a valued assistant to our surgeon on my ship." Lucas said, making it clear that he thought very highly of Catherine and her newly found skills.

"Ah, Lady Treadfast, perhaps you have something to say on the matter. Did you not mind tending to the wounds of the Captain and his crew?" Madame Aline asked, fascinated.

"I did not, in fact I came to enjoy it and find a real purpose in helping them." She assured Madame Aline and the people that were beginning to gather around them. Catherine stood between Alaric and Lucas. She looked up at Lucas who could not take his eyes from her. She continued to impress him. He resisted the urge to put his hand on her back, knowing that they were already causing quite the stir.

"You may be far more knowledgeable in areas that other Ladies are not. However, I believe you are still far too naive to the ways men. Despite the amount of time you have spent with them of late." Lady Camille said, eyeing Catherine.

The room around them seemed to fall silent at the sharp response.

"That may be so, Lady Camille, but a Lady can be too familiar with the ways of men. Do you not agree?" Louise spoke up, stepping forward through the crowd of people.

After the crowd of dinner guests, dispersed the party seemed to move very quickly. Lucas stayed as near to Catherine as he could, not wanting Lady Camille to have another chance to humiliate her.

They retired for the night to their chambers. Lucas led Catherine to hers, reluctant to let her out of his sight. "Get some rest. In the morning I will show you a little more of France, then we will be going to another dinner party, though this one is a bit more important. Monsieur Dupont will be there." He held Catherine's arm as they reached the door to her chamber.

"I enjoyed myself tonight and you are right, the Duke and his wife are wonderful friends." She shifted her gaze to the ground, "I am nervous for the dinner party tomorrow evening. I hope that the Marquis listens to you and he decides against the plantation."

"I have no doubt he will. When Alaric and I spoke to the Duke today, he seemed confident that we should not have a problem with persuading Monsieur Dupont." Lucas said, placing his hand gently under her chin. He bent his head down slowly and softly touched his lips to hers. "You were magnificent this evening." He whispered against her lips. "Good night, Catherine." He walked down the long hall to his awaiting chamber.

That next morning they awoke and headed down to the dining area where trays of fruits, breads, cheeses and meat were laid out on a long table that sat against the wall. They ate and headed out into the courtyard where their carriage awaited. The Duke had a pressing matter of state he had to attend to and Louise had plans for tea later with a few of the other Ladies.

"I am going to take Catherine to see more of the city and to check on the men that are still on board the ship. Would you care to join us?" Lucas asked, helping Catherine into the carriage.

"No, thank you, you go on. I will meet you back here this afternoon to ready for the evening." Alaric closed the door for them and signaled for the driver to be on his way.

Lucas and Catherine arrived at the docks after spending the day exploring the city and stopping to have a meal at one of the taverns. "Ol' Shorty, how is everyone holding up?" Lucas asked as they approached the plank that led up to *The Trinity*.

"Fine, fine, Capt'n. All yer patients are healing up nicely and are gettin' back to work, Miss." He grinned and saluted. "How did you enjoy yer first French dinner party, Lass?"

Catherine was happy to see the old sailor again. "It was quite entertaining, I must say and I am pleased to hear the men are getting back on their feet."

"Captain Harding, is that you?" A boisterous voice asked from behind them.

Lucas turned to see who was speaking, his heart leapt into his throat when he saw the man standing a few feet away from him.

The man came walking over to them, "It is grand to see you looking so well, I was worried when we saw the storm behind us. We guessed you and your crew must have gotten caught up in it."

Lucas tried to find his voice again. Catherine was busy talking to Ol' Shorty still and had not noticed. "Lord Benedict, it is good to see you again. Yes, we did indeed get caught in the storm, it was, uh, one of the worst I have experienced." He stammered, still trying to figure out how the Baron came to be standing in front of him. Lucas caught movement out of the corner of his eye. Judging by the gasp he heard behind him, he guessed she had now noticed her father. Lucas cringed as the Baron's face turned alarmingly pale as he took in the sight of his daughter.

27

"Father?" Catherine choked. "Father, I.." She ran to him and wrapped her arms around his neck, emotions swarming through her. "Oh, I have missed you." She pulled away from him and glanced back at Lucas and Ol' Shorty who was still standing on the plank near the ship with his mouth hanging open in surprise.

Lucas walked up next to Catherine. "Perhaps we should go on board *The Trinity*. I am sure you have many questions, Lord Benedict." Lucas guided Catherine and her father onto the ship and into his cabin.

Lucas and her father sat at the Captain's desk, she preferred to stand. She walked over to the small window and thought of all the times that she had stood at that very window and watched the ocean's waves roll. Inhaling, she needed to collect her thoughts. She was not ready to say good-bye and feared that her father would insist on her traveling back with him as soon as can be.

"Father, I am sorry that I frightened you. I know our butler must have sent you a letter by now explaining my disappearance." She sighed, turning from the window, and watching her father's reaction. He sat back in the chair, opposite of Lucas who sat quietly, allowing her to begin her story.

"I left some letters in my room, I knew Emma would see them. I wanted all of you to know the reasons I left and that I have had all intentions of returning." She stepped around the desk and walked to the middle of the cabin, unsure of how to begin.

"I was desperate to get out, Father. To see more of the world. I had asked you if I could join you on your voyages many times and I was never allowed to accompany you." Emotions stirred in her. "Then you promised me to Lord Anderson and I got very upset and knew if I was going to have a chance of seeing other places like the ones in my books, then I had to leave before my marriage to Lord Anderson. I needed a chance to find myself. I dressed as Allen, our stable boy so I would not be recognized and made my way down to the docks where I intended to board a passenger ship."

She let out a small laugh, "I wanted an adventure, father and a chance to find out who I really am. Mistakenly boarding *The Trinity* was the best thing that could have happened. I have met incredible people and made friends that I will never forget," She said, meeting Lucas's eyes for the first time. "I have learned more about sailing then I thought I ever would, I was splashed by whales, seen breathtaking islands and waterfalls. I helped sail through a storm, and ate iguana on the beach," she did make sure to leave out a few details, unsure of how her father would take them at the moment.

"I learned a lot of new skills from Cook and Doc. Father, I learned how to mend injures and take care of people that are wounded. Think of how many times one of the plantation workers cut themselves or came down with fever, I could help them now, Father." She knelt beside him, her hands resting on his arm. "All of this that I have learned, discovered and seen was all because of Captain Harding and the rest of the crew on The Trinity." Exhaling, she awaited her father's response, which turned from shock to anger, disbelief, fear and even a glimmer of pride.

He looked down and his hands, shaking his head. "I never received a letter. I sent a few though, letting the household and you," he pointed to her, "know that I was alright." He ran a hand over his face. "But I did not know where I was headed to next. I have had a lot of business to attend to this trip, far more than previous times." Suddenly, he stood up, the color in his face rising slightly. "How dare you disobey me? How dare you go behind me, lying to me. Promising me you would be at the estate, planning your wedding when you were really planning your escape." His voice rose with each word.

Tears slipped down Catherine's cheeks, shaking with anger, frustration, and hurt. "How dare I? How dare I? Father! I am not the only one here who has been hiding the truth or who has been pretending. Even now you won't speak the truth. You say you are here on business. Does that business have anything to do with you finding a partner for the plantation? You lied to me and pretended everything was fine, for years." She dropped her shoulders, "so how dare I." She turned away for a moment, attempting to compose herself.

She turned to face her father again who was staring accusingly at Lucas. Lucas stood, his fists resting on the top of his desk. His eyes were grey and no longer the stunning blue that they had been earlier. He held the Baron's hard gaze. "Do not forget who's ship you are on, Sir." He hesitated, "As for the information about your plantation, I did not say a word to her. She found out on her own. She was dressed as a young lad while she was aboard my ship. Do you recall a cabin boy, pouring our drinks and serving our food that night you dined on my ship?"

Her father took a step back as if he had been struck. His brow furrowed and he looked from Lucas to Catherine. "I did not even recognize my own daughter." He scratched his face, pain and confusion clear in his eyes.

Catherine took a step closer to him, resting a hand on his shoulder. "You did not expect I would be dressed as a lad and on board a privateer ship. So you did not think to look for me, therefore did not truly see me."

Her voice was softer now, "The Captain is right, I heard you speaking of the plantation that night. Sometime later the Captain found out I was indeed a woman and not a small lad and sometime still after that, he found out who my father is. Father, please," She urged. "There is more we need to discuss and so much more I need to tell you but we need to make it quick." Her father and Lucas both looked at her taken aback. "The Captain and I are due at a dinner party tonight and I do not wish to be late." She said, shrugging her shoulders slightly.

The next hour was spent filling her father in on their plans with the Marquis and all that they knew as well as most everything that had happened while she was aboard The Trinity.

They left the ship and headed for the coach, "Lord Benedict, if it is alright with you, I will come and see you early in the morning. If all goes right this evening, I hope to be sailing back to the West Indies tomorrow, but before I do, I would like to speak with you and let you know what happens with the Marquis." Catherine watched Lucas bow to her father, then wait for her at the edge of the coach.

"I am overjoyed seeing you again, Father. I have missed you very much. I am sorry I lied to you and I am glad I have been able to explain everything to you. We will see you in the morning." She placed a kiss on her father's cheek and wrapped her arms around him.

"I am too, my dear. You go, enjoy your evening and let us

pray the Captain can talk some sense into Monsieur Dupont." Her father allowed her to climb into the coach. Catherine was relieved that her father had not disagreed with her going with Lucas to the dinner that evening. She had desperately worried that he would have been so furious at her actions that he would have immediately taken her back to Barbados. At some point in their discussion, he must have realized that Lucas and her going to the dinner party was his last hope for saving the plantation. Though it would not save it completely, it would only buy him time to try and find a partner.

Catherine and Louise walked down the long staircase together. Despite it being such an important night, Catherine could hardly control her excitement at going to another dinner party. She thought it funny how she had grown so tired of the ones back home, but now looked forward to going to another.

"We will meet you there, Catherine." Louise said cheerfully as she climbed into one of the coaches as Catherine climbed into the other, with Lucas and Alaric.

They arrived at Monsieur Fontaine's estate. It was not quite as large as Duc de Choiseul's, though there was no doubting it's grandeur. Lucas squeezed Catherine's hand as he helped her out of the coach. She looked up at him, the importance of the evening suddenly weighing heavily on her nerves.

"Try not to worry. We have it all in hand." Lucas whispered in her ear. "And in the morning, with luck, we will be sailing back to Barbados." He smiled at her, causing her heart to do a little turn.

They followed a line of people into a room that was already near full. A man stood smartly at the entrance, announcing each new person or couple that arrived. "Ah, see that man over there?" The Duke pointed to a man standing in a circle of guests. He was drinking a glass of wine while he nodded along with something one of the other guests was saying. "That is Monsieur Dupont," the Duke nodded in the man's direction.

Catherine saw Lucas and Alaric exchange glances before the Duke took them over to be introduced. Louise guided Catherine over to meet a few women she had not had the opportunity of meeting the evening before. She curtsied as she was introduced to them. She glanced over her shoulder to see what Monsieur Dupont's reaction was upon meeting Lucas, but she could no longer see the men through the crowd of guests. She returned her attention to the Ladies until it was time to be seated. When she sat in her assigned seat, she was directly opposite of Lucas, which made her feel a bit more comfortable. One of the men that sat next to her was a Monsieur Clery.

"It is Lady Treadfast, is it not?" Catherine looked over to the man who sat to her right. He leaned in closer to her. "It is an honor to make your acquaintance, Lady Treadfast. Unfortunately, I was unable to attend the dinner last evening. I am sorry I missed it. I have heard tell that you became quite the sailor on your voyage to France. Is this true? If so, I would love to hear more about these adventures you have had." He eyed her with a look that made Catherine feel incredibly exposed.

"That is correct, Monsieur Miller. Lady Treadfast showed great courage and intelligence while aboard my ship." Lucas spoke up firmly, holding the gaze of the man. "She proved that she is no simpleton and a more capable sailor then many men."

"Not to mention she saved my life, as well as many others on board." Alaric added, from further down the table.

"Oh my! That does sound rather heroic and brave. I do not think I could stand being on a ship long at all, certainly not when so many dreadful things can happen." A woman commented from somewhere along the table.

"There is no doubting Lady Treadfast's bravery, I heard stories of her adventures while dining at the Duc de Choiseul's estate yesterday evening." Added one of the Lords that had sat next to her the previous evening. "Captain Harding, I believe you spend most of your time near and around the West Indies. Would you mind sharing with us what it is like there?" He asked.

"Ah, not much to tell that you have not already heard." Lucas lifted a hand briefly before setting it down again on the table. "It is very green, the brightest colored flowers and birds you will see anywhere, but it is also hot and the air is often times wet."

"And what of the sugar plantations? What of the plantation I have been offered by the Governor?" Monsieur Dupont asked, leisurely taking a bite of his food and watching Lucas curiously. Catherine sat up a bit straighter. This was the moment. She switched her gaze to Lucas, unsure of what to do next.

"There are many of them throughout the islands." He paused, taking a bite of his meal then looking back up the table at the Marquis. "Most of them provide a splendid crop each year. I have visited several of them and am aware of how the best ones are run," he explained. "As for the one the Governor is offering you, I would not be so sure the fair price he is offering you is worth it."

"Is that so? Why is that?" The Marquis waved his fork in the air. His grey wig making him look paler and older.

"Simple," Lucas sat forward in his chair. "It has not produced much of a crop, if any, the last few years. It may be one of the largest plantations on the islands, but it brings in the least amount of profit." Lucas shrugged, finishing off the last of his meal.

Monsieur Clery scoffed, "You could do far better than an old and useless sugar plantation, Monsieur Dupont. Leave that to the English Lords." His comment causing a ripple of laughter and agreements along the length of the table.

"I take it, Captain Harding, that you brought the deed with you?" The Marquis asked.

"Yes, I most certainly did." Lucas replied, not seeming the least bit worried. Catherine felt her stomach turning. She grimaced when she looked at the plate of food. She had hardly been able to taste any of it because of her nerves, but now she had completely lost her appetite.

After dinner, they flowed into a nearby sitting area, though, most of the guests seemed to prefer to stand. Catherine one of them, she did not feel much like sitting still. She had watched Lucas, Alaric and the Marquis go into a separate room. It had nearly been an hour since they went in and she had no idea if the conversation was going in their favor.

28

"You know for a fact that this plantation has not been proving profitable, then?" The Marquis asked, looking over the deed.

"I do indeed. Many of the English Lords that own sugar plantations in the West Indies do not actually stay at their plantation or even visit. They depend on a manager or a foreman that they trust and know will keep the plantation running as it should. However," he continued, "these plantations are providing a decent crop, the manager is easily able to keep the plantation running smoothly. With a sugar plantation that is producing little to no crop though, you will have a hard time finding a man that will be willing to take on such a task." Lucas turned, taking a few steps, looking around the room. "Not to mention, you will be getting nothing in return, you will not likely see any profit for a few more years, if any at all." Annoyance flickered in the Marquis' eyes. "The price the Governor is offering the plantation for is not that fair after all. He wants a powerful and rich French Lord on his side, and he is hoping you will be none the wiser when it comes to the plantation. Will you let him play you for a fool? If you purchase this plantation that is exactly what will be happening." Lucas challenged him.

The Marquis rolled the deed up and handed it back to Lucas. "I will certainly not be played a fool, as you say it, and most certainly not by some measly Governor. He can keep his worthless plantation. Now if you will excuse me." The Marquis responded, nodding to the two men before turning and leaving them in silence.

"I'd say that went remarkably well." Alaric said, staring at the door.

"Aye, I'd have to agree." Lucas tucked the deed safely in the inside pocket of his coat.

"Oh Lucas, I cannot believe you did it," Catherine beamed. They were in the carriage, headed back to the Duke's estate. "How will I ever repay you?" Lucas could tell from the sound of her voice she was trying to hold in the emotions that were spilling forward. He wanted nothing more than to pull her into his arms at that moment.

The next morning Lucas got up before the rest of the household. He wanted to meet with the Baron privately. The carriage took him to a small Inn that sat near the docks. It was not as fine at *Le Merle* but it was not one of the worst Inns either. Lucas walked in, looking about the room. The tables were filled with sailors, waking early to get ready to load or board different ships.

"Ah, Captain Harding, please come sit. I am eager to hear how the evening went." The Baron sat at a table near the corner of the room. "Where is my daughter?" He asked.

"She is well. I left before the rest of them awoke. Madame Choiseul will see that she is taken care of until I return." Lucas assured the Baron, taking a seat at the table with him.

"You have taken great care of her, I cannot thank you enough for all you have done for her," Lord Benedict said. "From the moment I lost my beloved wife, I have feared losing Catherine. That is why I never allowed her to leave the plantation grounds unless she was accompanied by me. I realize now that was too harsh and insensitive of me." Lord Benedict confessed. "Pray tell, were you able to convince Dupont to not take the plantation?"

Lucas pulled the deed from his pocket, handing it over to its rightful owner. "Tell me, Lord Benedict, why is the plantation doing so poorly? What will it take to get it back to its original state?" Lucas asked, leaning forward on the table.

"I thank you, deeply." He replied, placing the deed in his pocket and patting it. "I confess, I did not get much rest last night for fear you would not succeed." He let out a sigh, patting the deed in his pocket again. "In truth, it will take some work to get the plantation doing well again but the fact is, I cannot seem to keep a foreman on for any amount of time and the ones that I have managed to bring on and keep for more than a month or two, have proved to be incompetent and unknowledgeable. If I was able to find a reliable foreman and one that knew the work needed for the plantation, then it could be restored and fairly quickly."

Lucas nodded, looking around the room as it became more crowded. He looked back at the Baron. "You will also still need a partner, is that correct?"

"Yes, yes, unfortunately, none of it is possible unless I come into money somehow or find a partner willing to fund the plantation until it can fund itself again. I have spent far too much on it already and cannot afford to spend more. I just do not have anything more to put towards it, that is why I would need a partner." He explained, defeated all over again.

"I see," Lucas breathed out. "Lord Benedict, I have given it a considerable amount of thought and I would be interested in not only being your partner for the plantation but also taking on the task of foreman," He sat up straighter. Ever since he heard the Baron speak of his situation and then even more so once he found out just who exactly Catherine was, the thought had budded in his mind. The more time he spent with her the clearer the decision had become. Then when they were speaking with the Duke and Alaric suggested Choiseul be the Baron's partner, Lucas had realized that Alaric had not been speaking to the Duke at all but instead he was suggesting Lucas take it.

"I can see that you have, Captain Harding. I would be honored to have you as my partner and foreman." He smiled and reached his hand out to shake Lucas's.

"One more thing, please do not mention this to Catherine, I would like to tell her myself," Lucas added.

Lord Benedict sat back in his chair and studied Lucas, "I see that you care for her and her you." He finally said. "I will not say a word."

"I do care for her, a great deal. She did tell me of her engagement to Lord Anderson. What will you tell him? He likely called on her while she was gone, and I reckon he has heard by now of her disappearance. Is it likely he will call the wedding off?" Lucas hoped that he would call the wedding off but Catherine's father being a Baron and owning a large plantation, Lord Anderson may insist to continue on with their plans.

"When we arrive in Barbados I will speak with Catherine. If she truly does not wish to marry Lord Anderson then I will not force her hand. The engagement was never formally announced and can be passed off as simple rumors." The Baron searched Lucas's face. "What about you? If she chooses to no longer be engaged to him, will it be you that will be offering after her?" Lord Benedict asked, folding his hands together, atop the table.

"I have not spoken to Catherine of it. If the engagement is called off, I will ask her then." Lucas had no doubt that

Catherine did not wish to marry Lord Anderson but he was not entirely sure she would wish to marry him either. The thought caused his stomach to tighten uneasily.

Lucas and Lord Benedict spoke for a few moments longer before Lucas headed out to fetch Alaric and Catherine. They bid farewell to the Duke and his wife who had grown quite close with Catherine. They made their way back to *The Trinity* where the crew was busy finishing loading the ship up with plenty of supplies to make it to Madeira and then continue until they reached Barbados.

"What of my father? You spoke with him this morning. Did he not insist I sail back with him?" Catherine asked Lucas, clearly seeming confused at why Lucas was leading her on board his ship and not her father's.

"No, he agreed that you will be far safer aboard my ship where I am more equipped to fend off anyone that might try and take the ship. On his merchant ship, there is little protection." He explained, guiding her up the plank. He saw the surprise and shock in her face. "And do not worry, you will have a chance to say good-bye to him. He is on board right now, in the surgery, speaking with Doc. He wanted to meet him after hearing all the things you have learned from him." He allowed her to go below to find her father.

Lucas turned to Ol' Shorty to see how close they were to sailing. He looked around for Alaric as well, seeing if he had made it on board. Normally he would be overseeing the loading and charting of the sailors and goods but today Eddie and Ol' Shorty were taking care of it. Alaric stood at the railing, looking out at the ocean. Lucas began to approach his friend but was interrupted by Catherine and her father coming back on deck, closely followed by Doc.

"I have sent a letter, letting the butler know you are safe, and we will be heading back to Barbados. Though we will be on separate ships and may not arrive on the same day."

Her father held her arms gently as he spoke, pulling her into one last embrace before parting. "You take care of yourself, my dear."

"You as well, father. I will see you again in a couple weeks." She kissed his cheek and stepped back, standing alongside Lucas.

The two men shook hands. "You take good care of my daughter and bring her home safely, Captain." The Baron commanded, the emotion clear in his voice.

"Have no worries, I will keep her safe, you can be assured of that, though we both know she is capable of looking after herself." He smiled down at Catherine, feeling pride swell within him, partly towards Catherine and partly towards being trusted with her safety.

"That she can," the Baron replied, the pride in his voice matching Lucas's.

Lucas and Catherine watched as her father stepped onto the dock and the plank was pulled back onto the ship. "Aweigh anchor!" Lucas bellowed, his eyes locking onto Alaric's who still stood at his spot at the railing. Lucas knew there was not much he could say to his friend just then but wanted him to know he knew what was on his mind.

This voyage back was going to be far different than any other, Benjamin had been a part of the ship, more so than any other sailor ever had. He could feel it in the air amongst the crew, they felt the same and it would take time for everyone to adjust, especially Alaric.

"I suppose I should go and see if Doc or Cook need any assistance." Catherine said, tearing his mind away from his thoughts.

"I suppose you should, Lass." He grinned and pulled her closer, his lips locking on hers.

29

Catherine awoke, rolling over to feel the Captain's warm body near hers. The rhythm of his chest steadily rising and falling, his breathing even and low. Taking the opportunity, she closely examined the muscles of his chest and arms. His shirt draped open lower than usual, the strings that held the front of the shirt together had come undone while he slept, exposing more of his stomach and chest.

"Enjoying what you see, Lass?" He asked in a low, husky whisper. His eyes were still closed, a grin playing on his lips.

Catherine's face flamed." And what if I am?" She replied, unsure of what to say next.

Lucas chuckled and rolled over, propping himself up with his arm. There was a knock on the hatch. "What is it?" Lucas asked, loud enough for the man on the other side to hear.

"Capt'n we are readying to anchor. We have reached the island." It was Joseph, Catherine recognized his accent being much like Lucas and Alaric's.

"Island? Which Island?" Catherine asked.

"Well now, this island is a favorite of mine. It has the most delicious iguanas and if I recall correctly, a particularly lovely little pond back in the jungle. With water clearer then you will see anywhere else and a waterfall that will take your breath away." His grin broadened.

"I did not realize we would be stopping here again." She squealed in excitement, throwing the covers back and leaping out of the bed.

Lucas laughed, "We need fresh water and could use some fresh meat and fruit. I believe I mentioned last time that even if our ship had not needed repairs, we likely would have stopped." He watched her brush her hair down. Louise had been kind enough to get her a brush before they left.

After several more weeks at sea, they finally arrived back in Barbados. Catherine was thrilled to be back, but dreaded the moment she was to say good-bye to the ship and the crew. Every time she thought of parting with the Captain, whom she had fallen in love with during the journey, it felt as if she was losing a part of herself. She had grown to love sailing, love everything about being on board the ship and had become closer with the crew then she had ever been with anyone else, except for Emma.

"Alaric, I will meet you at the *Rusty Anchor* in the morning. There is something I want to talk to you about." Catherine heard Lucas say as he approached her.

"I expect this Emma that you have spoken about so many times is anxious to see you again." Lucas said, they both stood at the railing waiting to step off the ship.

"I expect she is and I her." The sadness was evident in her voice. Several minutes later, the plank was slid down. Catherine with her belongings was ready to set foot back on the island she called home. Inhaling deeply, smelling the familiar sent of the sea, fruit, fish and sand.

"Let's take a carriage to your plantation, after all, I have heard so much about it. Since it nearly cost my crew and myself our lives. I would not miss an opportunity to take a tour of it." He grinned and helped her into a carriage that sat nearby on the dock. Catherine nodded, she was too afraid to ask how long he would be staying or if she would have a chance to properly say good-bye to the crew.

The carriage jolted and swayed, causing them to bounce around in their seats. She had not realized just how different the carriage rides were on the island, compared to the luxurious ones in France. Eagerly, she waited to see the plantation come into view.

When it finally did, her breath caught, she had never truly looked at it from the gate. It was grand and beautiful and lined with rose bushes. As the carriage turned, pulling up alongside the estate, she wiped away a tear. She felt Lucas watching her and smiled when he gently took her hand and squeezed it. The door of the estate opened and the staff came out to greet her. The door to the carriage opened, Edward, one of the footmen, lowered the stepping block and helped her down. She felt her heart swell at the sight of so many faces she had missed.

"Welcome back Lady Benedict, we all have missed you a great deal." The butler said, speaking for the entire staff. With all that she had been through she did not see any reason to be formal with the staff. She ran over to the butler and wrapped her arms around him. Tears rolled down her face as she turned to Emma. They embraced, reluctant to let one another go.

"Oh, Miss Catherine, I was so worried. I feared the worst." Emma whispered, still holding onto Catherine's hands.

"I am perfectly fine, as you can see." Catherine sniffed.

"You must be exhausted, come in and let's get you cleaned up and then I will have some refreshments brought to you," Emma instructed.

"Thank you," Catherine smiled. "Has my father arrived yet?" She asked, turning to the butler.

"No Miss, not yet, but I am sure he will arrive in a day

or two." The butler turned to Lucas, "You must be Captain Lucas Harding." He bowed to Lucas, "It is a pleasure to meet you, Captain."

"Aye, the pleasure is mine. I have heard great things about all of you and this magnificent plantation." He replied, gesturing wide with his arms.

"If you do not mind, we will have our refreshments in the garden. It is a lovely day and I have missed the smell of the flowers." Catherine told Emma as they walked in the house. Catherine looked over her shoulder, making sure that Lucas was following them.

"This plantation is spectacular," Lucas said, taking a small bite of fruit.

"It is funny, I never knew just how wonderful it is, until I saw it when we first arrived." Catherine said, looking around at the flowers near the table they sat at.

"Well," Lucas said, standing, "I would like to freshen up, before it is time to properly dine, especially since the Baron will be arriving any day." He reached down, running his knuckles softly along the top of her hand. He started walking down the path that led away from house.

Catherine stood up, "Lucas, where are you going?" She asked.

"The Foreman's house," Lucas shrugged. He winked at Catherine and chuckled, continuing down the path to the small, white, wooden house which stood just in front of the first rows of sugarcane, sitting against the tall, lush trees.

End of Book 1

Epilogue

Alaric sat at one of the old wooden tables inside The *Rusty Anchor*. He looked around at the men that sat inside, talking, eating and gambling. Most of the sailors were from merchant ships or other privateer ships, a few of them pirates. Others were fishermen or men that worked on the island, all of them looking about as rough as the man sitting next to them.

Alaric twisted the cup around on the table, watching the last bit of ale swirl inside it. Unable to sleep the night before, his mind would not let him forget all the times he had come into port and had taken Benjamin out to see the sights of the island or let him explore the ship, before he was old enough to be a part of the crew. Once he had been old enough and they would return to the island, Benjamin scarcely left Alaric's side, afraid he would miss some exciting moment or adventure.

"Here, luv. Have another ale," One of the women that worked in the tavern sidled up to Alaric and poured more into his nearly empty cup. "No man that is as handsome as you should look so troubled."

Alaric glanced up at the woman that stood next to him, one hand carrying a large jug of ale the other resting on her hip. "Thank you."

"You let me know if there is anything else you need," she said, sliding her hand along his arm as she turned to tend to other customers.

Alaric watched the tavern door; Lucas should be at the tavern soon. The door swung open just as Lucas entered the room. He sat down at the table and waved a hand, asking for a cup of ale as well. "You alright, Mate?"

Alaric knew Lucas understood exactly how he felt. He had no words to express his anguish and frustration. He let out a slow breath, raking his hand through his dark hair.

A half smile formed on Alaric's face. "I am glad you decided to become the Baron's partner on the plantation and you will make a fine foreman. I am happy for you, truly." Alaric's smile widened. "Have you asked for the Lass's hand?"

Lucas sat back in his chair. "Not yet, but I will." He chuckled, "she was quite taken aback when I told her I was going to get cleaned up and started heading for the Foreman's house."

Alaric laughed, "I am sure she was surprised. She was afraid of losing you more and more each day as we neared the island." Alaric looked down into his cup again.

"Alaric, I want you to take *The Trinity*." He sat up and leaned his arms on the table. Alaric studied his friend. "I will need to be here for the next several months at least. Getting the plantation going again. I am not sure when I would be able to sail again." Lucas explained, his expression serious. "You need to go after Thomas. I do not want to hold you back. I am only sorry I will not be there to see you kill the bastard."

"Lucas, are you sure about this? You are *The Trinity's* Captain." Alaric said, shaking the surprise from his face.

"Not now I'm not," he shook his head. "We have sailed together for many years and you are just as much that ship's Captain as I. Take it. Find Thomas, for Benjamin." Lucas' voice was steady and hard.

"Alright, mate." His voice filled with emotion. He raised his cup. "For Benjamin."

"For Benjamin," Lucas mimicked.

CPSIA information can be obtained
at www.ICGtesting.com
Printed in the USA
LVHW040233230223
740164LV00002B/260